Loving ROSENFELD

LEIGHANN HART

First paperback edition January 2021

Cover Design © Designed with Grace

Copy Edits by Justin Williams

ISBN 978-1-7376130-0-8

PLAYLIST

Introspective - Oliver Tree
Dream Boy - Beach Bunny
Novocaine for the Soul - Eels
Out of My Element - Sure Sure
Bad Ideas - Tessa Violet
Looking for Love - The Chain Gang of 1974
Coffee - Jack Stauber's Micropop
Emotional - Anthony Hall
Solitude is Bliss - Tame Impala
Two Points for Honesty - Guster
It's Alright - Mother Mother
Backyard Boy - Claire Rosinkranz
Ice Cold - half alive, Kimbra
Anxious - Hippo Campus
Yule Shoot Your Eye Out - Fall Out Boy
She's Got You High - Mumm-ra
Listerine - Dayglow
Goodie Bag - Still Woozy
I'm Fine - Daisy the Giant
OK - Wallows

She Drives Me Crazy - Fine Young Cannibals
Might Might Not - Sure Sure
Mushy Gushy - Chapel
Adulthood - Jukebox the Ghost
Maybe - half alive
Bitch Theme - Bratmobile
Coloring Book - The Regrettes
So Alright, Cool, Whatever - The Happy Fits
Peach - The Front Bottoms
Overthinking IT - Willow
Good to You - Marianas Trench
Alive - Chai
Crying Like a Church on Monday - New Radicals
Next Best Thing - FLOOR CRY, Vansire
Hands Down - The Greeting Committee
Going Away to College - blink-182

For Justin,
who never missed deadline—including my curfew.

"We are all just coming and going in this life.
We are just a lost star.
We are a spark on the horizon."

—*Gregg Alexander*

1

BAD TIMING

Closed.

The chunky block letters on the coffee shop's door mocked Peter, urging him to defy its declaration. A glance at his phone indicated the time as 6:56, four minutes before closing.

Four minutes. If it had been four minutes until deadline at the newspaper, he would have a sliver of a window to submit his work. Why, within the same span of 240 seconds, was he denied a medium cappuccino with 2% milk steamed at 180 degrees?

Hands cupped around his eyes, he peered inside the shop. The track lighting illuminated two employees who were preoccupied cleaning. Peter did not recognize one of them. Sizing her up was a luxury his limited time could not afford. Kendall, his regular barista, worked alongside the new girl. Bulky headphones hugged the crown of her head, likely blaring some heavy metal nonsense.

Irritation bubbled at his core, begging him to find a nearby stone and bust the floor-to-ceiling glass windows. A caffeine migraine commanding the wrath of hellfire raged in Peter's skull. The sludge they served at Town Hall made radioactive waste an appealing alternative. That tarrish muck would not cut it. He yearned for the real deal, for the rich, seductive flavor of espresso.

"Dammit." Kicking the dirt on the sidewalk, Peter ran his tongue along the inside of his teeth.

He was en route to a city council meeting. Not that he cared about being late to such a boring assignment. As much as he loved being a journalist, the subject matter of the articles failed to ignite a passion within him. This disinterest did not hinder the quality of his stellar reporting. Even so, Peter possessed no desire to change the world through his work. That daunting task was better left to the Glenn Greenwalds of the world.

His objective?

Cruise through life, one miserable day at a time.

Upon rushing out of the office, the black brick exterior of his favorite coffee shop, 'The Roast,' had caught his attention. Peter's disgruntlement reigned supreme at being hurried off to a meeting that one of his co-workers pussyfooted their way out of covering. Caffeine proved his only hope of surviving the nauseating, hour-long affair. But that hope departed in the face of the shop's closed doors. The promise of a cappuccino vanished as quickly as this assignment fell into his lap.

"Hey!" he yelled, fists pummeling the glass storefront. His arthritic hands soon ached from the fervency of their motion. The startled employees searched for the source of the disturbance, their collective gaze flitting to but not resting on Peter. A white wire weaved around the new barista, implying the use of earbuds. It was a wonder either of the women heard his desperate knocking; pounding, rather. "What's the deal?"

They regarded Peter for a nanosecond before returning to their tidying. Were they really going to ignore him, one of their most loyal patrons?

"Should we call the cops?" Ryleigh threw a soaked dish rag onto the nearest table. It landed with a wet 'thud.' A mean stack of psychology work awaited her at home. She had no time to deal with this hooligan.

"Call the cops on Peter, the coffee purist? Don't worry about him. We're cool. And the last I checked, he's only capable of verbal assault."

Kendall steadied the mop she wielded, replacing it in the neighboring bucket of soapy water. The light refracted off the silver barbell anchored in her eyebrow. "He's a regular. It's by the grace of some weird stroke of luck that you haven't served him yet."

"I know you can hear me, Ken. Come on." Peter paced in short spurts, a restless caged animal. Hands planted on his hips, he looked skyward and shouted a string of colorful obscenities that would have given the most foul-mouthed sailors pause.

Ryleigh resumed wiping the tables. A hundred rounds of handwashing would be mandatory to rid her fingertips of the stale water stench. "He seems a little high-strung."

"I won't lie to you. He can be a real dick sometimes," Kendall said before turning to the bothersome man outside. "Dude, we're closed. Go back to work."

Peter slid his middle finger along the glass, producing a hair-raising squeak as he disappeared around the corner.

A swell of nausea overwhelmed Ryleigh as she trekked through the main corridor of Victory Hills High, navigating the crowd of students bolting in competing directions. Anyone else would have ducked into a bathroom and ralphed away their stress. Not her. She had a perfect attendance record to uphold, which, by a recent mandate, included tardies.

Each locker-lined hallway represented a new gateway to her recent academically induced anxiety. Make no mistake, school kindled the flame of her existence. Ryleigh received every ribbon, won every award; she was *that* girl.

The shifts at the coffee shop had disrupted the impeccable rhythm of her studies. The result? She drowned in readings, fell behind on packets, fumbled with presentations.

If a roaring social life had contributed to this academic decline, it would be an easier pill to swallow. Ryleigh Branson was a boyfriend-less virgin who preferred the company of Langston Hughes to the living, wheezing likes of her idiotic male peers.

Her commitment to the part-time position had thrown the rest of her life out of whack, which extended to failing to dress herself properly. Ryleigh glanced down at the awful outfit she wore: a graphic t-shirt, dark-wash skinny jeans, and checkerboard slip-ons.

Utter disaster.

Emitting a groan, she ducked into her biology class. Andrea, her best—and only—friend, sat at one of the lab tables lining the rear of the room. Ryleigh chucked her mustard backpack onto the spotless black countertop and perched on one of the metal stools.

"I didn't know we were doing a middle school throwback look today. You should've texted. I could have broken out my plaid vest," Andrea teased, eyeing the horrendous outfit. As an 'it girl' of Victory Hills, she was qualified to give the fashion diagnosis. The unofficially elected position required that she always be put together, fully made up and wearing a stylish new boot or en vogue blouse. Ryleigh contracted a migraine thinking about what lengths her friend must go to getting ready each morning.

"Laundry day." The lie escaped her lips as if it had the priority clearance of a breath. The tiniest of white lies did not sit well with Ryleigh. Why had she delivered this mouthful of deceit? The acquired dishonesty was an unlisted perk of her new job. She excavated her biology notebook from her bag, along with a pen and highlighter.

Andrea placed a palm on her cheek, resting an elbow on the table. "Homecoming is Friday, in case you forgot. I know you're swamped lately, and that's why I took it upon myself to ask around and secure some date options. There are some worthy candidates who are *very* interested in taking you."

Never had there existed a friendship more diametrically opposed. Social functions were the pinnacle of one's existence, loathed and avoided by the other.

Ryleigh flipped through her notebook, turning the pages with unnecessary force. Under which circumstances did she think a celibate bookworm would be interested in attending such an obnoxious event?

"Andy, I'm not going to that dance. I think it's great you're on the court for a second year. I helped you with your campaign posters; I am fully supportive of your involvement with this. So, as my best friend, I would appreciate it if you support my decision to not attend after-school social gatherings."

"If you would give one of these guys a chance ..."

"Look around this room," Ryleigh urged, lowering her voice. "These are not guys. These are not men. These are boys. I have no interest in spending an evening with any of these immature dweebs."

Ryleigh never understood the allure behind boys their age. Holding a conversation with one guaranteed the loss of precious brain cells; a full-blown relationship would surely have dire consequences. If anyone were to come along and sweep her off her feet, he would be an older, sweater vest wearing, sonnet reciting, foreign film watching gentleman.

"You know, I hate that I won't be around to witness your exploration of older men once you're at UMich. You'll have banged your way through every professor, from anthropology to sociology, by the time you graduate."

"That's seriously disgusting."

Andrea tapped her foot on the stool's inner ring. "My thoughts exactly."

Peter devoured a microwave meal in front of his computer screen, hunched over the keyboard. Had anyone walked in on the scene, they might have likened it to Quasimodo raiding the dumpsters of Notre Dame for edible scraps. The frostbitten, mushy alfredo penne glued to the plastic tray paled in comparison to the sight and smell of his coworkers' homemade fare.

An unkind purgatory welcomed those who were single in their mid 30's.

His tenure at *The Harris Chronicle* spanned 13 years, during which time he had not once eaten in the staff lounge. He avoided this room like the plague, uninterested in interacting with his colleagues anymore than necessary through collaborative efforts as they pieced the paper together each night.

He ate in silence, hands flying across the keys between heaping forkfuls of spongy pasta. Peter's typing speed had not waned much despite the terminal stiffness of his crippled digits. Arthritis, carpal tunnel, and eye strain had not been in the job description when applying to this publication. A disclaimer should have come attached to journalism.

Warning: chronic pain and loneliness lie ahead.

A couple of overnights needed his immediate attention and hard-wired concentration. Peter spared no room for mediocrity. The events he reported on were starved of excitement and intrigue, but he wrote about all of them as if they were the Academy Awards. He could not pick up a woman in a bar or tell you how many innings were in a baseball game, but he could write the hell out of anything thrown his way.

This overachiever aura bit him in the ass when his prehistoric boss, Mr. Roberts, took special interest in him. Now, he had higher expectations for Peter than anyone else. Knowing someone believed in him created a peculiar sort of comfort. He had given up his own high expectations for himself long ago.

"Peter?"

He dropped the fork and craned his neck to get a glimpse of the guest. Mike Corso, a fellow staff writer, loomed in the doorway.

"What can I do for you?" Peter generally steered clear of small talk. He had no energy to waste on nonsense.

"I'm stuck with homecoming court coverage."

Mike was an unmarried, balding man in his early 40's. His unwed status became a lot less mysterious when one factored in all of the inappropriate comments he aimed at the unsuspecting women around the office. Of all the riff raff working at the *Chronicle*, Mike landed at the bottom of the totem pole.

"I don't like where this is going." He minimized the seven running browser tabs and spun around to face the nuisance invading his office. Peter's chair screeched as he lurched forward. He steepled his fingers, a weak suppression of annoyance. "Look, I helped you out Monday by covering that godforsaken meeting. Don't expect me to give you an out all the time."

He had been late reporting to Town Hall due to the unfortunate debacle at the coffee shop. Peter had not returned to the cafe since the incident, as a means of protest. But he could only resist the charms of espresso for so long.

Mike shuffled his dress shoes against the tacky seaweed carpet. "You know I hate covering high school shit."

"Not my problem, Corso."

Slackers were unworthy of his sympathy.

"What if I sweeten the pot? A trade. I'll take one of your assignments."

"I can roll with that." Peter scribbled something which ticked the box of illegible on a sticky note and slapped it in his co-worker's hand. "Protest at Planned Parenthood. Have fun."

He groaned, turning to leave the office. Peter wanted to gloat, to drink in this glorious moment of defeat, until—

"Hey," he prompted, halting Mike in his tracks. "Which school?"

"Victory Hills. Friday night at seven."

2

AN APOLOGY

The pervasive aroma of bacon wafting throughout the Bransons' home marked Friday's arrival. This day guaranteed three things: the heartiest breakfast of the week, the commencement of the weekend, and a chance to play catch-up with school assignments. Ryleigh followed the delightful smells all the way to the kitchen, bag slung over her shoulder.

"Morning, sweetie," her mother chirped as Ryleigh claimed a seat at the table.

Her mother pulled three prepared lunches from the fridge, setting them on the expansive island. She moved about the kitchen in her scrubs with purpose. Every second mattered, much like at the ER. In keeping with the same philosophy, their home was organized to run at its highest efficiency. Nothing was ever out of stock or out of place. Charlotte Branson made sure of it.

"Morning." Ryleigh's backpack strained as she hooked it onto the back of the chair. A thick tome of William Carlos Williams was to blame; a collection she would have loved to rip out and read from while devouring her savory breakfast. Beautiful poetry lurked behind her, inaccessible.

Prior to the start of this school year, chapbooks were no strangers to the Bransons' dinner table. But her parents had drawn up an executive order banning books of any kind from mealtime. Yet, her father read *The Harris Chronicle* every morning. The hypocrisy left her seething. Who read print news anymore, anyway?

"Work today, Ry?" her father inquired without tearing his eyes away from the unbanned newspaper he held dangerously close to his face. Dexter had needed reading glasses for several years but refused to acknowledge his diminishing sight. A typical man defending his typically impenetrable pride.

"Yeah, I'm closing."

Ryleigh had almost forgotten about that afternoon's shift. The weekend would have to wait.

"Seems I'll make it home before you then." He smiled, folding a corner of the paper to gloat at his only child.

Dexter tortured children for a living under the guise of pediatric dentistry. He owned a private practice, a small office on the edge of town. Suffice to say, they were the house that handed out pencils at Halloween. Receiving pencils as a treat was much scarier than the cheap thrills elicited by their neighborhood's DIY haunted houses.

"Don't antagonize her, darling," Charlotte chided, refilling her husband's coffee. A dusty blonde wave broke loose from her hand-constructed ponytail. Her mother always pulled her hair back with her fingers, never bothering with a brush. Charlotte's tired eyes twinkled in sync with her smile. "We're so proud of you, honey. I'm sure you're doing a great job. They're lucky to have you."

Ryleigh's concern did not lie with where she stood at work. This job was impermanent. Her slipping performance in school, on the other hand—her parents would give her an earful if they caught wind of that development. Rising from the table, she chugged the rest of her coffee. "I have to go."

"Drive safe," Charlotte offered as her daughter swept out of the kitchen. An edge of apprehension dimmed her chipper tone, something that often accompanied these posthaste phrases; the concerned voice of a mother who was too hard on herself.

"Always," she sang.

Peter locked the front door to his condo, depositing the keys into the pocket of slacks so recently ironed that they were warm against his thighs. The contents of his worn leather messenger bag jostled as he galloped in descension of the steps. October's palette of warm-toned colors had splattered itself across town, and with the recent decline in temperature the walk to the newspaper office became somewhat appealing. Anything to avoid risking his hunk of junk car falling to pieces in the middle of a busy street. Though, busy was the last word one might conjure when asked to describe Harris.

A timid autumnal breeze greeted him as he opened the door at the bottom of the stairwell; the cool air whooshed inside to mingle with the building's artificial warmth. Peter wore his signature attire: a dress shirt, slacks, belt, argyle socks, and beaten up brown loafers which were in desperate need of replacement. He readjusted the uncomfortable weight of his work bag, fishing inside an outer compartment to make sure he remembered his cell phone. Not that anyone ever called him besides his mother.

Few people littered the path to the office. A tall woman in athleisure struggled to keep control of an eager golden retriever, who sniffed Peter in passing. Had the keen canine detected the shower he opted to skip? An elderly man rocking a fedora ambled along clutching two brown sacks of groceries. He struggled to keep the hat on his bald head in the blustery weather. An enraged lawyer spewing legal nonsense into an earpiece bumped elbows with Peter, offering no apology as they went their separate ways. Time is money, the lawyer might have said.

Exchanging niceties with strangers was not his forte. This had been a problem when he first started working for the *Chronicle*. Offering a casual hello to someone on the street and interviewing someone for an article were distinctive ball games. The second scenario had procedures in place to ease Peter's anxiety. A glimpse of the person was granted pre-interview; bits of information, their name, their relevance.

The unknown is what troubled him.

After seeing the man with the groceries, he made a mental note to hit up the 24-hour market later that night. His refrigerator and pantry looked as if they had made it out the other side of an apocalypse, barren and destitute wastelands where food had once resided.

Fingers curled around the entrance to the *Chronicle*, though he stopped short of pulling it open. Peter glanced across the street at the buzzing coffee shop. Could he breach his weeklong protest? His vacant stomach pointed to a resounding yes.

Peter swallowed his pride and entered the crosswalk. As he conquered each of the white rectangular bars, the reason for his protest of the shop resurfaced at the forefront of his mind. Shame shadowed the recollection. What a cranky bastard he had been. *You owe Kendall a grand apology after that scene you caused.*

The mind-numbing whirring of the blender drowned the noises within the shop. When Ryleigh cut off the ear-grating appliance, the ruckus inside the cafe resumed in all its glory, volumes and tones contrasting like a band out of time. Headache medicine would have been a useful companion during her shifts at *The Roast*; she never had the foresight to bring any along. Cue the suffering.

She poured the caramel freezer into a plastic cup, but she tipped the blender mouth too fast and some of the frozen coffee spilt along the outer walls of the cup, pooling on the counter. Ryleigh snapped a lid on it, dropping it off at the pick-up area where a uniform clad, private school princess awaited its arrival. The teen stuck up her nose, shooting Ryleigh an 'are you serious' scowl.

"Um, can I get a napkin?" The girl enunciated napkin as if it were two words, an overkill of emphasis. Ryleigh sucked in a cheek, teeth gnashing on the tender flesh. Customers did not often annoy her, but these Mercedes driving, Ralph Lauren wearing, Ivy League chasing snobs made her blood boil without fail. She scooped up a small stack of napkins and relinquished them to the girl who thought her prep school queen bee status extended to this civilian coffee shop.

Upon clocking into work, Ryleigh fell into the barista role as if it were second nature. She slid her apron on in the blink of an eye and set to it. That $11.00 an hour would not earn itself. Sure, the shop could be a breeding ground for migraines, and some of the customers were a handful—a select few were several handfuls, including this abhorrent 'napkin' girl—but she loved the hours she spent in the cafe.

Ryleigh lost herself in the fast-paced rhythm of the job, finding comfort in the level of attention it required. The focus she dedicated to fulfilling incoming orders temporarily relieved her of burdensome thoughts surrounding school, homework, and the granddaddy of anxiety: college. But as she fell into the melodic, repetitive task of making drinks, her stress dissipated.

That stress returned with astonishing urgency as a familiar man entered the shop. Pressure bottled in her ribcage, poised to explode like an aggravated aerosol can. Peter the coffee purist entered the cafe, boasting the nonchalance of someone who thought they owned stock in the establishment. What an act to follow the prep school princess. If the scene from Ryleigh's closing shift bore any indication, this interaction would be a nightmare.

But the Peter who presently stood in the shop seemed nothing like the man who had pounded on the storefront window. A billowy cloud of sereneness hung around him, making his presence less intimidating. Perhaps that serenity would meet an abrupt end whenever he opened his mouth to order. Ryleigh jumped at the toaster oven's high-pitched dinging. Regaining composure, she stole another glance in his direction. A weathered bag sat anchored to his shoulder, left hand glued to its strap as if it were a lifeline.

Good, he's going somewhere. Maybe I won't have to put up with him long.

An unwelcome realization wiggled its way into her subconscious: he was not unattractive. At this, Ryleigh's heart raced and head swam, all major organs competing in a triathlon to manage this unexpected observation. Peter crouched by the half-size refrigerator containing premade items. Precious few details were on display with his back turned: the vertical seam on the rear of his dress shirt, the battered heels of his shoes. The chestnut, windswept curls stood out against the rest.

Pesto and turkey on ciabatta in hand, Peter approached the counter. His vacant stare traveled past Ryleigh to the kitchen space like she did not exist. A discernible redness clung to his waterlines, exhaustion at its finest. He pushed the boxed sandwich toward her. "Is Kendall around?"

"No, she's off." The normal confidence in her tone faltered. Ryleigh wished her co-worker would have swooped in to take the order, but Oscar dallied in the storeroom collecting inventory. She blinked in rapid succession, disappointed when he did not vanish.

Peter's gaze flickered between her face and silver-plated name tag. "You're new, right?"

Words evaded her but she saved the interaction by employing a swift nod. Ryleigh averted her eyes from the man towering over the counter, afraid that a peep at him might turn her to stone. Why did her first transaction with a regular customer have to be with *him*— this good-looking, yet possibly deranged, guy?

"I'll take a bagel and a medium cappuccino. 2% milk steamed at 180." He rummaged through his back pocket and produced a wallet in worse shape than his shoes. "And the sandwich, obviously."

Ryleigh fought the urge to verbally question his carb intake, striking it as inappropriate conversation to broach with a semi-stranger. She had three weeks of coffee-making experience under her belt. The prospect of preparing an espresso drink for this maniac of a man ranked above the realm of terrifying.

She punched in the order. "What kind of bagel?"

Peter leaned across the counter, face poised a dangerous foot away from hers. A hint of his heady cologne permeated the air. He lowered his voice, giving way to a hoarse whisper. "I don't remember specifying, so that would imply I expect a plain bagel, yeah?"

Threads of self-satisfaction were woven with such care into the retort, a twisted grin should have succeeded its deliverance. *Who does this guy think he is?*

"We have plain, everything, raisin, blueberry, and chocolate chip," Ryleigh stated, ignoring his condescending tone and waiting for him to make a selection.

"Chocolate chip?" Do people seriously order that?" he asked, borderline offended by the creation of the flavor. Peter adopted a pained expression and muttered something unintelligible under his breath.

The persistence of his attitude amused her. She had to suck in her cheeks to prevent a smile. "They're popular with children, mostly."

"Plain. No cream cheese; it makes me sick." He swiped his debit card, pushed a few buttons on the payment pad, and vanished the wallet.

"Can I have a name for your beverage?" Ryleigh plucked a permanent marker from the bucket of sticky, syrup-covered writing utensils. She seized a paper to-go cup from the towered stack beside the register, almost scrawling his name on the cup before he spoke.

Nice going. That would've been great.

The corner of his mouth twitched. "You ask a lot of questions."

"Only the necessary ones."

"Peter." He regarded the barista with a curious gaze, scrunching his forehead to forge wrinkles. Ryleigh scribbled on the cup and set it off to the side, pretending to not notice his studious look. Those sleepy eyes bore into her, as if to channel additional acknowledgement. *Don't fall for it.*

"You can wait for your order at the end of the counter, sir." She motioned to the drink pick-up area.

Peter's lips formed a trained smirk. "You really have no clue how often I come here, huh?"

"Like you pointed out, I'm new." Ryleigh bit her tongue as the words flew from her mouth.

His face neutralized, lips parting as if to speak but hesitation winning out. Peter fiddled with the cuffs on his dress shirt. While she had welcomed the sleepy stare, this new look had her on edge. He brought a hand to the back of his neck, "That was you, then, wasn't it? Last week?"

If you're referring to your meltdown, then yes.

"No hard feelings."

"I'm not usually like that. Rough night."

Why had he taken the time to explain his behavior? Kendall had warned against his douchebag tendencies, but the extension of an apology seemed to contradict the alleged persona. Ryleigh mulled this over as she popped the bagel into the toaster.

As the espresso brewed, she caught a glimpse of Peter admiring the pastry case. He leered at the treats with an unnatural yet endearing degree of lust. This man had a love affair with carbs.

She slipped a temperature gauge into the milk-filled steaming pitcher and placed it under the frothing wand. The hand on the gauge made its steady rise. Ryleigh cut off the pressure at precisely 180 degrees. Her chest tightened upon realizing she had to surrender the order, thereby getting rid of the handsome customer. *At least he's a regular.*

"To-go for Peter."

"If your cappuccino skills are any good, I'll have to kick Kendall to the curb."

The faint smile Peter gave as he grabbed the coffee and bagel rendered Ryleigh to a pool of pink, glittering goo. Within seconds, he was gone, fading from her memory with the annoying agility of a mesmerizing dream.

She could withstand a parade of private school brats if 10 minutes of her shift were dedicated to serving him.

Peter wedged his foot in the path of the closing elevator door, slipping inside while he had the chance. Lydia, their opinion editor, retreated into the corner, as if Peter's presence posited danger in the tight space. He had zero fucks to give about Lydia and her opinion-based bullshit columns. The only thing that mattered in those 22 square feet? The piping hot cappuccino; the torch that would guide him through the night ahead.

He blew through the oval cutout on the lid in anticipation of taking the first sip. Peter tried to brace himself for the worst-case scenario. Trusting a bull in a china shop had a greater chance of success than having faith in a new barista to not screw up your coffee order. The scalding hot cappuccino cascaded over his tongue like the finest silk; espresso and milk mingling together in luxurious harmony. *Perfection.* Had Lydia not been in the elevator, Peter may have elicited a moan at this blissful, inaugural sip.

"Damn, that's good," he whispered.

3

SEXUALLY (IN)ACTIVE

The key difference between the work week and the weekend? Peter traded the stuffy office-mandated slacks for sweatpants. Keeping busy on days off justified the neglect of the social and romantic sectors of his life. Extra assignments meant no time to stress about dating, which equaled no worries. He held a black belt in the fine art of rationalization. Peter would rather die single than unleash his scarred heart onto the vicious battlefield known as love.

Muffled strumming of an acoustic guitar resonated among the sofa cushions, breaking the dead silence of the condo. Peter waded through the feather-stuffed fabric until he located his cell phone, retrieving it from its mysterious hiding place. Checking the caller ID would have been an unnecessary formality.

He answered without pretense. "Hey, mom."

"Peter," Janet cooed, "how are you, darling?"

"Amazing." He emphasized each syllable, achieving the cadence of a bored cheerleader.

"Oh, please, don't bore me with all the details."

His mother accepted his tempestuous attitude, affectionately calling him her 'little storm cloud' as a teenager; his father did not find the act amusing and bemoaned the world for having dealt him a moody son.

"You know me, always working." He dragged out the last half of the sentence while sifting through the piles of paper crowding the coffee table. Peter cradled the phone against his shoulder, thumbing through the stacks. The paper in question surfaced—a xeroxed police report. He jumped at the chance to report within the crime beat, likening himself to a suave detective in a noir film. Though, Harris's general lack of miscreants made this opportunity scarce.

"It's the weekend. You need to go out and have fun. Go for a walk, get some fresh air." Concern and sincerity cried out through Janet's rather calm insistence; a friend on the surface and a worried parent drowning below.

She's just looking out for you. Relax.

"The paper doesn't cease circulation for the sake of me having a weekend to myself, mom." The exaggeration did not aid his cause. There was no fooling his mother.

"I happen to be aware that you're *off* Tuesdays and Saturdays, Peter Zayn Rosenfeld."

Countless memories were tied to the cadence of his full name rolling off her matriarchal tongue. Of these mischievous incidents, Janet discovering his stash of dirty magazines in college took the cake. She uncovered the tasteless publications peeking out between the mattress and boxspring while changing his sheets. 'Don't bring this kind of filth into my home. Look at it on the internet like everyone else in the 21st century,' she had said.

"I know very well they don't expect you to work from home on your days off."

"What else am I supposed to do?" Eager to change the subject, Peter asked, "How's dad?"

Awful as it may have been, he did not care one bit about his father's well-being. The inquiry slipped out on pure reflex, a standard branch of his and Janet's conversation whose deviation never lasted. Gideon Rosenfeld had been a difficult man to grow up around; the supreme leader of ball-busting fathers. Every decision Peter made?

Wrong. Every interest he had? Misguided. Even as an adult, he remained a victim of Gideon's unyielding scrutiny.

"Your father's great. He's out back staining the deck." A bullet had been dodged. Peter would live to see another day. "Your father and I have been throwing around the idea of coming down for the holidays. If that's alright, of course. We understand you're busy with work, honey, but we miss you something awful."

"You're coming here for the holidays?" Peter echoed, processing the repeated phrase. "My place is pretty cramped, but we can make it work."

The thought of playing host to his family's holiday festivities incited near cardiac arrest. What choice did he have? He could not tell his mother no. Peter had managed to avoid his parents the last three Christmases. Not that he disliked their company, but Christmas with the Rosenfelds was an ordeal and a half. Peter and his father engaged in raucous shouting matches and tallied up the KOs while his mother wept into her umpteenth glass of cabernet sauvignon.

"I'm so glad to hear you'll have us. It's been too long, dear," Janet shrieked into the receiver.

Two years qualified as 'too long' in her book.

A couple of summers ago, he visited them for a week that felt more like a month. He was in no hurry to recreate the terror that plagued every parental visit; rehashing the same tired, unchanging subjects.

Peter did not have much to show for his 13 years of post-college independence. Once he had a few years of experience at the *Chronicle*, the plan had been to move to a larger metro area, somewhere he could advance his career. But Peter developed an attachment to Harris, a city where people minded their own business, where he could exist in the background. A larger city would mean more people, summoning an influx of uncomfortable situations: improv proposals for dates, invitations for drinks with co-workers.

Consensus? Not worth it.

A tightness enveloped his chest. Soon, his belligerent complacency would be on full display to the two most important people in his life.

"I can't wait to see you guys." A metallic taste spread in his mouth, as if blood had been stolen in penance for the lie. Peter pinched the bridge of his nose. "I'm going to let you go. I'm finishing up a few things."

"Okay. Enjoy your weekend, sweetheart. I love you."

"Love you too, mom." Lips pressed into a thin line, he hung up.

The drive across town to Sherman's Drugs always filled Peter with immense dread. This monthly journey meant venturing into the suburban side of Harris, a place infested with picture-perfect families, luxury vehicles, and high-class homes; a cookie-cutter hub overrun by hot-shot CEOs and their tanning bed bunny wives.

Though these people were raging narcissists who bathed in their own vapidity, they had achieved something that evaded Peter to no end: a relationship. He coveted what they shared, simultaneously unsure if he could accept that kind of love if it ever came his way.

Red light.

A breeding ground for unwelcome thoughts.

Peter fiddled with the knotted drawstring of his hoodie in a weak bid to distract his manic mind. Hours had passed but the phone call with his mother rang fresh in his mind. In a matter of weeks, the Rosenfeld men would come face to face, doomed to repeat the toxic cycle of the three R's for the duration of the visit: rile, ridicule, recuse. Hurling oneself off a cliff yielded less risk than enduring an interaction with his father.

Green light.

Two months — then, this unavoidable dread would become relevant. Peter could bury it until then.

"Why does this place always smell like it's been freshly mopped with a bucket of bleach?" Andrea's lip curled. The malodor assaulted their senses while passing through the automatic doors of Sherman's Drugs.

"It's a pharmacy. It's supposed to smell sterile," Ryleigh said. They skimmed along the expansive aisle of greeting cards en route to the rear of the store. "I should've stopped by after school yesterday. Sorry to drag you along."

"I wasn't about to stay behind and let your dad talk my ear off about gum tissue grafts." She had wanted to be a dentist since they were little kids, and Dexter chatted her up about the subject whenever the opportunity presented itself. Ryleigh envied Andrea's clarity about her future. "We should pick up snacks for our movie marathon. I love your parents, but some of that organic stuff they buy skeeves me out."

"Good luck sneaking your junk food contraband past them."

"Did I tell you what happened in fifth period yesterday?" Judging by the gleam in Andrea's eyes, it had to be boy related. "Colin finally said something to me after weeks of eye-flirting in calculus. He came up to me after class and asked if I wanted to get together and study sometime next week."

"Yeah, I'm sure studying is all he has on his mind." Ryleigh flashed a devilish grin.

"Oh, shut up. Apparently, he's not very good at calculus if he thinks I'd make a decent study partner."

"Again, not the reason he asked."

Ryleigh's appearance at the pharmacy window attracted the attention of an older employee. 'Heidi' was embroidered in vibrant red stitching on her white coat. "What's the last name and date of birth?"

"Branson. 9-3-2000."

"Okay. I've got it right here. Give us about half an hour and we'll have it ready. Are you signed up for our text alerts?"

"I'll be in the store."

The pharmacist may have still been within earshot when Andrea butted in with her two cents. "I can't believe your mom let you get on the pill. I've been trying to convince my mom for like a year. No luck. It's ironic, really. I'm the one who's sexually active."

"That is the absolute worst phrase ever invented. Can we not talk like clinicians?" Ryleigh squeezed her eyes shut. "My mom let me get on it for my skin."

"Bullshit. You haven't had a speck of anything on your face since the eighth grade. Plus—"

She snagged Andrea's forearm, jerking her into the safety of the office supply aisle.

"What are you doing?" she demanded.

"Shh." Ryleigh peered around the end cap display.

Peter.

He accepted a paper bag from Heidi. The collective hum of their voices came out garbled, like a static-stricken radio station. Every muscle in Ryleigh's body tightened, breathless at having encountered Peter the coffee purist in the wild. But, he lacked the dapper attire of the coffee purist. A slight frizz distressed his curls. Loose-fitting sweatpants. Slip-ons. Perhaps today, he was simply Peter.

"What gives, Ry?" Andrea peeked at what lay beyond the end cap. She whispered, "Hey, I know that guy."

Ryleigh wrestled her into the aisle. "You know him?"

Andrea crossed her golden arms and cocked her head to the side, employing the 'it's not an interesting story' act. "Yeah. He interviewed me for homecoming court. He's like a reporter or something. So, what?"

"He's a regular at my work."

Ryleigh chanced another look at the pharmacy window. He exchanged pleasantries with the pharmacist as he paid for the medication. Peter's lips hinted at a smile he seemed too exhausted to manufacture.

"Oh my God." Andrea's arms fell limp at her sides, mouth agape. "You're crushing on this guy."

Is it a crush?

Is that why her pulse lunged into her throat?

"If he hears you, I swear, Andy."

The corners of her mouth stretched to their limit to reveal blinding white teeth. "Go talk to him."

"No way." Ryleigh's eyebrows knit together. "Besides, isn't this the part where you incessantly mock my interest in older guys?"

"I've known you for 10 years. Not once have I ever seen you freak out like this about seeing someone. You have my blessing. Now go before he leaves."

"You have a good night, Heidi." Peter swiped the stapled paper bag from the counter.

"You too, hun."

With seven years of rapport between them, he let the distasteful nicknames slide. Only Heidi and his mother could get away with something as appalling as 'hun.'

The temptation to purchase a pack of cigarettes seduced his weary spirit. Smoking was as far removed from his life as sex. But, whenever dealings with his father neared, the itch for nicotine cropped up. *You're better than this.*

Peter emerged into the area near the registers, losing all interest in the plastic-wrapped boxes behind the glass case. A familiar visage rendered him immobile.

The new barista.

She studied the drugstore's pitiful Halloween display, turning over a pumpkin-printed mug in her pale hands. Her name eluded him. *Something with an R...*

"Hey." She replaced the mug on the shelf.

Shit. You can't even remember her name.

Peter clutched the paper bag for support, resulting in a distasteful crinkling noise. A corner of his mouth hoisted to form a shy smile, "Rachel, right?"

Her lips parted long before she made a sound. "Ryleigh."

Idiot.

"I'm usually good with names."

Embarrassment engulfed him like tar, thick and inescapable. Her neutral stare extended an invisible hand, pulling him from the depth of humiliation. Ryleigh's features relaxed in a manner which welcomed their beholder. Her liner-smudged, blue eyes trained on him, unfaltering. Peter failed to discern whether a coy smile played at her lips, or if they rested with a natural wryness.

"Do you live around here?"

Yeah, that wasn't creepy at all.

"If you're trying to stalk me, I'm afraid you've blown your cover." She tucked a section of flowing black hair behind her ear, revealing an appendage riddled with silver earrings. He counted five piercings. "It's Harris, aren't we all a hop, skip, and a jump away from each other?"

Heidi's soft voice spoke over the screeching intercom, "Ms. Branson, your prescription is ready for pick-up."

"That's me," Ryleigh pointed to the ceiling. "See you around, Peter." His stomach hardened at the casual use of his name. Backpedaling, she tapped her lips. "Or was it Patrick?"

4

FOR HERE

"*I*'m leaving the scene." Peter rode his brakes down the traffic-ridden street. An ambulance wailed its screeching siren, using the shoulder to zip past the line of cars.

"Did everything go well? Did you get the interview?" Cliff Roberts' senior citizen status did not preclude him from wearing the hat of an intimidating boss.

And he wore it well.

"Yes, sir, I did get an interview." Peter paused to navigate a sharp corner. "It may not be the one we were shooting for."

"Spit it out, Rosenfeld."

Peter swore saliva pelted him through the phone.

"The authorities wouldn't let any of the press speak to the individuals involved in the crash, and that order extended to family members. I spoke with an EMT and a witness, both of whom provided useful accounts of the accident."

Mr. Roberts' exhalation sent an unpleasant crackling static into Peter's ear. "Alright, do what you do best and make something out of nothing."

"Will do, sir." He terminated the call, flinging the phone onto the passenger seat.

Cliff could be quite particular about the angle in which certain stories should be presented. He wanted firsthand accounts, a reconstruction of the nitty gritty details. Coercing people to relive something as horrific as a car accident turned Peter off. Instead, he interviewed a small sampling of individuals and weaved engaging articles anchored in fact.

Sensationalism had no place in Harris.

Upon returning to downtown, he stalled in his parked car. Returning to the office under Mr. Roberts' duress did not appeal to Peter. He had been chewed out through the phone; he would rather not go for round two in person. The coffee shop on the corner buzzed with activity, drawing him in with its warm light.

"Ah, what the hell." Jaw set, he snatched the laptop bag from the backseat.

Patrons sipping lattes, conversing, and working monopolized more than half of the tables in the shop, but no one occupied his preferred spot.

Corner table, two chairs, an outlet.

Peter stood in line and impatiently waited for the indecisive couple in front of him to confirm their order. Poisonous words bubbled in his larynx, an ever-churning ocean of toxic waste raring to flood.

All contemplation halted when the couple stepped aside and revealed the newly hired temptress. The ambiance from the track lighting enshrouded Ryleigh's face in a cloak of ethereality as she scribbled something on a napkin beside the register. Peter could not embarrass himself in front of her again, not after the drugstore.

"A medium cappuccino, to go?" Ryleigh punched the order in before he opened his mouth. "2% steamed at 180. Or are we feeling adventurous today?"

"Your exceptional memory must go a long way at this job."

"Are you always this pleasant?"

"You caught me on a good day. That cappuccino is for here, by the way." A psychology textbook nestled beside the register caught Peter's eye while he rummaged for his wallet. "Psych major or just an elective?"

Ryleigh spied the worn book. "It's an elective, I'm undeclared for now."

"No kidding. I rode the coattails of undeclared until junior year. College is such a cruel joke ... making decisions that will influence the rest of your life at an ill-equipped age."

"You basically summed up my thoughts."

Peter glanced at her as he swiped his card. "Hemlock?"

Hemlock College was a private school, a 20-minute drive outside of Harris. A few years earlier, he went out with a graduate student at Hemlock—someone he interviewed while doing a spotlight on the swim team. The disastrous evening shattered any shot at a subsequent meeting. All for the best.

"Yeah. I'm a freshman."

Undeclared. Equipped with this knowledge, he should have understood she was either a freshman or sophomore. Ryleigh's eager eyes conveyed her low mileage.

She must have noticed him lingering near the register like a complete imbecile. "I'll bring your coffee out when it's ready if you want to find a seat."

Ryleigh recognized the impropriety of lying about college. How could she say no to those sleepy, long-lashed eyes? She planned to use her break to submit an application to a safety net school. That agenda now seemed shady, given Peter would presumably still be in the shop.

She watched him get situated as the espresso brewed. While his laptop started up, he unpacked an unfamiliar device along with earbuds, a notebook, and a pen. Fixated on Peter's every movement, Ryleigh failed to notice the espresso flowing over its shot glass and into the machine's grates.

Balancing brimming mugs on saucers topped her short list of irksome things that went along with being a barista. Ryleigh imagined tight-rope walkers felt the same kind of pressure. Peter's coffee made it to the table, safe and sound.

"Thanks, you're a doll." His hand automatically reached for the mug handle.

Why did her heart not soar at the saccharine remark?

Proximity.

Their closeness flustered Ryleigh, the usual separation of the counter absent. Gray beams highlighted Peter's golden eyes, an odd but arresting combination. His messy brown hair and five o'clock shadow betrayed the niceness of his ironed dress clothes.

"Didn't your mother teach you it's rude to stare?"

"Let me know if you need anything else." *Like my number, perhaps?*

Peter sipped the steaming cappuccino as he transcribed the two interviews from the accident. Every so often, his attention wandered to Ryleigh. A mussed braid contained the wonderment of her thick hair, identical in style to his last visit. When his focus returned to the laptop screen, a slew of blue and red squiggles revealed the extent of his distraction.

"Goddamnit," he mumbled into the mug.

Maybe the coffee shop had been a poor choice.

He found himself drawn to Ryleigh's animated aura, the sort radiated by a person who lived their life in full color. Her technicolor vibes intimidated Peter's spent black and white reel.

Ryleigh sauntered back to the table as he scanned the transcriptions for pull quotes. She collected the empty mug. "Can I get you anything else? Thought I'd check on you before my break."

"Unless you can make this article compose itself, I don't need a damn thing. But thanks, anyway." Peter did not cease his rhythmic typing, but his gaze pulled in her direction. The hem of her loose dress halted at the mid-thigh. "You better cover those Casper legs if you're heading outside. It's 44 degrees."

"Didn't your mother teach you it's rude to stare?"

Peter's lips clamped together at her recycled line. "I wasn't staring. Peripheral observation."

"Just so you know," she slid out the unoccupied chair across from him, "this is *my* table."

Had anyone else claimed the seat, he would have objected to their outright brashness. Why did he not turn her away? Peter needed confirmation that this scene was anchored in reality. "I have seniority rights to this table."

"Ageist." Ryleigh's eyes flicked upward. She cracked open a portable leatherbound notebook and produced a pen out of nowhere. The writing utensil sailed along the page. Her shoulders drew closer to her body, as if those words were a secret that necessitated protection. Pen aimed at his recorder, she asked, "What's that?"

"What are you writing?"

"I asked you first."

"It's a recorder." Peter crossed his arms. "Your turn."

"Uh, it's a poem." She tightened her grip on the pen before releasing it. A playful grin materialized, flushing any residual embarrassment. "Why don't you record your interviews on your phone?"

"Guess I'm old-fashioned. Why don't you write your poems on the computer?"

"Touché."

His screensaver populated on the laptop screen; had it been that long since he touched the article? Peter refused to let a cute college student influence the quality of his writing.

You think she's cute, now? This is the last thing you need.

Ryleigh snatched the journal and moved it to her lap, letting it rest against the table's ledge. Colorful band stickers littered the cover. A jean-wearing bunny caught his eye.

"You're a Blink fan?"

"They're one of my favorites."

Those words must have been eating her alive, because she wrote like someone held the cold mouth of a gun to her temple. Even after bilateral carpal tunnel surgery, he winced thinking about how much his wrist would ache if he were to replicate her ferocity.

"I saw them with Silverchair a few months after Enema came out."

That got her attention.

"No way." Ryleigh's pen halted as a menacing grin blossomed. His heart raced at their penetrative eye contact, but something inviting shone in her pools of blue and Peter lingered longer than he normally would have. "That album's ancient."

Fingers flexing above his keyboard, he joked, "I'm admittedly a little ancient."

She searched his face, eyes darting here and there, before returning her focus to the journal. "You wear it well."

Heat traveled up from beneath the collar of his dress shirt, along his neck, and onto his face. *Is she into me? No, she thinks you look good for your age, that's all; which is ironic because she doesn't know how old you are.*

He refreshed his laptop's screen and ventured a safer avenue of conversation. "So, you're going to school here. You don't strike me as a local."

"You're wrong, there. Born and raised." Ryleigh's thumbs tap danced on her phone's digital keyboard. Was she telling off a throng of boys? Tweeting? Peter supposed it did not matter, except the sudden interest had him miffed. Mischief backlit her squinted eyes. "You, on the other hand, you're definitely not from here."

"Californian transplant. What gave it away?"

"Your accent isn't up to par to audition for Damn Yankees, that was my best hint. California's a world away."

"That was kind of the idea." *And your presence at this table is shattering all the progress I've made.* Peter shut the laptop, rising to his feet. "I better head back. Busy night."

The subtle biting of her lip urged him to stay, but he could not fall victim to another charming woman.

Not after college.

5

TRY ME

All hell broke loose during third period biology in light of Mr. Fisher's absence. Quiet chatter hummed throughout the room, igniting further exasperation from the incompetent substitute who just wanted to know 'if anyone could work the projector.'

Andrea fanned herself. "Guess who asked me to the football game tonight?"

"God, I don't know. You're making it so difficult," Ryleigh mocked. "Let me guess, Colin from calculus?"

During all of their conversations, Ryleigh always referred to him as 'Colin from calculus.' Never Colin Halstock, or even Colin. Andrea would likely not approve of the catchy, alliterative nickname if things panned out between her and this new guy.

"Yes," she shrieked, clasping a hand over her mouth. The substitute glared at the girls when the strange celebratory noise erupted from their table.

Ryleigh shrugged at the disheartened substitute, mouthing, "Sorry."

"Will you go with us?" Her lower lip poked out.

"I'm not going to crash your first date."

A pen danced between Andrea's fidgeting fingers. "I don't know if I'm counting this as our official first date. What's more casual than hanging out at a football game? I would be way less nervous if you were there."

As much as Ryleigh wanted to say no, she could not ignore Andrea's desperation. They were like sisters. Anytime one needed the other, they were there. No excuses. She would have to suck it up and go.

"Luckily for you, I'm off work tonight. Text me the details when you get a chance and we'll meet up in the parking lot before the game."

"You're a lifesaver, Ry." Genuine happiness glistened in her topaz eyes. Andrea nudged her friend's ribs. "Who knows, maybe your reporter will turn up tonight. Extra, extra, local student Ryleigh Branson has a crush on a living, breathing guy, not a fictional character."

She has a point. Ryleigh might have laughed at the comment if not for the dread it manifested.

How had Peter come to spend his night sandwiched among the greater Harris area's sports reporters, under the disorienting lights of a high school football stadium? Two words: stomach flu. Matthews, their sports aficionado, called out sick, and Mr. Roberts tasked Peter to take his place.

"You see that scrawny kid in the #47 Creek Bend jersey? Best kicker in the state, they say. Hoards of colleges are fighting over him."

Peter detested sports, yet the inane conjecture by a fellow journalist bothered him. These kids played on teams, but a select few were given superstar treatment. Sure, they should be recognized for their talents, but why leave the other teammates in the dark? Did their roles carry no meaning?

He sampled his cappuccino; a consolation prize he had picked up on the way to Victory Hills for being made to suffer through an assignment in this uncultivated beat. A bitter tang spread within Peter's mouth as he returned the cup to the cement flooring of the bleachers. If someone happened to kick it, they would be doing him a favor.

Kendall's cappuccinos had been satisfactory until Ryleigh came around. Peter could not work out how their drink-making process could be different enough to warrant this discrepancy. A more plausible explanation? His infernal interest in Ryleigh laced her drinks with a placebic effect.

While his colleagues recorded notes on their laptops, Peter's aching fingers urged him to stave off typing until it became necessary. His election of a notebook and a fountain pen resulted in odd looks from those working around him.

A photographer examined the press badge pinned to Peter's sweater. He boasted a thick mustache that would have given a push broom a run for its money. "Ah, you're from the *Chronicle*. I didn't recognize you. Filling in for Matthews, I see."

Why yes, and I begged not to be here.

"I'm not particularly adept at covering sports."

He waved a hand. "There's nothing much to football."

Lies. Every play in the game confused Peter. Semi-familiar terms inched forth from the recesses of his memory: fumble, touchback, safety; if only he could remember their significance. Eavesdropping on the other journalists' remarks seemed like a good strategy to clarify important moments of the game. Peter found no success. They may as well have spoken a foreign language.

Attempting to detail a critical play from the first quarter proved disastrous. Crafting a catchy opener breeded agony. Peter operated on a mediocre cappuccino and overwrought brain cells, neither of which aided his ineptitude. The game had all but started and he was primed for a break.

Ryleigh cursed herself for agreeing to this third-wheel disaster as the trio scouted out seats on the crowded bleachers. If not for her and

Andrea's figurative blood oath, she would not be on this wingwoman suicide mission.

"What's up, Branson? Your date didn't show?"

Colin was the stark opposite of Andrea's clean-cut, preppy persona. He embodied the skater boy, give the finger to figures of authority type. Razor cut, shaggy blonde hair fell short of his eyes. But Colin was far from a bad boy, to Ryleigh's knowledge. Good grades. First string on the soccer team. These must have been redeeming qualities to Andrea.

Ryleigh ran her tongue along her teeth. "I'd rather drop dead than go out with someone at this school."

"It was a joke."

Highly doubt that.

"You're going to have to explain everything to me. I watch games with my dad sometimes, but the details sort of go over my head." Andrea's voice pitched, like she had inhaled a small dose of helium.

"Nah, this isn't football. You want to see *real* football? Come to our games in the spring."

For Christ's sake. Why didn't you bring a book to read, or your notebook? Where's your foresight?

Colin wrapped an arm around Andrea, and she leaned into the affection without hesitation. They looked like they had been matched together on some cheeseball dating show. It was enough to make Ryleigh gag. "I'll be back."

The lovebirds were too wrapped up in first date fantasyland to acknowledge their companion's exit. Several guys' enthusiastic whis-tles harassed Ryleigh as she ascended the bleacher steps. Some of them made innocent kissy faces while others mimed jerk-off motions. *Animals.*

Since she failed to bring anything along to occupy herself, she would have to improvise with what she had access to. No paper, no problem. Napkins would suffice. Ryleigh had written poems on napkins in the cafe, in a pinch. She ripped a handful from the metal dispenser and spun on her heel to ponder the attainment of the next item: a pen.

As if on cue, she spied Peter tossing a to-go cup into a nearby receptacle. An iciness more bone-chilling than the night's fall wind cocooned her. He wore a pewter sweater, pastel blue dress shirt layered beneath. Wild curls contained by gel. The hair on his face exceeded the classification of stubble, evidence of a trying week. Ryleigh's stomach twisted.

"Peter." Calling his name felt like swallowing a sword.

"Ryleigh? Hey." His cheekbones raised, but the warmth did not last. He motioned to the bleachers. "I have to get back. I just stepped away for a second."

Ryleigh dashed to stop him. "Can I ask a favor?"

"Depends on what the favor entails."

Flirtation edged his tone. *No, he's not flirting. That's how he always sounds, isn't it?* Is this what it meant to like a guy: transforming into a giddy schoolgirl flustered by low stakes chitchat? Ryleigh registered the idiocy of the question as it was verbalized. "Could I borrow a pen?"

Peter slid a fountain pen from his pocket. He held it out to her, and right as she tried to grab the pen, he retracted it. Ryleigh shivered when his gaze dipped below her face.

"This is my favorite pen. I expect you to take good care of it." He surrendered the sacred writing utensil, backing away toward the bleachers. "I also expect it back at the end of the night. I'll be out front."

Poetry sprouted wings and departed her mind. Ryleigh's possession of this wonderful pen gave her an excuse to see Peter again that night. That was more than enough to get her through this stupid game.

Once the crowd died down, Peter set up camp on a bench outside the stadium. His glaring inexperience murdered each new line in this catastrophic article. The late hour sharpened the breeze, numbing those who dared to step in its path. And he had neglected to bring a coat.

"Hey, stranger."

Ryleigh, coming to return his pen, no doubt. There were two culprits for the imminent termination of his job: this tanked story, or his newfound distraction. She had the story beat by miles.

"Hey, yourself. I have a bone to pick with you." Peter glanced at her amidst his typing, eyes bouncing between the notebook and computer screen to ensure he transferred the correct player's statistics.

"Don't worry, I have your pen."

"Nevermind the pen. You left me to suffer through a subpar cappuccino. I'll have you know your co-worker's shoddy craftsmanship is having a negative impact on my performance tonight."

She joined him on the bench. Even from a couple of feet away, the fruity smell of her perfume almost sent him into a coughing fit. Frayed rips in her black jeans widened when she crossed her legs. "If you want my schedule, just ask."

"Noted."

"Do you usually report on sports?"

"Hardly." He released a crude laugh. With a final stroke of the keys, he granted her his undivided attention. "What are you doing at a high school football game, anyway?"

"I have a cousin who goes here. There's this guy she likes and they came tonight sort of on a date. She asked me to tag along because she was nervous about hanging out with him for the first time and—why am I telling you this? You're busy. You don't want to hear about this kiddy drama."

Ryleigh's magnificence made his insides flush. The pen had been returned. Why she would stay to converse further befuddled him. "What are you doing here?"

She whipped her hair, exposing a glimmering studded ear to the biting wind. "What do you mean? I just told you."

Peter extended an arm over the top of the bench, shifting toward her. "I mean, what are you doing *here,* on this bench, talking to me? Shouldn't you be out at some rager, chugging a cheap drink while two guys fight over you, learning how to master the fine art of beer pong?"

"You want to know what I think?"

"Try me."

She slid along the bench, the space between them so narrow that their pants could have created static electricity. Featherlight arousal tantalized Peter's senses. Their closeness inflicted corporeal pain, testing restraint he no longer possessed.

"I think you leveraged your precious pen as an excuse to see me again tonight. Sue me for coming around to repay you for your generosity." Ryleigh brought her lips to his ear. Her hot breath emerged like steam, tickling his skin. "And for the record, you described the antithesis of my ideal evening."

She leaned into him and nothing else mattered.

Peter did not care that 11 p.m. neared. He did not care that his garbage story was due in half an hour.

Hushed, heated exhalations passed between them as their mouths collided. Her brazenness made him light-headed. Peter's thudding heartbeat flooded his ears with deafening palpitations.

Two years—it had been two years since he felt the tender embrace of a kiss. *Now's a fine time to reminisce about Kendall while you're making out with her co-worker.*

Flames crept up his calves and welded him to the spot. The thrill of this impromptu affection paralyzed him, but he did not mind. Peter supposed he could spend an eternity on that bench connected to this wonderful, witty woman.

Her lips parted when his chilled fingertips grazed her cheek, the sweetness of her trespassing tongue poised to induce a toothache. Ryleigh's mouth moved against his like they were accustomed to each other's rhythms.

They hardly knew each other, and yet she performed the intimate act with unsettling confidence.

His cell phone rang and interrupted their spontaneous bliss. Ryleigh pulled away, yanking on her sweater sleeves. Peter produced the device from his pocket and slid the green bar.

"Hey, Cliff. Still working on it."

"Are you coming back?" Mr. Roberts asked.

"I'm going to finish up and send it in. Pretty close."

"Alright. Watch the time."

Peter tapped the red icon on the display. Ryleigh stared at him, curling a strand of hair around her finger. He gestured to the phone. "My boss." Skin flushed, inarticulateness took hold. "That was — "

"Payment for the pen." She pushed off the bench.

A heaviness weighed on him in the face of her departure. What did Peter expect, exactly? That she would stay and chat as he finished the article? That they would ride away into the moonlight together upon its completion? He had learned his lesson about letting people in, no need to let history repeat itself.

Ryleigh backtracked toward the parking lot, calling, "Oh, hey, the next time you come by the shop, your drink's on the house. You know we have a satisfaction guarantee, right?"

"I'll take you up on that."

The kiss, pleasurable as it may have been, would be an isolated incident.

He would see to it.

6

PAGE THIRTEEN

Swathed in sheets, Peter rolled to the unoccupied side of the bed. His fatigued eyes attempted to decipher the red pixels on the dusty digital clock: 11:32 a.m.

Unwelcome bursts of reality greeted him as he adjusted to the daylight. Guilt weighed heavy like an anvil on his chest. The unexpected kiss with Ryleigh left him conflicted. She was a freshman in college; 18, no more than 19 years old.

He had gone out with younger women, but this age difference surpassed the realm of what was justifiable. Not to mention what a nightmare it would be if he brought someone Ryleigh's age home to meet his parents—or if she brought him home to meet hers.

Analyzing himself out of any potential romantic attachment had become an acquired skill, one that served as a shield for his fractured heart.

Nothing terrified him more than the institution of a relationship. Two people commit to each other, initiating a painful waiting game to see who will screw up the union. Peter had played that game once, and he had lost. The aftermath of which spawned the move to Connecticut with a few hundred dollars to his name and a broken spirit to boot.

He dressed for work while half-listening to the local news. Peter knew his damnable interest in Ryleigh prompted the unwanted trip down memory lane. No way could she be as vicious, as heartless, as … His fingers trembled as he fastened the last buttons on his pin-striped dress shirt. How had his life undergone such drastic changes since relocating to Harris? In California, he had a girlfriend, a close circle of friends, and his family.

Here, he had no one.

Whether he cared to admit it or not, his existence had become isolated and predictable. Something tugged at Peter's heart the more he pondered the subject. He turned up the volume on the news broadcast to drown out his self-reflection.

"Did I tell you Colin drove me home after the game? It was the sweetest," Andrea said as she and Ryleigh traversed the student parking lot.

"Yes, you've mentioned it three times now." An excited flutter spasmed in her stomach at the mention of the game. Andrea did not know Peter had been there, or about the pen, and definitely not about the kiss. She would have rather dived into traffic than interrupt Andrea's gushfest over Colin from calculus. Ryleigh fished for the keys buried in her backpack, wincing when her finger caught the sharp edge of a plastic folder. "Also, you two rode together so under what circumstance would he not drive you home?"

Ryleigh and Andrea had carpooled to and from school since junior year. Their neighborhoods were off the same road, and her parents appreciated the gesture. Despite Andrea's straight A's and good girl exterior, she misbehaved the second her parents turned their heads.

A car of her own? Not happening.

"My parents offered to pick me up, but we were having such a good time. I'm surprised they were cool about me riding home with him so late. You know how they are." Andrea buckled her seatbelt. "He invited me to the movies next weekend."

"He seems nice enough."

"What's that supposed to mean?"

"Most guys our age are immature jerks," Ryleigh neutralized her tone. Their differing opinions about guys resulted in tension on occasion. She adored crow's feet, whereas Andrea had a fascination with biceps; to each her own.

"Not all of them. Colin has his moments, though, I'll give you that," Andrea said. "Isn't today your first catering thing? And to think, a few weeks ago, they thought you couldn't be trusted with such great responsibility."

The catering event. Ryleigh had almost forgotten.

Her brain had been a mushy mess of nostalgia all day, replaying the way her and Peter's lips had aligned like they were custom made for each other. The soft scratch of his stubble bristling against her smooth skin. How his eyes seemed to beg for more once it was all said and done. Sweat collected in Ryleigh's palms, fusing her hands to the steering wheel.

"I wouldn't say they trust me, necessarily. I was their last resort. Oscar was going to handle it, but he had a family emergency. Kendall's staying behind to run the shop while I'm gone. Apparently, my boss trusts me more to go on a solo catering gig than to man the shop alone."

"You'll be fine, as long as you don't spill coffee on anyone," Andrea winked, gathering her belongings from the floorboard. Trekking up the Fuentes' driveway, she called, "See you tomorrow."

Ryleigh let down the passenger window. "I'll text you later and let you know how many people's skin I singed."

Everyone at *The Harris Chronicle* looked forward to the weekly staff meeting. Everyone but Peter. Ahead of the hour-long affair, the gossiping bunch of his coworkers crowded together to dish on the latest office-related drama. He likened his colleagues to wild animals permitted temporary relief from their usual state of captivity.

He swung by his office to drop off his bag and start up the computer. Behind him, a chorus of quiet voices hummed as people congregated in the conference room. Peter suppressed a yawn, raking through his thatch of curls. Weariness wore to his bones. Paying a visit to *The Roast* that afternoon would have been a mistake. How could he face Ryleigh and Kendall on the same shift, knowing that he had shared some form of intimacy with both women?

Their youngest reporter, Leo Asher, addressed Peter when he ducked into the hallway. "Today's the day, I can feel it. Roberts is going to give me a real assignment."

"Scholarships are real assignments."

"I've been on scholarships for months. I can be trusted with something a little more high profile." Leo was a junior in college, but his serious case of baby face could have fooled anyone.

"Do you know how long Roberts had me on scholarships when I started? Six months. I'd get comfortable if I were you." As they neared the central hub of the office, the entrancing aroma of fresh coffee assaulted his senses. The prospect of caffeine filled Peter with an artificial dose of charity. "Tell you what, Asher, do you like football?"

"Who doesn't?"

"Next time Roberts tries to dump a game on me, I'll slide it to you. If he gives you any trouble, just tell him I'm responsible."

Turning his head away from Leo, Peter nearly crashed into Ryleigh. *What is she doing here?* Breaths caught in his chest, in no hurry to seek freedom. She mouthed, 'Hey,' steadying the stack of dishes she held. Rubbing his jaw, he gave her a fractional nod. He wanted to smile at her, to ask how her weekend had been. The jaded recess of his soul dissuaded him from doing so.

From his seat, he watched Ryleigh waltz around the conference table, filling up the white coffee mugs. Several pieces of hair maneuvered their way out of her braid as she poured the coffee, from one person to the next. When she arrived at his mug, a whiff of that fruity perfume infiltrated his nose. Peter concentrated on her delicate hands steadying the carafe, fighting off the memory of her soft lips, the way she had whispered in his ear like a licensed seductress.

As much as he would have loved to forget the incident, his puzzlement surrounding it stalled him. She was young, gorgeous, witty.

What could she possibly want from him?

Two chairs later, the carafe ran dry. Ryleigh went to the refreshment area to refill it, giving Peter's neighbor an excuse to run his mouth. Though, the absence of an excuse had never stopped him, either.

"Completely non-conspicuous placement of your hands." Mike glanced at Peter's lap. "Nice to know you have blood running through those veins of yours. You know her?"

"Drop it, Corso."

He refused to indulge his colleague, who may as well have been accompanied by a club and a giant turkey leg.

"Alright, ladies and gents." Mr. Roberts slung his behemoth planner onto the table. His coarse white hair strayed from its usual parting, sticking up as if he had tumbled around in a field of dryer sheets. "I don't want to be here anymore than you do, so let's get this over with."

"Earlier today, I was informed Matthews is extending his leave. Since Rosenfeld can't tell a damn tennis racquet from a baseball bat, I need somebody else to pick up the slack in sports this week."

Peter's ribs compressed like an accordion. Ryleigh squeezed her lips together, but it did not aid in shielding her profound amusement. He could have died right then, inadequacies on full display.

"I'd like to take a stab at it, sir," Leo said.

"There's a lot of moving parts when you cover sports. It'll make your pretty little head spin. Your time will come, Asher." Mr. Roberts scanned the staff. "What about ... Corso?"

Peter's gaze split between Mr. Roberts yapping about the schedule and Ryleigh idling in the corner. Enduring her hour-long presence was like a recovering heroin addict confined to a room with nothing but a needle. As much as he craved to inject her affections into his veins, that stellar high would be riddled with side effects he was unqualified to handle.

Having retained nothing from the meeting, Peter returned to his office hoping to stifle his panic stricken inner dialogue with the melodic clicking of the keyboard. Ryleigh packed up and left the conference room short of the hour wrapping up. The tension in his chest lingered long after she had gone.

As he sifted through his e-mail, a knock reverberated on the door. *Could it be her?* No, it was Mike. He leaned on one side of Peter's desk and jutted his chin out.

"You alluded, not so subtly, to my erection in front of the entire conference room. You think I want to talk to you?" Peter keyed a response to the head of the farmer's market, who had inquired about coverage for the close of their season. "This better be important."

"C'mon Pete. What's the story with you and that girl?"

"Call me Pete again and you're permanently banned from my office. She's my barista. What's it to you?"

"Provided that you don't have anything going on with her, I thought maybe you could get me her number, put in a good word?" Mike managed to come off as a complete creep, as per usual.

A wicked seed of an idea planted itself inside Peter's mind, so wicked that he hesitated to follow through with it. Keeping weirdos like Mike at bay seemed like a sufficient reason to deliver the forthcoming white lie.

"I'd stay away from her unless you're trying to land yourself on page thirteen." While he found the joke humorous, Mike did not seem to understand it judging by his immovable grimace. "How long have you worked here? You don't know what's on page thirteen? Mugshots galore. She's in high school, Corso."

You're going straight to hell for this.

"Damn, that blows." Mike's testosterone-driven enthusiasm deflated. He paused midway to the door. "Not to knock you down from your holier than thou high horse, but need I remind you, *you* were the one with tight pants over this girl."

7

ETHICS LADDER

*D*ays without seeing Peter morphed into weeks. Each chime of the door's bell incited a higher degree of dread as someone other than him entered the shop. By the end of the third week, she was sure he was avoiding her.

Ryleigh had cleaned the same table for five minutes. The aching in her wrist from the repetitive, circular motion did not disrupt her fleeting subconscious. Had she been wrong to kiss Peter? He certainly had not come back for seconds. Why had he hung her out to dry? Her mental state crumbled and eroded like ancient rock formations as she tried to answer these questions. Questions only he could answer.

She had to see him.

Kendall danced at the sink while cleaning the blenders. The heavy bass line of hard rock droned on in her headphones, creating a static hum in the shop. Upon her migration to the espresso machine, Ryleigh urged, "Hey, I'll clean that. I'm making a drink on the way out."

She let her headphones rest on her neck. Kendall's forehead scrunched, wrinkling her sepia skin. "You're going to see him, aren't you?"

"I'm just bringing him coffee." Her hand rubbed along the side of her jeans. "And maybe my phone number."

45

"I gave him my number, once upon a time."

Spots obscured Ryleigh's vision. Had they been ex-lovers, their hostile attitudes toward each other now made perfect sense. A pulling sensation hooked in her gut. Kendall and Peter were much closer in age.

"I didn't know you two had history. I don't want—"

"I'd barely clock it as history, and we're still friends, somehow, in spite of it." She shrugged into her leather jacket, lagging by the door. "Big sister advice? He's a whole lot of mess for someone your age to try to deal with."

Kendall meant well, but Ryleigh had already made her decision. One brush with Peter's coarse lips had transformed her into a lovesick teenager. She refused to let him slip away, not when she had barely skimmed the surface of everything that could be. When would she meet a guy like this again? A sharp dresser with a smart mouth and a knee-buckling smile.

Her years of abstaining from the barbaric ritual of dating had not been in vain. She had been waiting for him.

Adrenaline raced through Ryleigh and overshadowed any fear of rejection. Once the cappuccino was made, she ripped a page from her poetry journal, folded it, and placed it in her jean pocket. She stepped outside, bounding across the street with her heart on her sleeve.

Ryleigh grew ill at the prospect of seeing Peter. The initial excitement had fizzled out. Alone in the elevator, she had a hot drink and cold feet. Not to mention the poem nestled at her rear; the one she had written that day in the shop when he stole her table. The sliding of the chrome doors sealed her fate. Nausea held her in a vise grip as she crossed the threshold into the bustling workspace.

A woman with a comically long neck eyed her the moment she invaded the office. Short, choppy hair framed her face, which retained a spectacular angle for her age. She was one of those women who you were shocked to hear were 15 years older than they appeared.

"May I help you?" The woman unscrewed the cap on a bottle of white-out, elbows resting on a desk calendar. A metal plate on the desk declared her as 'Ms. Walters.'

Ryleigh presented the cappuccino. "I wanted to drop this off for Peter."

"Which Peter would that be? We have two."

She had seen his last name a thousand times on his loyalty account, she had overheard it at the catered meeting, and yet it evaded her. "He's tall, curly dark hair ..."

"Odd. Cranky Peter never gets visitors." Ms. Walters looked Ryleigh up and down as if she were an alien lifeform. "Rosenfeld's office is 307. Down the hall, take a left, second door on the right."

Cranky Peter? *Some reputation this guy has.*

It turned out the instructions Ms. Walters provided were unnecessary. A gold placard mounted to the left of each door proclaimed the office number and its occupant. 303, Greene, closed door. 305, Asher, light off. 307, Rosenfeld, door wide open and light on. No Peter.

The computer chair had been rolled away from the desk. On the monitor, the cursor blinked, awaiting the formation of ensuing words. There were no personal mementos, save the amusing 'Trust me, I'm a journalist' coffee mug.

Discomfort blazed through Ryleigh like flame conquering a kerosene-soaked rope. The walls of the space closed in and immobilized her in a circle of inaction. She could not stand there forever, stressing the possible appearance of a man whom she had kissed once.

Just put it on his desk and bolt.

Her paddle ball heartbeat pummeled against her chest. Placing the cappuccino and poem beside his keyboard felt criminal. Ryleigh stared at her cherry red boots. What would her parents say about her gallivanting around with someone who knows how much older than herself?

Peter's scratchy voice froze her hand as she reached to retract the coffee. "Didn't know you guys delivered."

Ryleigh turned around. "You've been avoiding me."

Fine, red lines had constructed highways in his tired eyes. His thin face drooped like a flower thirsting for rain. Cruelness marred the usual frailty of his smile. "Oh, you noticed that, huh?"

Ryleigh's lungs constricted at his staggering audacity. How dare he speak to her like this after the transcendence they had shared. Had he not felt the same, extraordinary, toe-curling spark when their lips met?

"Maybe I shouldn't have come." She tried to move past him but he caught her below the shoulders. Her muscles weakened despite the lightness of his touch, and her limbs trembled when he let her go.

"I'm sort of glad you did."

"You can't kiss me like that and then act like I don't exist." Ryleigh swallowed her embarrassment. He could hear her out. He owed her that much. That headstrong act faltered as she whimpered, "I have feelings."

A balding guy passing through the hall snorted. "Page thirteen. Good one, bud."

"Beat it, Corso," Peter shouted. His thumb and index finger did a split across his forehead. "Look, I understand you have feelings, alright? I'm keeping my distance out of respect for your feelings. Because, emotionally, I'm unavailable."

Ryleigh grabbed a fistful of his sweater, resulting in a clumsy collision of their bodies. "If I asked you to kiss me again, right here, right now, would you?"

"No. No, I-I can't."

"I should go." She surrendered her hold on the sweater.

"What's that? A love note?" Peter alluded to the folded paper, recovering from a stuttering imbecile to the prince of snark in record time. And while his pointed remarks normally made Ryleigh's nerve endings tingle, this one left her gutted, numb.

"Take it as it resonates."

Mike's derisive mention of page thirteen triggered a cacophony of neuroses. High school joke aside, a college freshman hardly qualified as a higher rung on the ethics ladder. She was practically half his age. Peter knew he liked her, and that horrifying admission complicated everything tenfold.

"Emotionally unavailable. That was the best you could come up with?" Peter muttered to himself after she had gone.

The bullshit excuse sounded a hell of a lot better than 'I'm terrified of anything with a vagina.'

Of course he had wanted to kiss her. How could he not with those doll-like eyes and smug lips angled up at him? Kissing would lead them to the messy tango of other intimate dealings, experiences that were better left untouched. Peter had endured enough sexual humiliation for this lifetime.

A meticulously crafted heart in the center of the cappuccino's foam stared back at him, making him regret how he had handled the situation. The remnants of the artwork disappeared throughout the course of the hour, fading into the lake of coffee like it had never existed.

His nervous stomach deterred him from drinking it.

The night crept by as he grappled with the Ryleigh dilemma. He edited the same story three times before submitting it, only to have one of his co-workers send it back to his desk flagged with careless errors. Thoughts of her clouded his ability to focus on correcting the article. Ryleigh's hurt had engraved itself into his brain, as if it were his own. Her watery eyes pleaded with him, her cracked voice recounting, 'Take it as it resonates.'

When he opened his eyes, his gaze wandered to that pastel pink slip of paper. No one had ever written him a love note. Maybe it was presumptuous to refer to it as such.

Peter figured he may as well read it before throwing it in the trash. Her smudged cursive filled the page, the same looping penmanship in which she scrawled his name onto his many to-go cups.

Eyes haunted by fatigue
Rings of fire guarding graying amber fossils

Brows lay flat in surrender to the mundanity of life
Arches vanished in the absence of having anything to contest
An inexpressive mouth conceals the wonderment of his perfectly imper-
fect grin
When those thin lips part to expose crooked teeth
His face blooms, a spring garden shaking off winter's burden
Crow's feet take up roost, glorious creases of skin mimicking sharp talons
Laugh lines surround the smile, mirroring rippled water
Just as tranquil
But summer's heat is merciless
The once hopeful buds of spring were never meant to last

His fingers ghosted over the lines. Why had she wasted these lyrical words on him? Peter's cool olive complexion blanched as he deciphered the string of digits beneath the poem.

Her phone number.

"So, what's the big news you've brought us here to discuss?" Andrea, ever the gossiper, did not waste time with formalities. Ryleigh had invited her to their favorite lunch spot under the pretense of filling her in on 'guy-related developments.' She predetermined to omit the part where Peter acted like a dick. "Are you still pining after that news guy?"

"I brought him a cappuccino after my shift the other night." Ryleigh swirled the straw in her cup. "I can't believe this place still uses straws. They must not watch the news. These are killing marine life, you know."

Andrea choked on her soft drink. "You just showed up at his office? Unannounced? That's psycho."

If she knew about the kiss she wouldn't say that.

Ryleigh shoved a guacamole-laden chip into her mouth, a display of innocent indifference. "I was going to leave it on his desk and get the hell out of there, until he walked in on my not so stealthy opera-tion." She paused for a beat, debating whether she should reveal the more damning part of her quest. "This is going to sound like I've gone insane, because it's so off-base for me, but I gave him my number."

"Who are you and what have you done with my best friend?" Andrea's eyes bordered on popping out of their sockets. "How old is he, anyway? Never mind. It's your life. Did you hear from him?"

"No, not yet. How did your date go?"

"Fine." Andrea wrinkled her nose, as she did whenever an unpleasant topic arose. "He tried to make out with me halfway through the movie, and I totally shut him down, which pissed him off. Don't get me wrong, I like him, a lot. That's why I'm trying to take it slow."

"He shouldn't get pissy with you for not wanting to do something that makes you uncomfortable. They make PSA's about guys like that."

"Exactly. That was our first official date, and he was reaching for privileges he has yet to earn, if you catch my drift."

Ryleigh's phone created an unpleasant buzzing against the wooden booth. She flipped it over, throat going dry at the display. The lock screen illuminated with a message from an unsaved number. Each word contained within the notification escalated the already discon-certing rate of her pulse: *Had I read the poem first, I might have kissed you.*

8

PROOF

Ryleigh came in through the garage, wiggling out of her boots and shrugging off her coat. Her fuzzy socks muffled her descent to the kitchen. Anticipation ruled each step. Peter texted her the same time every afternoon, like clockwork, as she arrived home and he headed to work. Their secret, technological connection spawned euphoria.

It was all hers.

Her mother stirred something in the slow cooker, aka whatever Ryleigh and her father would be eating for dinner. Charlotte sported loungewear, savoring each minute of tranquility before reporting to the hospital later that evening. The alternating series of three days on and three days off either left her anxious to get back to the emergency room after idling at home, or exhausted when returning from a string of night shifts.

"How was school?"

"Barely made it out alive." Ryleigh snagged a bottle of water from the refrigerator. It was comical how health conscious her parents were, but no matter how hard she tried, there was no convincing them to become environmentally conscious. She hopped onto one of the stools lining the island.

"Believe it or not, I'm going to miss that sarcasm when you move out." Charlotte propped an elbow on the counter and adopted a speculative stare, marking the distinct transition into snooping parent mode. "Is Andrea still seeing that new guy?"

"Colin? Yeah, they're attached at the hip, hence why I'm cooped up in the house lately." She eased her phone out of her jean pocket to peek at the screen. A new message from Peter had arrived seven minutes earlier.

P: Kendall is 100% done with my beverage remaking shenanigans. Why is it that my coffee tastes exponentially better when you make it? I'm convinced there's some extra step or secret ingredient you're keeping from me. At any rate, I think it would be beneficial for the three of us if you sent me your schedule.

R: i'll send a screenshot for your convenience. as far as your conspiracy theory goes, i guess you'll never know.

"When are you going to bring around a Colin?"

"Trust me, mom, whenever I finally do bring a guy home he won't resemble Colin in the slightest." Ryleigh scrolled through her photo album until she located the picture of her schedule. "Speaking of, how would you feel if I went out with someone older?"

R: here you go, grumpy pants. plan your trips accordingly.

Charlotte perked up. "Dad and I would have to meet him, see how he behaves around you. But we're talking a few years older, right? College aged?"

"Of course."

P: Text me when you're on your 15 tomorrow.

R: hold on a second … did the emotionally unavailable Peter Rosenfeld just admit to missing me?

P: I may miss you, but my walls are up. Solitude is bliss.

"Thank god you found someone close to your age. And here I thought you'd never come off your affinity for wrinkles." Ryleigh wanted to slam her face against the granite at that remark, but then Charlotte would have spent 10 minutes examining her for possible injuries. "So, who's this mystery guy that has you rapt? Would I know of him?"

"No, I've never mentioned him." *At least it's not a lie.* She sensed her mother's calculating mind darting from place to place. Ryleigh shimmied off the stool before Charlotte could unload any more questions. "I'm going to head upstairs and do some homework. Calculus is endangering my GPA."

Peter's jarring sunny disposition frightened his coworkers. The random acts of kindness he initiated around the office turned heads, which extended to taking on unwanted photo assignments—never mind the fact that he was the worst photographer on staff. Ryleigh's virtual company cushioned whatever transpired in real time. Her frequent communications had him so high, he might have volunteered to cover an entire weekend of football.

Felicity shot down to his marrow whenever the brewing coffee text tone played. He could not recall a time he was this caught up with a woman, because he had never been this caught up with anyone.

His last relationship had not incited this visceral reaction. Heather Barnes had waltzed across the quad of their college campus, hair blowing in the breeze like a model, and asked him out. This bold action should have told Peter all he needed to know about her, and all of his assumptions rang true throughout their relationship. Heather was bossy and quick to make decisions for both of them, whether he agreed or disagreed with the outcome.

While he had not quite fallen in love, it was his first and only serious relationship. The pairing meant something to him; it bore significance, even if he could not define it.

Ryleigh had him under the influence of something akin to inspiration. Peter poured more effort into his stories than he thought possible, even the god awful county fair piece. He grimaced while writing a line describing a pie in the face game that forced him to ponder the value of his existence.

"No errors tonight. Are you trying to run me out of my job?" Levi, the senior copy editor, said as he passed Peter's office.

"On cloud nine over here."

It was inconceivable how one small change could bestow upon him this renewed vigor for everything in his life. The next message that came through dampened his upbeat attitude and brought back the familiar, neurotic personality he had developed during adulthood.

R: even solitary guys need dates. are you free saturday?

P: How's your night going?

Not acknowledging her previous text was a dick move. He did not have the heart to outright deny the request, but he could not go along with her invitation without experiencing a tsunami of guilt and self-doubt.

It was better this way.

Peter understood with great anguish that it was too late to implement the tried and true barrier of distance, for each day he found himself more drawn to her companionship. Ryleigh had latched onto him like a parasite. If only she knew of the tortuous grip she had on his pitiful heart.

Every fiber of his being wanted to tell her yes. Physically, he would not allow himself to type that single, damaging word and press 'send' with a clear conscience. She kissed him. She gave him her phone number. *And yet.* He felt sick to his stomach staring at Ryleigh's text.

In the following seconds, the universe offered guidance in the form of a cruel twist of fate.

"Karma is a beautiful thing, don't you think, Pete?" Mike swept into the room, unannounced. He gripped a rolled-up newspaper. "You didn't proof last night, did you?"

"Whatever innocuous thing you barged in here to present me with can wait. It's not the best time. And what did I say about calling me Pete?"

"There's nothing innocuous about this. It's wholly relevant to you and your predicament." A hard smile ironed itself onto his face as he slapped the paper onto Peter's keyboard. "Flip to Asher's piece."

He thumbed through the pages in search of the scholarship section. "You're infuriating, Corso, you know that? I'm slammed tonight, and if you think—"

Heat rose behind Peter's eyelids, each letter of the headline branding itself into his skull. Star Student: 2018 Recipient of Beckwith Poetry Scholarship.

Below the title was a picture of none other than Mr. Beckwith, shaking hands with a certain charcoal-haired barista. His stomach lurched at the implication the article brought forth, but dysphoria soon weighed down that unease. The bold cutline stated, 'William Beckwith congratulates Victory Hills senior Ryleigh Branson.'

She had braces in the photo. *Braces.*

"You've got to be fucking kidding me."

9

CUTLINE

yleigh perched on the curb outside the shop, ass frozen to the asphalt. The tights she had chosen for the day were much too thin. Bumps prickled her skin beneath the icy caress of the November afternoon. Looking nice for Peter had trumped any consideration for the weather.

She would have waited an eternity like that, freezing and miserable, for a chance to catch a glimpse at one of his lop-sided smiles. One which bared his wonderfully semi-misaligned teeth. Peter's smile was the most beautiful thing she had ever seen, the unofficial eighth wonder of the world.

R: i'm on break.

Uncertainty weighted her fingers as she composed the brief message. He had ignored her invitation for a date, and that stung more than she cared to admit.

"I've noticed you and Peter are getting on well. He's been uncharacteristically cheery." Kendall slouched against the street sign, pulling a heavy drag from her cigarette. She turned her head toward the street and exhaled the smoke. A slow smile built in her profile. "Did you fuck him?"

Ryleigh could have disappeared into the sewer at her feet. The connotation of the word 'fuck' and its linkage to Peter made her insides flip flop. "What?"

"Point blank. Did you fuck him?"

"Jesus. No. We text. That's it."

"What I'm getting at is, I know you like him, and I'm sure it's only a matter of time before something happens between the two of you. In the name of full disclosure, we kind of had a one-night-stand."

Her mind involuntarily wandered to Kendall and Peter in such a scenario. Ryleigh's muscles tightened as the hot current of jealousy flowed through her veins. "How do you *kind* of have a one-night-stand?"

Kendall flicked the cigarette into the gutter. She pulled the shop's door ajar. "Let me know when you've been in bed with the guy, and then we'll talk."

Ryleigh brimmed with the urge to press for details, but a towering man advancing toward the cafe caught her off guard. Peter's long, slender legs carried him at an unthinkable pace in her direction. She could not decipher if his face strained as a result of the uncompromising sunlight, or if it came from a place of indignation. Sticking around to find out seemed like an ill-inspired idea. She stood and brushed off her tights, retreating inside The Roast.

"Ryleigh," she heard him shouting as he proceeded to trail her into the shop.

Hurrying behind the counter, she slid on her apron and pretended to settle back into work.

Peter appeared frowzier than usual. His curls were askew in every direction, a byproduct of the unforgiving wind, and his clothes needed a good ironing. Even in this disheveled state, she found him criminally attractive.

"Can I help you, sir?" Ryleigh asked as he reached the register. She knew he would not be amused by the feigned cluelessness, but was encouraged by her love of agitating him.

"Did you not hear me calling you outside?"

"Of course I did." She spoke a notch above a whisper.

"You could've acknowledged me."

"I could say the same." Ryleigh blamed residual envy for her onslaught of pettiness.

"Why do you think I'm here, standing in front of you?" Peter gestured around the shop. His shouting lacerated the hushed bubble guarding their conversation and gathered every patron's interest. He lowered his voice, lids raised at half-mast over his red-rimmed eyes. "I'm not trying to embarrass you, alright? But we need to talk. Now."

"Can you two break up after I order my caramel latte?" The woman crossed her arms and adjusted her handbag, tapping the polished concrete floor with a flat-clad foot.

Peter oozed faux cordiality. "What's your name?"

"Suzanne."

"Well, you know what, Suzanne? You can fuck off." He pointed to the exit like he expected the poor woman to obey the command. Planting a hand on his paper-thin waist, he continued, "I have some business to attend to, and I'm not leaving until it's straightened out. Take a hike, lady."

"I'll take her order," Kendall whispered to Ryleigh, replacing her station at the register. "Why don't you and hothead step outside? Talk things through."

Suzanne shot Peter a scathing scowl as Ryleigh yanked the cuff of his dress shirt, tugging him along like a misbehaved child. Her thoughts soon matched the tempo of her erratic heartbeat. Though their contact was minimal, she felt the vibrations of his fury as if they had been bonded on a molecular level.

Saliva pooled in her mouth as she guided him through the storage room where they emerged in the alleyway. The hold she had on Peter's lithe wrist should have sent her stomach into a frenzy of flutters.

But Ryleigh was too pissed to feel butterflies.

"Are you crazy? Are you trying to get me fired? What's your deal, anyway? I should be the one who's angry. I asked you to hang out and you ignored me."

The flash flood of accusations rushed from her mouth, but they hardly registered with Peter. A deep berry was smeared across her lips, and, having never seen her in lipstick, he selfishly wondered if she had worn it for him.

He stood against the black brick wall to put some space between them. Because, in spite of the truth stowed away in his pocket, his adoration of Ryleigh had not waned. His heart and mind waged a nasty custody battle. Winner takes all. On the surface, he decided it was best to play defense.

Nails biting into his palms, he snapped, "We're not hanging out this weekend, or next weekend, or any weekend. Forget it."

"I don't understand." The sentence came out stilted, broken. Those desperate syllables fought to be heard through her breathiness.

He rummaged in his khaki pocket for the folded piece of newspaper, thrusting it into her hands. "Would you mind telling me what the *fuck* this is?"

She unfurled the paper. Realization flickered across her features before reverting to their guarded neutrality. If she confessed now, it would not make a difference.

Honesty did not count as an afterthought.

Ryleigh toyed with her fishtail braid. "I did that interview before we met. I didn't think they would run it this late. I completely forgot about it."

"We must be running low on material because *there* it is." Peter fired a finger at the article in her trembling hands. "You must have seen this yesterday. I'm sure your parents have it taped to the fridge."

"They don't … nevermind, it doesn't matter." Her pale complexion lost its radiance. "Peter, I'm sorry."

He snatched the page from her. "Are you? Were you, at any point, planning to tell me that you're in *high school*? Did it occur to you, even once, that crucial detail may be of interest to me? You don't realize how much pushback I could get for this."

"When were you going to tell me about Kendall?"

Peter's breathing abated at the name drop. Humiliation reared its ugly head whenever he thought of that night. Hopefully she had spared Ryleigh the specifics.

"What happened between us is irrelevant. I don't owe you an explanation." Tongue in cheek, he gratuitously inhaled. "You, on the other hand, have a lot of explaining to do."

Shuffling forward in her combat boots, she halted an inch from his worn loafers. Ryleigh bore no indication that his height or flinty stare intimidated her. "If anything, you encouraged me to lie with your assumption."

"Just because I saw your textbook and asked a question *thinking* you were in college doesn't give you an out to lie about it."

"Okay, your good looks and adorably cynical remarks may have swayed my judgment. When you thought I was in college, I went with it."

Peter crouched to the ground, blurting, "We kissed, dammit. If I had known—for God's sake, I have a reputation to uphold."

"Your reputation is safe from scandal. I'm 18. It's not like I'm underage. Wouldn't that be worse?"

"Wouldn't that be worse? Listen to yourself."

Ryleigh stared down at his hunched form. Adoration shone in her eyes, but that unabashed sweetness twisted itself like a knife in his gut, eviscerating everything that comprised his 160 pound being.

She could never know the depth of that hurt.

Wanting her in the way he did may not have been criminal, though in regard to morality it yielded a red octagonal sign.

"You're a nice girl, and you're one hell of a barista." A painful tightness apprehended his throat, as if choked by the finality of the speech. "But I don't think it's the best idea for us to explore beyond our usual roles. Do you understand what I'm saying?"

Her powerless voice concurred, "Loud and clear."

1 0

MALE LEAD

*P*eter perched at the espresso bar, looking on as Kendall flew to the different coffee apparatuses, hustling alongside Oscar to curb the after-school crowd.

It was not yet time to head into the office, but he had come to favor the shop over the numbing silence of his condo. The stillness that usually brought him comfort wreaked havoc on his frenetic psyche.

At least the buzzing customers and whirring appliances succeeded in keeping thoughts of Ryleigh at bay.

He had obtained her schedule from Kendall so as to avoid unnecessary run-ins. The mere memory of her face made Peter's chest ache; who knows what physiological horrors would plague him if he were to see her again, in the flesh.

A dark blue mug on a matching saucer inched toward him across the counter. His eyes flitted up to where Kendall stood on the other side of the bar. She nodded at the cappuccino, donning her 'are you alright?' look which pinched her brows together and tugged at the corner of her mouth.

"Drink up, sourpuss."

And then she swept off to deal with the squadron of prep-school regulars.

One sip of the beverage turned his stomach, taste buds set off by an unmistakable, though decidedly slight, discrepancy between Ryleigh's and Kendall's cappuccinos that had bugged him for weeks.

He spoke a notch above the noise, loud enough for Kendall to hear despite the sputtering steaming wand. "Did you know? About her being in high school?"

Swapping the to-go cup for a glass of water, she cleaned the frother, lashes fluttering his way. "I swear, man, I had no idea. She doesn't seem like a high school kid though, does she?"

"I see what you're trying to do Ken, and while I appreciate it, I've already played the justification game."

"But you're into her, right?" Kendall dispensed a swirl of whipped cream onto a frozen drink, snapped a lid on it, and placed it on the pick-up counter, calling out, "Medium pumpkin pie freezer, almond milk."

Peter reclined in the barstool, fists in his pockets. He snorted, "Oh, sure, I *was*, before I found out that she's basically a child. I feel like a real creep. I'm no better than Corso."

She tipped her head toward the ceiling and unleashed a sardonic laugh. "Don't you ever compare yourself to that animal co-worker of yours. Believe it or not, underneath that unapproachable, sandpaper exterior, you're an alright guy, Rosenfeld." In a lower voice, she mumbled, "Even if you have the stamina of a teenage boy."

Christ, can't we get past that? His eyes closed momentarily as a beet red swarmed his cheeks.

"Excuse me," came the nasally voice of a prep-school kid. Callista Morales. Peter had recently interviewed her for placing four consecutive years in the state's extemporaneous speaking competition. She was a senior, same as Ryleigh. But his stomach did not perform kick-flips as he glanced at Callista in her pressed uniform, because he was, in fact, not a creep.

Ryleigh was the exception to the rule. That was all.

Glossy pink lip curled, she said, "I ordered almond milk. Do you really think I wanted whipped cream? I'm *vegan*."

Kendall popped the lid and started spooning away the offensive topping. "I apologize. Whipped cream comes on all of our freezers. We're happy to exclude it if you let us know while you're ordering."

Callista narrowed her hazel eyes.

"Are you serious? You're just going to skim it off the top and expect me to drink it, pretending all the while there aren't dairy microbes infesting my coffee? I don't think so."

Managing a curt nod, Kendall replied in an unbelievably even tone, "I'll remake it for you. Not a problem."

One could not afford to be impolite with rent due in New England.

"She's young, so what?" she asked while scooping ice into the blender. Thick spoonfuls of pumpkin puree, espresso, almond milk, and syrup joined the ice. "She's single. You're single. Give it a shot."

Peter fished a five out of his wallet, setting it beside the coffee he could not bring himself to drink. He wanted to heed Kendall's advice, but at that idea, an ache rang out in his hollow body.

Because he could never have something casual with Ryleigh; she would get too attached and he would wind up hurt. Again. Or worse, he would hurt her.

"Yeah. That's not happening."

"What's up with you tonight? You're totally bummed." Andrea flicked a piece of popcorn at Ryleigh, and it bounced off her cheek.

Saturdays were designated sleepover nights: popcorn, ginger ale in champagne flutes, and a cheesy romance movie marathon. A long-standing tradition.

Ryleigh refreshed the lockscreen on her phone for the millionth time. A crack splintered in her soul with that blank screen staring back at her. She had royally screwed up.

"It's not a big deal."

"You're a pathetic liar, Ry." Andrea aimed the remote at her television. "Clearly, it is a big deal, because this movie has your most hated type of male lead, and not once have I heard you mockingly ask if he conditions his beard or if he dry cleans all of that plaid."

The breath Ryleigh pulled in nicked her insides like tiny shards of glass. Would Andrea understand? Perhaps that did not matter. An ear to vent to sounded nice.

"I told Peter I was a freshman at Hemlock. He noticed my psych book one day and I panicked."

"Excuse me, you what?"

"He found out I was lying, of course, right? But it wasn't my pathetic lying skills that nailed me. He found my scholarship article. God, he brought it to the shop and presented it as evidence, like I was on trial."

"You should've told him from the start. At least you're 18, though." Andrea bit her thumbnail.

"That's what I said. Let me tell you, he was none too impressed with that defense." Ryleigh stared at the comforter, startled by memories of the confrontation. The bit with Kendall may have stung, but she had overreacted. He had been right. He owed her nothing. "He was … furious."

She sat criss-cross, chin resting on her palm. "Sounds like an asshole, if you ask me. I mean, yeah, you lied, but it's not like you guys did anything."

The pilot light of Ryleigh's embarrassment roared and flayed her skin to a crisp. When Andrea figured it out, she was left to wonder what gave it away: the dead silence or the pink, perspiring skin.

"Jesus, how much shit have you been keeping from me?"

"We made out the night of the Creek Bend game. Don't get your hopes up, I don't have any crude details to report."

"Hold on." Andrea scrambled for the remote and turned the movie off. The brooding lumberjack had lost his novelty. "You have to give me something after dropping that. Was he a good kisser, or what? 'Cause he kind of seems like a dork."

Melancholia swirled in the pit of Ryleigh's soul. The mere mention of that kiss simultaneously made her toes curl and heart crack, knowing that she may never feel those lips again. "The best."

A small rock pelted against Andrea's window, preceded by another. And another.

"I told him not to come by tonight," she mumbled as she undid the latches and lifted the window. Ryleigh migrated to the pneumonia hole, praying that whatever idiocy Colin had on display might distract from her internal pity party. Andrea glanced at her. "Christ, he knows Saturday nights are sacred."

Colin had on a t-shirt and cargo shorts in full defiance of the early December night. His skateboard lay discarded on the grass. Even from the second floor of the Fuentes' house, the girls could see his slack expression, as if he were a recent victim of lobotomy.

"What are you doing here? Did you not read my messages?" Andrea whisper yelled.

"I missed you," his voice blurted, stupid and too loud. He rubbed his eyes, squinting up at his girlfriend like she was out of focus.

She huffed a pathetic laugh. "You saw me this morning, and you'll see a lot more of me at school this week."

"Just let me in, Andy."

"Do you want my dad to kick your ass? Go ahead, ring the bell." Colin, unable to register sarcasm in his zonked state, moped toward the front door. Andrea halted him. "You're obviously stoned out of your mind. I can smell you from here. Go home. Call me tomorrow."

Ryleigh's chin poked forward at her friend's election of 'call me tomorrow,' painfully aware that Peter would not be reaching out to her anytime soon.

"Is it that time of the year already?" Dr. Kennedy chuckled as he waltzed into the examination room, closing the door behind him.

"I guess so."

Peter was in no mood to put up with Maxwell Kennedy and his

tenor chuckle, his too white coat, his jolly disposition. He wanted to return home and mourn the loss of a girl who was never his.

"I know you're not too terribly fond of these visits, so we'll make it quick." Dr. Kennedy readied his pen and clipboard. "Do you feel as if you've seen any improvement over the last 12 months?"

He had gone through great lengths to avoid the yearly check-in to get his medication refilled. Once, he managed to get an emergency prescription by phoning the nurse and explaining that he could not afford the annual appointment. Peter's keenness to cheat the system backfired, though, when he realized that the temporary supply would only stave off his appointment one extra month.

"No." Peter tilted his head from side to side. "Not until recently."

"What caused the sudden shift, if I may ask?"

"The answer is horribly cliché." He paused, debating whether he wanted to sound weak at the feet of his own psychiatrist. "I met a girl."

"Hey, good for you, that's great news," Dr. Kennedy manufactured a cheerful response, attention diverted from the papers scattered atop his lap. "We can scale back to 60 milligrams a day if you think you're ready. If you're not feeling right after a few weeks, we can switch back to your usual."

His mother had persuaded him to surrender to the help of medication, especially after his 'incident,' as she preferred to call it. Sitting here discussing a potential romantic entanglement was ludicrous considering a woman had landed Peter in this office in the first place.

"I'll stick with the 80. I just met this girl, I don't want to scare her away."

What are you talking about? Do you hear yourself?

Peter had essentially handed Ryleigh an eviction notice from his heart, and here he was yammering on to his psychiatrist like she was this crucial, albeit new, part of his life.

Dr. Kennedy offered an uncharacteristic bit of wisdom as he handed Peter the script. "You have to hold onto whatever happiness you find in this world."

11

SEVENTEEN YEARS

Peter's silence made Ryleigh's poetry skew in an agitated direction, but she had never been more prolific. Bitter verses flowed from the tip of her pen, a relentless fountain of spite. She had no shortage of words to describe his stubbornness and her stupidity.

Ryleigh remained expectant her phone would ring, that Peter would somehow reach out to say he had changed his mind.

The message never came. The phone never rang.

Cue the greasy hair and three-day-old socks. She supposed this is how romance worked in the movies: getting all hung up on a guy and granting permission for the entire flow of daily life to stop or go based on their say-so.

"Meet me downstairs in five," Charlotte called from the hallway. Seconds later, her ballet flats clicked on the wooden staircase.

Ryleigh slipped on fresh socks and spritzed her mess of hair with dry shampoo. Not much could have been done to rescue her fatigued appearance in five minutes. She would have to roll with disaster.

The thought of leaving the house was unappealing, but this instance was non-negotiable. Once a week, she accompanied her mother to the grocery store. The routine sanctity of the shopping trip became their ritual since they were unable to spend much time together between their busy schedules.

An indistinguishable song whispered through the speakers in the Bransons' SUV. Ryleigh kept quiet as her mother drove toward Murphy's Market.

Colonies of bare trees blurred in her peripheral. She felt a kindred spirit with those naked branches, as if Peter had stripped away all the brilliance that made her whole.

Purple rings hugged Charlotte's eyes, a visual display of her exhaustion after two night shifts. She broke the stillness as they neared the store. "What's been going on with you lately?"

"Nothing." Ryleigh further chiseled at her chipped nail polish, the flakes dispersing in the car's pristine cabin.

"It must be something. You've been in your room the entire week. I know it's exams, but you can't possibly have spent all of that time studying." Her denim eyes cut to her daughter. "We're worried about you."

"It's a guy."

"When we had our little chat, I assumed this guy was hypothetical. Is it the one in college?" Charlotte inquired, pulling into a parking spot.

She was not in the mood to ad-lib details. "Maybe."

Once they parked, Ryleigh let her seatbelt slingshot away from her body and bolted out of the car. She cursed herself the entire walk to the entrance. Sure, the lying was eating her alive; but luring her mother anywhere near the truth was a more dangerous game, one she was not ready to play.

"Whoever he is, dad and I need to meet him. I agreed to let you go out with someone a few years older with that stipulation. I think that's reasonable." Charlotte retrieved a cart as they entered the frigid grocery store. "This guy must be something special if you're this torn up."

"I'll be fine." *Another lie. Add it to my tab in hell.*

"Oh, I forgot to tell you," her mother began, trifling through her bottomless brown leather bag for the list. "I saw Andrea and her boyfriend at the emergency room last night."

Ryleigh reanimated on a dime. "Is she alright? She didn't mention anything about it."

"She's fine. Her boyfriend had an accident at the skate park, nothing a few stitches couldn't fix. Andrea ought to buy him a helmet for Christmas."

Stoned out of his wits, no doubt.

"No kidding."

She envied what Andrea and Colin shared; she wanted that with Peter. But she doubted he would ever give her the time of day again after her transgression.

They finished up in the produce section and headed for the bread aisle, nearly colliding with another shopping cart in the process. Charlotte apologized to whomever she had almost annihilated. "I'm so sorry."

Ryleigh's breath hitched at the sight of Peter standing just a few feet from them. Their separation did not seem to affect him in the way it had rocked her. His sharp face was clean-shaven, and he wore office clothes beneath his open peacoat. She wished she had changed; the yoga pants and oversized sweatshirt swallowed her petite figure, not doing her any favors in the shapeliness department.

"That's okay." He gave a lazy, obligatory smile and cast a look at Ryleigh that silently asked if her mother knew of their connection. If so, he did not wait for a cue. "Hey, Ryleigh."

Even if the greeting was out of pure politeness, which seemed very un-Peter-like, it melted her aching heart.

Charlotte's fingers grazed the base of her neck. "You two know each other?"

"From work," she intoned as if her mother should have arrived at the conclusion on her own. "He comes by practically every day."

"Oh." A shaky laugh escaped her mother's lips.

"It's true. Your daughter makes a mean cappuccino." He extended a hand, which Charlotte shook with relative uncertainty. "Peter."

"Charlotte." She mirrored his forced amiability.

"It was nice meeting you," Peter said, then regarded Ryleigh, "I'll see you later in the week."

She was not sure if he said this because her mother formed a barrier between them, or if he would actually start coming to the shop again. Her pulse slowed as Peter rounded the corner to another aisle, pulling his ringing phone from the depths of his coat.

No less than two seconds after he left, Charlotte belted her daughter into the hot seat. "I don't like the way that guy looked at you."

Ryleigh played it off. "He's a caffeine addict who probably associates my face with coffee by now. It's basic psychology, mom."

"Maybe this after-school job wasn't such a great idea."

"Because of Peter?"

"Because of guys *like* Peter," she specified, giving her daughter a sidelong glance that suggested, 'I was your age once, and not that long ago.'

"He's harmless."

"Maybe he is, dear." Charlotte swiped a loaf of 15-grain bread from the shelf. "I'm just not in love with the idea of 40-year-old guys visiting you at work."

It occurred to Ryleigh she had not the faintest clue of Peter's age. Not that it mattered. Her deep-seated adulation of him could not be halted by a number.

"They're there for the espresso, not for me."

"It's my job to worry about you," her mother said, as if the line somehow justified her paranoid rant.

No amount of motherly concern could dispel the pink cotton candy cloud of infatuation blanketing her brain.

"I have to go to the bathroom."

Charlotte quirked a blonde brow. "You hate public restrooms."

Ryleigh's thumping heart drowned out her mother's skepticism as she sprinted along the aisle.

As if running into Ryleigh and her mother had not turned his day sideways, the mysterious forces of the universe decided Peter could stand to suffer some more.

'Leo Asher' lit up his phone's display.

Leo, the man who had inadvertently outed Ryleigh's lie. Leo, the man he should have thanked for shedding light on such a pivotal fact but whom he mostly wanted to strangle.

His tongue lodged between his molars. "Do you realize you're calling me two hours before work? This better be a Cat 5 emergency. I swear, you and Corso are like cantankerous growths."

"Sorry to bother you. It can wait."

"Consider me bothered. And you've already got me on the phone, so you might as well get on with it."

"I think I blew my interview."

The miniscule concern hit a new low of unimportance.

"The one with the basketball coach? I skimmed it when I proofed last night. It was fine. Interviewing isn't something you pick up overnight."

Something prevented him from moving any further as he knocked cans of crushed tomatoes into the two-tiered cart. Ryleigh rested her foot on the bottom bar, a smirk playing at her lips.

Peter held up a finger. "Stop by my office tonight if you get a chance. I'll give you some pointers. Oh, and Asher? I won't be as gracious the next time you dial me outside of hours."

"We really need to discuss your eating habits." She beheld the collection of cans and sleeves of bagels with genuine concern. Her laugh raised goosebumps on his forearms. The familiar, breathy sound may as well have sent him into cardiac arrest.

God, he missed her.

"I'm a single guy hurtling toward middle age. Pray tell, what kind of stuff do you think I'm capable of cooking?" A more vibrant blue radiated from her irises, unobscured by their usual shadows. "You look better without all of that crap around your eyes."

"It's called eyeliner. And for the record, I don't wear it for other people. I wear it because it makes me feel good."

At last, she stepped aside and permitted him to advance down the aisle. Unrelenting in her pursuit to talk to him, she followed at his heels.

"You can't do this." Ryleigh's protest tugged at his reserve of remorse. "Don't you realize I miss you?"

The phrase channeled helplessness, as if she were a stray animal Peter refused to take home. It also crossed the rubicon of things that did not sit well with him. Those words signaled attachment. They encapsulated everything he feared.

How could she possibly miss him when they barely knew each other? The idea was absurd.

Another part of him thought he might have missed Ryleigh, too. But there were too many conflicting emotions where she was involved to trace any of their origins.

"Listen." He brought the cart to a halt. Peter lowered his tone to an almost inaudible volume. "I like you, and that's saying a lot because I basically hate everyone."

Her face fell in the wake of his extended pause. "But?"

"I can't get caught up with someone so young."

"You can't or you won't?" Ryleigh's softness contradicted the demanding question.

"I won't. If you were in college, maybe—"

"I'm legal. And next fall, I'll be in college. For real."

Peter did not love that they were having this conversation in the middle of the grocery store. Was she forcing him to discuss this in public as revenge for his theatrics at the coffee shop? Her curled shoulders and wet eyes pointed to no.

"You don't get it. There's more to consider. It's not so black and white." He rubbed the back of his neck. "Let me put this in perspective for you: I'm 17 years older than you. *17.*"

"Why does it matter? It doesn't bother me."

Naivety plastered onto her face, glowing with the earnestness of a neon sign adorning a shop window.

"Think about it. I was born into the Reagan administration. You were a baby when I graduated high school."

"That's a backward way of thinking," she volleyed, bare lashes aflutter. "We're both adults."

"You're an adult by technicality, not by experience."

Ryleigh's pursed bottom lip reminded him of their kiss and how desperate Peter was to recreate that magic. His stomach clenched, knowing he had made a big deal about their age difference to dissuade himself more than her.

A dinging notification on his phone rescued him from the intimacy of their tension-filled moment.

Saved by the pharmacy.

"I have to go," Peter clipped. When he looked up, the electricity in her eyes had fizzled out.

"Was kissing me a mistake?"

How did women manage to do that? Say something like they can see into your goddamn soul.

He glanced over his shoulder as he turned to leave. "As I recall, you kissed me."

Kissing you back was the most blissful mistake of my pathetic life.

12

A FAVOR

Nat King Cole's crooning voice swelled as Ryleigh bounded downstairs to assist her parents, who had been retrieving plastic storage containers of Christmas decorations from the garage all evening. The stifling scent of cloves and cinnamon sticks could have knocked her unconscious once she hit the landing.

Ryleigh gathered her hair into a bun when she came upon the sitting room. "The neighbors called. They're begging for us to nix the potpourri."

"Told you it was too strong," Dexter said.

"I may have gotten carried away with the cinnamon sticks." Charlotte fiddled with the sleeves of her cardigan. "We weren't sure if you were coming down."

"I was reading."

She had actually been sobbing senselessly into her pillow, but the particulars were immaterial.

Holiday decorating abided by a tried and true process: Ryleigh aided her mother in decorating the house and her father cussed while assembling the 8-foot artificial tree. After the branches were fluffed, they would join him in untangling the lights and adding the ornaments.

He had made decent headway with the faux spruce. The pink, peach, and teal tipped metal of the branch bundles indicated her father had three more layers to install. PVC pine needles sprinkled the hardwood as he finessed the individual branches. "Remember when we used to get real trees? Those were the days. You know, this stress isn't good for me in my old age. What's the harm in switching back to the old tradition?"

"Dexter, that tradition is old for a reason. Your daughter is allergic to Christmas trees. I'm convinced you broach this subject every December for no other reason than to antagonize me." Charlotte narrowed her eyes.

"Maybe next Christmas we can get a real tree. Something tall and full. I didn't buy a house with vaulted ceilings to stare at the same stumpy, clunker tree year after year."

Ryleigh adored her parents' low-stakes bickering. Arguments were scarce in their 21 years of marriage, but the holidays ushered in a unique breed of stress. Yuletide commanded a certain *je ne sais quoi* that had the nicest of people at each other's throats.

"Do you honestly think she doesn't plan on coming home for Christmas?" Hands planted on her denim-covered hips, she turned to her daughter. "You'll be home for Christmas, won't you, dear?"

"Every year."

She helped her mother lay out the silver charger plates, snowflake-shaped napkin holder, and silver glitter-covered pine cones that had been used to set the table for the holidays for as long as she could remember.

Dexter ventured a change in subject to avoid further backlash. "You're going to freeze in Michigan. I remember those Ann Arbor winters like they were yesterday."

"Really? I've heard it's not much colder there."

Interacting with her parents had become a burdensome chore. Her mind lingered elsewhere, led astray by a constant feeling of regret she could not shake. Peter refused to return any of her messages, and he spared no exception to the day they ran into each other at the supermarket.

He had just been cordial for the sake of cordiality.

"We'll send you off with plenty of warm clothes." Charlotte directed the comment at her daughter but sassed Dexter in the process. Her snappy attitude faltered, face growing serious. "It's going to be so different next year."

She made the remark as if realizing for the first time that her little girl really was leaving. It was no longer a far-off apocalyptic date on a page in her planner. At some point over the past few months, years even, her baby had morphed into a young woman, one who was on the cusp of welcoming adulthood with open arms.

"It'll be weird for me, too. I'm moving somewhere I've never been, and I won't know anyone." As she said it out loud, the concept did not appeal to her.

What was she gaining in moving to Michigan—how different could it be from Connecticut? More importantly, was it worth leaving her parents and Andrea behind? Then her thoughts pivoted to Peter, and how she hungered to have him in her life. If he would have her.

You can't change your college plans over a guy.

Her chest caved in when the 'extra, extra' ringtone sounded from her phone. She had purchased the tune and assigned it to Peter's number as a joke, knowing he would never call her but thinking it would be hilarious if it ever went off. Standing there in front of her parents, it was far from humorous.

"What kind of ridiculous ringtone is that?" Dexter snorted while tending to the final branch bundles.

Her mother's stare could have cut through steel.

She knew.

Ryleigh placed her hand over the blaring device in her rear pocket, toeing toward the staircase. "I'll be back."

Ahead of his parents' arrival the next morning, Peter had taken the day off to prepare his place. Between keeping his distance from Ryleigh and the impending doom of interacting with his father, he hardwired his remaining focus into work, aiming to quell the anxiety chipping away at his nerves. The condo provided a visual representation of this shift in priorities.

Dirty clothes lay wrinkled on the bedroom floor, few of them having made it into the hamper. A sour malodor clung to his towels, past due for a wash along with his bedsheets. The slate floors amplified every trace of dirt or imperfection, an art exhibit showcasing the scuff marks from his loafers.

Avoiding Ryleigh had impacted him on a larger scale than he could have foreseen. Cleaning provided a convenient distraction from his quasi-romantic misery.

As he scrubbed the bathroom baseboards, she infiltrated his not so carefully guarded thoughts. The facts had been laid bare at the grocery store: he was 17 years her senior, and in a few months, he would be twice her age. And yet, he could no longer deny Ryleigh's interest. She had made it abundantly clear.

His phone vibrated against the counter. The rubber glove resisted removal, barricaded by sweat as Peter peeled it off.

J: Hello sweetie, will you pick up a case of cabernet sauvignon for the festivities?

P: No problem.

Her message may as well have read: 'Peter, be a dear and pick up some wine. You know I can't stand to be around you and your father sober.'

He did not fault his mother for her excessive alcohol intake during family visits. How else would she survive her non-negotiable referee duties? Although Peter would rather not spend the week with his father, he was looking forward to seeing his mother.

Family had always come a distant second to his father. Gideon rushed from closings, to open houses, to out-of-town conferences at the drop of a hat, opting to miss out on his son's events rather than lose an opportunity to advance his real-estate career.

For a fleeting moment, Peter mused that his present life was not a dramatic departure from his father's. He overworked himself of his own volition, and ignored things which carried the potential to brighten his harried existence.

He began slipping the glove back onto his hand when another message came through. Ryleigh's name on the notification screen instigated heart palpitations.

R: you can't ignore your problems forever

Peter could not help but laugh at the proverbial nature of her words, sounding as if they had been cracked out of a fortune cookie. A selfish notion manifested and goaded him to call her rather than reply to the text.

Three terrifying rings later, she picked up.

"Did you dial me on accident?" Ryleigh asked as if there were no other circumstances under which he would be calling.

"100% intentional. How've you been?"

"I hope you're joking." A quiet respiration crept through the receiver. "Not great since you left me stranded in the canned goods."

"Sorry about that. I had to get to the drugstore." Peter's insides performed a noxious plummet, an elevator crashing at the bottom of its shaft. "To be honest, I didn't call you just to chat. I wanted to ask you something."

"Anything," Ryleigh urged.

"Hold on a second."

He placed the phone on the kitchen counter, grimacing at the sticky residue from the lemon cleaner. Peter located his favorite plaid mug and set himself to the task of preparing a pot of coffee. The dark roast released its addicting fragrance as he measured the grounds and poured them into the filter. Once the water had been added to the reservoir, he pressed the button signaling the medieval coffee maker to brew.

Peter returned the phone to his ear while grabbing a carton of half and half from the refrigerator. "Hey."

"Did you put me on hold to make coffee? Don't tell me you're too old to know what speakerphone is."

"That's cute, real funny." He hooked his pointer finger in the collar of his t-shirt. Peter's leg involuntarily shook. *Just ask her. What's the worst that could happen?* "I was wondering if you could do me a favor."

"Of course."

"Would you mind coming over to my place Saturday night? My parents are coming into town, and I don't get along particularly well with my dad. It'd be nice to have someone there as a buffer."

"Mmm," she purred in consideration. Her sultry rumbling inundated Peter with unbridled warmth. "And what are you going to do for me if I agree to this heinous plot?"

He was not wrapped around her finger, he was fused to it. "Whatever you want."

"And you won't say no?"

"I won't say no."

"Can we hang out one night?"

This is a horrible idea. His willpower had already been spread thin. Surviving an evening with her would be a terrible undertaking. But she had agreed to his ridiculous request and he had stupidly offered her anything in return.

"Consider it done. This drip coffee is disgusting, by the way. Doesn't hold a candle to yours."

"I think that's the nicest thing you've ever said to me," Ryleigh teased. Static rustled on the line as she shouted a muffled 'be down in a minute.' "I better go. Text me your address for Saturday."

"Will do. Wear an ugly sweater."

13

WORKING ON IT

Ryleigh checked her reflection in the rearview for the zillionth time. After fixing stray eyeliner smudges, reapplying overzealous layers of chapstick, and fluffing her mess of waves, she had run out of excuses to remain in the safety of her parked car.

Head falling against the headrest, she shut her eyes and swallowed hard. The funny thing was, her nerves were not borne out of the unorthodox arrangement of meeting Peter's parents. Her anxiety stemmed from being in close quarters with him for the duration of the evening, and in his home of all places.

High-pitched whistling startled Ryleigh as she got out of her car. Peter crouched on the trio of steps outside the condo building.

"Look who made it."

Two coffee pots adorned the front of his red sweater, the white text proclaiming, 'Merry Christmas Pothead.' A faint flame persisted in the center of the cigarette dangling between his fingers. Ribbons of smoke curled into the air.

"Great sweater." She claimed the step below Peter, not trusting herself to occupy the same space as him. Her skin tightened beneath the cable knit when he brought the filter to his lips. "I didn't know you smoked."

"I don't." He contradicted the statement with a long drag accompanied by an even longer exhalation. "I lifted it from my mom. Spend 10 seconds around my dad and you'll understand."

"Your parents have been in town for how many days and you're already acting like a 13-year-old." Ryleigh snatched the cancer stick and suctioned her own drag before returning it to Peter. She choked on the fumes. "Why do people like this? It's horrible."

"We like coffee, some people hate it. Everyone has a vice." He flicked the cigarette onto the ground and extinguished the embers with his slip-on. "Really? Fa-la-la-la-llama?"

Ryleigh despised the scratchy, colorful sweater, decked out with ridiculous pom poms and threaded with glitter.

"It's awful. This isn't even mine, I borrowed it from a friend. It was the least offensive thing I could find."

"Let's get this trainwreck over with." Peter extended a veiny hand, which Ryleigh accepted with a bit too much ardor. His elongated fingers entwined with hers to maintain a secure grasp. The weight and texture of their hands differed, but twin flames burned in their palms.

"I was under the impression you invited me to prevent a trainwreck."

"With any luck, you'll slow down its inevitable demise." He swiped something on his keys against the door, and it emitted a loud buzz as they passed through its threshold. Though they were on their feet, he never surrendered her hand.

"Do they know I'm coming?" she asked as they ascended the stairs.

"No, because then they would've asked questions from the moment I mentioned you to the moment they met you. My dad's foot is permanently lodged halfway up my ass. I could do without a reenactment of the Spanish fucking inquistion."

His immediate release of her hand when they reached the landing on the sixth floor reminded her that she was there for moral support. Nothing romantic adhered to this favor.

Strangely, Ryleigh was okay with that.

"Last chance to back out." His feverish eyes begged her to stay while he reached for the doorknob.

She yearned to gather a fistful of his stupid sweater and devour his lips. That course of action may have been in poor taste with his parents just inside the unit.

Instead, she said, "I'm not going anywhere."

The door to unit 6A swung open, revealing a cozy, sparsely decorated space. An olive green couch occupied the center of the living room; a worn leather armchair guarded the corner to its right. Mismatched lamps beamed yellow light, casting warm shadows on the graphite walls.

"Peter, darling, is that you?" Janet called.

"Who else would it be?" Gideon mocked, bewildered at her foolish question.

Ryleigh's chest heaved as the Rosenfelds rounded the corner, coming face to face with Peter and herself. Janet had a few inches on her husband, tall and lean like her son. His father's face creased with wrinkles. Not the soft, lighthearted kind; these were harsh and ran deep, the consequence of someone who wore a permanent scowl. They donned matching green sweaters that said, 'Don't hog the nog.'

Peter snaked one of his long arms around Ryleigh's waist, thumb stroking her hip. Her heart fluttered at the intimate nature of the embrace. She was so high from his subtle dose of affection, she almost missed the absurd statement that followed.

"I'd like you to meet Ryleigh, my girlfriend."

She must have misheard him. Had Peter introduced her as his *girlfriend*? Heat flushed through her body. Everything within her tipped toward reaction. Ryleigh fought to control the tone of her greeting. "It's so nice to meet you both."

"You'll have to forgive our shock, dear. Peter didn't mention any guests." Janet stole a sip from her wine glass.

"You know me, I'm full of surprises," he deadpanned.

She wondered why his mother did not find the remark funny, as Ryleigh often laughed at his inane comments.

His father sunk onto the couch. "This is quite the treat. Our son never gives us the privilege of meeting his romantic acquaintances. Not that there have been many."

Romantic acquaintance? A girl could dream.

"We're in a serious relationship," he insisted. They had not moved an inch from the entryway, awkward inches separating them in their socked feet.

Janet waved a hand from the armchair. "Come on and sit down, you're making me nervous."

Ryleigh and Peter settled on the sofa alongside his father. Lowering herself onto the furniture yielded embarrassment. The cushions were less firm than they appeared, and she sunk not so gracefully into their facade of comfort. His joggers brushed against her jeans as he settled in, and it left her disappointed when he crossed his legs, unwilling to share whatever warmth he had to spare.

"Where are my manners?" His mother produced a clicking noise with her tongue. "I'm Janet, Peter's mom. This is his father, Gideon."

'Father' was a cold, distant distinction from the comforting casualness attached to 'mom.' It painted a picture of their family dynamic without any background.

"Peter really hasn't told me much about either of you."

He shot her a life-threatening glare.

Gideon's laugh accentuated the crease between his graying eyebrows. "That doesn't surprise me. He's not terribly personable."

Ryleigh had a knee-jerk reaction to speak up. "Not in the traditional sense. He has his moments, though."

Peter's father spoke about him like he was not in the room, and it made her feel sorry for him. His lack of reaction implied this was not an instance of irregularity.

No wonder he asked me to come.

Janet seized the bottle of cabernet sauvignon off the coffee table and refilled her glass. "How did you two meet? I'm a sucker for a good love story."

Thick brunette curls sprouted from her scalp like an overrun garden, much like Peter's out-of-control tresses. Ryleigh noticed, in particular, the pair shared the same bizarre eye color; and the elegant curvature of their noses was identical.

"We work across the street from each other," he stated as if there were nothing else to divulge.

"What was your first impression of him?" Janet prompted. A bemused smile played at her glossy lips as she sipped the red wine.

She did not hesitate launching into the assessment, remembering the day they met with more clarity than what she ate for breakfast that morning.

"He wasn't fake nice, like most people you run into. And I thought right away, there's something charming about this guy, how he's not afraid to be himself. The first time he looked at me, I mean really looked at me, I felt like I'd done an hour of high-intensity cardio. And ..." Ryleigh trailed off as her eyes locked onto Peter's. *And then, I lied to your son about being a college student and when he found out the truth he was pissed and we really haven't been talking since but here we are.* "And, of course, he's incredibly handsome."

Peter reclined against the couch cushion, influencing Ryleigh to readjust her position. She lodged in the crook of his arm, melding them together like two puzzle pieces. A breath bottled in her chest as his lips grazed her hair. The euphoria of the moment was shattered when his mother spoke, reminding her they were not alone.

"Young love," Janet sighed at her husband. "That was us, once upon a time."

"Now we have a pool to see which one of us will drop dead first," Gideon said. "Believe me, if you two make it together as long as we have, you'll do the same."

"Say, you don't have a nut allergy or anything do you? These have pecans," Janet asked while arranging a pile of white, powdery cookies on a disposable serving tray.

"Nope. No allergies," Ryleigh said.

She absorbed the sight of Peter's minimalist kitchen. The eggshell cabinets competed with the black countertops, striking a pleasing contrast. His place was pristine, devoid of dirt or clutter. Although, she realized, the clean presentation could have been a front to impress his parents.

"I'm surprised Peter hasn't mentioned you. He and I are quite close, in case he hasn't told you."

"We haven't been together that long."

"My son's miserly with his feelings. I hope you're willing to look past that, because I can tell you mean something to him." Janet flipped on the archaic coffee pot stationed beside the sink. She pulled four printed mugs from the cabinet, continuing in a lower voice, "I can see it in his eyes. It makes me so happy, so relieved to see that look again. He's been through hell and back; 14 years since his last relationship."

Striving to maintain an air of neutrality, Ryleigh distributed the coffee among the mugs. "That's a long time."

"It was a bad relationship, keeps it close to his vest even after all these years. He doesn't like to talk about it," she advised. Janet brought the tray into the dining nook. "Coffee and cookies, a seasonal Rosenfeld tradition."

Ryleigh carried the mugs two at a time, placing them on the dinner table. A pair of fold-up chairs discounted the presence of their formal counterparts.

She claimed the seat beside Peter. "What are these?"

"You work in a coffee shop full of pastries. You've never seen a cookie?" His crooked smile hid behind the safety of the coffee cup.

"That's no way to talk to your lady." Gideon's mouth corkscrewed, souring his already sullen expression. His face brightened while addressing his son's alleged girlfriend. "They're snowball cookies. Horribly addicting."

"That's super sweet," Ryleigh said upon sampling the pastry. A mustache of powdered sugar clung to her upper lip. Peter ran his thumb along the thin white line, gaze darting between her waiting mouth and earnest eyes. Gideon cleared his throat to burst their bubble of intimacy. "My dad would probably kill me for eating this."

"Why's that?" Janet asked.

"He's a dentist. He gets a little preachy about cavities and gum disease around the holidays, with all of the desserts floating around."

A dentist? While Peter did not have any preconceived notions about Ryleigh's upbringing, he was taken aback to uncover this mark of affluence.

Gideon thieved a second cookie. "We tried to get Peter to pursue something in medicine. He had other plans. But, as you can see, he's not homeless. Could've been worse."

"I'm sure your dad wanted something more out of you, too." Peter planted the heels of his palms atop the table. "Real estate agent? I'm sure that's not what granddad had in mind."

"Let's not ruin this lovely evening."

Janet's pleas were useless. This evening had been ruined before it began.

"I made an honorable salary," Gideon protested. Both he and Peter had abandoned their chairs; only the small dining table separated them. "I provided a good life for you and your mother. My father was proud of my work. That's more than I can say for you. You're almost 36 years old, what do you have to show for your life? You've been working at the same job since you got out of school, the same position, no raise, horrible benefits, low pay. We thought you'd at least be married by now. We'd like to have grandkids before we roll over and die."

"That's your problem," Peter spat, pointing a finger at his father. "You're always worried about how my actions reflect on you. You don't care about me, what makes me happy. All you care about is how it will affect *you*."

"Can we ever get through a visit in one piece?" Mascara-tinged tears flooded Janet's cheeks. She grabbed Ryleigh's hand. "I'm terribly sorry you had to see this."

Gideon further antagonized Peter. "I bet you yell at your girlfriend like this too, don't you?"

"She's not even my girlfriend," he bellowed. "I invited her tonight because I thought it would temporarily get you off my back. That went real fucking well, huh, dad?"

Janet's eyes widened at her son's revelation.

"Since you're so worried about me 'getting off your back' as you call it, your mother and I will stay at a hotel for the rest of the week." Gideon headed down the hall to gather their things. He shouted from the bedroom, "Come on, Janet, let's get out of his hair."

Peter stormed out of the condo, slamming the door. Her heartbeat slowed in the face of his abrupt exit. As much as Ryleigh wanted to excuse herself from the table and follow him out, she did not think it entirely appropriate. She had gotten a glimpse at the scope of Peter's fury when he uncovered the scholarship article.

He did not need rescuing. He needed to be alone.

Sniffing, Janet asked, "So, you two aren't together?"

"No," she presented an apologetic smile, "but I'm working on it."

14

TOO YOUNG

"You're not feeding yourself. You're as thin as a rail. Did I not teach you how to cook?" Janet waved around a freshly peeled potato. "When you were little, you were always in the kitchen, wanting to help."

Two nights in a hotel had done nothing to resolve their feud. His father was dead-set on not stepping foot in the condo ever again, but Janet gave him no say in the matter.

The Rosenfeld matriarch remained vigilant about keeping the two men separated. She recruited Peter to assist in the kitchen while Gideon lounged on the sofa, submerged in a recent copy of *The Harris Chronicle*. Peter would not have been surprised if his father took notes while reading, pinpointing everything he disliked about the paper and suggesting ways it could be improved.

"Apparently, I was too busy playing sous chef to have retained anything useful. My definition of cooking is throwing something in the toaster or the microwave," Peter joked in self-deprecation.

"Sweetheart, that isn't real food."

He peeled potatoes, rinsed them, and placed them beside the cutting board. The repetition of the task stunted his neurosis. But as the pile of russets shrank, his thoughts grew from a steady hum to a deafening roar. The way he had blindsided Ryleigh, the way he had behaved in front of her, he knew all of it was wrong. Last potato rinsed, he dried his hands and retrieved his phone from his pocket.

P: I owe you a night out for surviving my favor, as promised. When are you free?

"Are you texting your pretend girlfriend?"

Janet did not bother dancing around words to get the information she sought. That was the way she had always been: straight to the point.

"It sounds awful when you say it like that." He pulled a second cutting board from the cabinet. Peter's sharp chin dipped down, hovering close to his chest. "I'm afraid I messed up there."

His mother pointed her starch-coated knife at him.

"Would you care to explain why you didn't breathe a word of this girl until I flew 3,000 miles to see you? I'm getting older. You can't take me by surprise like that. It would've really been something if I'd had a heart attack that night," she scolded, keeping her voice low to avoid attracting attention from Gideon.

"We're not dating. Should I have told you anything? I've only known her for a few months. I'll admit, I enjoy her company. Though, I'd never tell her that."

Trying to vocalize his relationship to Ryleigh scrambled his brain cells. They were not quite friends, and far from lovers, but something indistinguishable connected them; a thin thread binding one to the other. No matter how hard Peter tried to snap that pitiful thread, it stayed intact.

"Isn't that sweet?" Janet grinned. She left Peter to finish cutting the potatoes while she tended to the pot of gravy on the stove. He knew by the slow, methodical way in which his mother stirred the sauce, she had an opinion to push. "I have to say, she does look awfully young."

He channeled his anxiety into the pressure he imposed on the knife blade. "I'm worried she's too young. She keeps saying it doesn't matter, but I have other ideas."

"How old is she?"

You can't lie to your mom, c'mon. "18."

"That's certainly unconventional," Janet swished the gravy-laden rubber spatula in the air. Peter pictured the thick, brown sauce splattering his pristine cabinets. She held his arm loosely, face upturned. "Regardless, I saw the way you looked at her the other night. Don't think for one second you can pull a fast one on your mom. You're smitten with this girl. And if you have any sense beneath that head full of hair, you'll do something about it."

White lights illuminated the Bransons' tree, giving select ornaments an exponential gleam. Snow flurries danced in the dark beyond the casement windows. A fire blazed in the brick hearth, creating a cozy atmosphere in the cavernous sitting room. The family huddled around the coffee table, slamming tiles onto a battered grid board.

"Triple word." Charlotte's hands shot skyward. "That'll be 72 points for yours truly."

Ryleigh adopted the role of scorekeeper from a young age, understanding neither of her parents could be trusted with the responsibility. As she scribbled down her mother's points, Dexter appeared to be searching for a scenario in which the math did not add up. *Typical.*

"Enjoy your 72-point turn while it lasts," he said. "But I'll have the highest-scoring turn of the game. You'll see."

"Settle down, children," Ryleigh admonished, placing a word on the board.

Her phone produced a crude buzz on the wooden floor while she replenished her stash of lettered tiles. She pressed her lips together to suppress a grin at the message.

. . .

P: I owe you a night out for surviving my favor, as promised. When are you free?

R: how's tuesday night? we need to talk about the fake girlfriend situation, btw, and why you neglected to mention the fine print of our deal.

Dexter hurtled a throw pillow at his daughter and it knocked the device from her hands. "I told you to put that infernal thing in your bedroom."

Charlotte kept her arms tight against her body, shooting Ryleigh a quick glance. The suspicious looks were growing in prevalence. She had a feeling her mother knew exactly whom she texted. And despite this, the confrontation never came. Ryleigh would have preferred a lecture to guilt-inducing leers.

She retired her phone to the entryway table.

P: Noted. I'll pick you up at 8. Dress warm.

Peter had held fast to his promise of taking her out even though his end of the deal had gone up in smoke. While it was technically not a date, the knowledge of the upcoming evening thrilled her to no end.

Ryleigh closed her eyes and covered her mouth in mute excitement before turning to face her parents. She crouched in front of the coffee table. "Sorry."

"At least she isn't completely attached to her phone, Dex," Charlotte said. "Not like Andrea. I don't think she ever takes her eyes off hers."

"That's a little dramatic."

"If you say so." Her face scrunched up as she assessed the letters on the wooden tray. Charlotte laid several tiles on the board in defeat and avoided direct eye contact with her husband, who gloated at the failed turn.

Ryleigh's mind drifted to the logistics of their outing. Andrea covered her for the ugly sweater party, but she could not be her scapegoat for every outing. She would have to tell the truth.

Well, at least a variation of it.

Without any pretense, Ryleigh plunged into the conversation she needed to broach, however unwilling she was to do so. "Could I go out Tuesday night?"

Dexter stared at his daughter over the top of his recently purchased eyeglasses, which had fallen down the bridge of his triangular nose. "Define 'go out,' because if your idea of going out entails doing keg stands until the wee hours of the morning or driving while under the influence of things that grow out of the ground, you won't receive any blessing from me."

"I think she means with someone," Charlotte interjected, saving Ryleigh from having to explain herself.

His sternness melted. "Our pumpkin is going on a date. Last year I might have objected to this, but you're going off to college soon and let's face it: I won't be there to monitor your every move."

Why must I endure this? Do it for Peter, do it for Peter.

"Dexter, if you mention her leaving for school one more time," Charlotte ground out. She gathered herself, inhaling with the force of a vacuum cleaner. "When will we be able to meet this guy, honey?"

Venom lurked behind the slathered sweetness of her inquisition. It was a challenge, as if to say, 'I know precisely what you've been up to, and we both know your father won't take kindly to it.'

"Soon."

Panic set in at the single, uttered word.

His father had somehow waited through the entirety of dinner before delivering his careful critique of Peter's place of employment. "You know, son, I was reading over some of your articles. Well, I was reading through the whole paper, really."

Peter half-listened as he accompanied his mother in clearing the table, stacking plates and bowls on the breakfast bar. They migrated to the kitchen to tend to the colossal pile of dishes that had accumulated throughout the night.

Gideon relocated to one of the stools at the bar, which provided a view of the sink. "The articles written by your staff are highly simplistic. Would it kill you to liven it up a bit, make the stories more interesting to read?"

"You sound like someone who's never picked up a small-town newspaper. And by the way, the last I heard, people don't read the paper for entertainment. They read it to catch up on current events. You want to be entertained? Try a magazine," Peter quipped, rinsing the dishes his mother passed along. "Don't expect the articles to be rich with detail or insights, because they aren't. They're straightforward and present the facts. I don't work for a prestigious, metropolitan paper where everyone takes themselves too seriously. This is Harris, and like you said, we're highly simplistic."

"So, that's it then? You accept the fact that you work for a local paper and make no effort to improve its status, or your status as a writer for that matter?"

He considered the rate at which his father's mind operated to churn out negative remarks at such unwavering frequency.

"I'm trying to pay off my student loans, not win a Pulitzer." Peter hung his head, possessing no strength to continue the ridiculous argument. "Could we possibly redirect the conversation to an area other than my never-ending list of shortcomings?"

Ripe for a reaction, Janet mumbled something inaudible and pressed on washing the shrinking stack of dishes.

Gideon squinted at his son. "Maybe if you'd take pride in something, I wouldn't step all over you."

"What do you want from me, honestly?" He threw a dampened

dish rag onto the floor like an enraged restaurant employee. "I went to college and got a degree. I have a decent job. I'm not an alcoholic. I'm not strung out on drugs."

"What I want is for you to be passionate about something. Anything. You half-ass everything in your miserable life."

Harsh as the jab may have landed, it rode the gray area between accusation and fact; and it cut deeper than Peter cared to admit. "When I stumble across the first thing that resembles passion, you'll be the first to know."

Two bottles of wine and several hours later, his parents said their final goodbyes and returned to the hotel. Gideon did not speak to Peter the rest of the night, leaving Janet to guide any discussion. He hated the awkward position in which his mother constantly found herself, caught between the two great loves of her life.

As soon as they walked out the door, Peter collapsed in an exhausted heap. The relief coursing through him from his father's exit outweighed the emptiness that gnawed his nerves as he said goodbye to his mother.

This time next week, he would feel fine. He had gotten used to the distance separating him from the only person he genuinely loved in this twisted world.

He would sure as hell be okay without his father.

Climbing into bed, he popped his fluoxetine and chased it with a swig of water. It was hardly 10 o'clock and he was between his sheets, begging for this day, for this week, to be over. All of his systems denied the plea.

Peter had never been more awake.

A supercut of the last seven days played on a tireless loop, feeding his shame until it was so thick, it became a second skin. Every detail rushed back, ugly and uninvited. His mother drinking the entire case of cabernet. His father spouting constant criticism. And then there was Ryleigh, caught in the middle of his familial mess.

How was she still speaking to him after what he had blindly put her through? One thing, he knew for sure.

He did not deserve her, in any capacity.

15

MULL IT OVER

*R*yleigh's anxiety about the evening ahead snowballed. Her stomach knotted more than the tangled mess of hair she had brushed to perfection.

An hour earlier, she had locked herself in her bathroom to get ready—though, most of that time was spent panicking on the edge of the clawfoot tub. It was a modest room, small but not cramped, encouraging its visitors not to linger. Its only bit of uniqueness was the light pink wallpaper her parents had put up not long after they moved into the house. Now, it cracked and peeled in several places. Would they replace it once she moved out? Redecorate? Would they do the same to her bedroom? These questions stung from the inside out.

Her time here was up, just like the tired wallpaper.

The early acceptance letter from UMich poked out of her purse, tucked neatly in its torn envelope. Peter had a right to know. They were not together, and their tentative friendship stood on shaky ground, but she could not withhold such vital information. Not after her devastating lie.

Peter had told her this was not a date, and yet she selected her sheerest dress, slipped on her hottest panties, and prayed to a god she did not believe in that tonight, she would be able to taste his lips again.

P: Be there in five. Parking down the street, as requested.

Without a second glance in the mirror, Ryleigh snatched her purse off the counter and flew downstairs, careful not to trip over the haphazardly tied laces of her boots. She peered around the corner on the bottom step to assess whether it was an opportune moment to make her move.

Anderson Cooper's smooth voice carried through the hall from the living room, where her mother folded a basket of laundry. Light shone from under the door of the half bathroom to signal her father's occupance. *Perfect timing.*

"I'm heading out," Ryleigh called, slinking toward the foyer. The last thing she needed was to endure a string of questions, all of which she would be forced to give phony answers to.

"Have a good time, sweetie," Charlotte shouted.

"Wait, let me get a picture of—"

She heard her father protesting as she slipped out the door, locking it with expert swiftness.

Ryleigh spotted the neolithic silver sedan parked three houses down and the earth skirted out from beneath her feet. Peter had a way of leaving her unsteady without trying. He stood in a slouched stance against the hood of the car, hands in his pockets. Smoothing her sweater dress, she strode in his direction. Seeing him on her street catalyzed a dangerous rush of air to circulate through her fragile lungs.

She wanted this. She wanted him.

No matter how much she convinced herself, the sinking weight of guilt encapsulated her. Ryleigh thought of the inevitable wrath of disappointment her parents would unleash upon her when they uncovered the truth about who she was seeing. But the truth could stay hidden one more night.

"Hey, you." Peter's gaze roamed over her form, the canary glow of the streetlight reflecting off his mesmerizing eyes. Ryleigh marveled at the way he stared at her, juxtaposed with his adamant inaction. His gentlemanly restraint made her heart swell. "You look nice. However, if you'll recall, I did send you a text requesting you dress warm. Here you are, dressed to seduce the flu."

"I guess that makes you the flu."

"You're a regular comedian. Don't expect a can of Campbell's and a get well soon card from me." He opened the door for her. "Get in before you freeze to death."

Competing notes of cinnamon and espresso mingled in the sedan's cabin. A navy and gold graduation tassel with an '05 charm hung from the rearview mirror. *You're alone with him. In his car. Holy shit.* Swallowing, she yanked the seatbelt across her chest, clicking it into place.

"Coffee?" Peter proffered, plucking a to-go cup from its drink holder. He held it out to her as he peeled away from the curb. "It's a caramel latte with almond milk, I hope that's right. I didn't know what your usual was so I asked Kendall. If it's horrible you can blame her."

Their fingertips brushed as she accepted the coffee, heat enveloping her ears. The high she experienced from their contact, however innocent, was indescribable.

"Thanks. How uncharacteristically sweet of you."

"I can be sweet. I reserve my sweetness for a select few."

"And I'm one of those lucky people?"

"Don't push it." He emitted a fake laugh. "Earlier, I accidentally mistook your drink for mine. I could feel my kidneys failing once it hit my tongue."

"You're so dramatic. It's not that sweet."

His right arm hung over the console between them, his long, skeletal fingers lying limp as he drove. An image of those wondrous digits tracing her tight-sheathed thigh flashed in her subconscious.

Peter's hands drove her nuts; large palms and mile-long fingers. Bass player hands.

They were sheer perfection.

"If it has sugar in it, it's sweet by definition. It's beyond me why people willingly ruin their coffee with all of these syrups, creamers, and artificial sweeteners. Have you ever had an espresso drink as it's meant to be? You're being robbed of your coffee-drinking experience."

Ryleigh admired his profile as he rambled. Passing headlights floodlit his dark, pin-straight lashes. A few days worth of stubble minimized the angling of his jaw. His curls had been tamed by gel, rescuing them from their signature erraticism. Her examination circled back to that wonderful, dangling hand. The memory of Peter helping her off the steps overrode reality, leaving her submerged in that night rather than this one. She recounted the rose petal softness of his skin, and how he held onto that small part of her like he never wanted to let go.

She snaked her fingers between his. Ryleigh suffocated in the confinement of the passenger seat when his thumb caressed her palm. Its pad traced her creases, injecting her with the white heat of want, a feeling her body had assigned to him and him alone.

"Is this your polite way of asking me to shut up?" His cheekbones became prominent, laugh lines accentuated by a tight-lipped smile.

"Peter, if I wanted to shut you up, I'd use my mouth."

"I have it on good authority that you're a voracious reader," Peter teased as the pair entered Park Brothers Books in the heart of down-town. An endless gallery of oak shelves filled the space, each one packed to the brim with paperback and hardback editions alike.

"And who told you that?"

"I'm a reporter. I happen to have excellent observational skills." He winked. "Plus, it would be hard to miss the book you keep by the register."

Peter made it halfway to the mystery section when he realized Ryleigh was missing. He peeked over his shoulder, puzzled as to why she had not moved from the foyer. She idled by the new release table, but she did not ransack its offerings.

"What are you doing?"

"Don't you love the smell of a bookstore?"

Ryleigh's face softened as she drew in a deep breath through her doe-like nose, eyes shut. The question buried itself in the trenches of his cerebrum when her liner-rimmed lids fluttered open and he lost himself in her sapphire irises. He wanted to tell her how stunningly beautiful she looked. Peter knew better.

"I've never noticed it."

She shook her head and waltzed along the main corridor of the shop. Before ducking into an aisle, Ryleigh pointed a finger, "You don't know what you're missing."

He lagged behind to investigate this alleged bookstore aroma. Inhaling, freshly cleaned carpet, crisp paper, and the slightest bit of vanilla greeted him. The scent was indeed one worthy of love. Perhaps what he found more worthy of love were all the miniscule details Ryleigh introduced him to, as if they experienced opposing versions of reality. Peter vaguely remembered what it was like to be young and invigorated by the tiniest pockets of bliss the world had to offer. Life was simpler without existential dread nipping at your heels.

He stumbled across Ryleigh snooping around the young adult section, transfixed with the description of a vibrant yellow book. His skin flushed beneath his sweater at the maddening serenity which circumfused her.

"I figured I'd find you lurking in poetry."

"You scared me." Her fingers fanned out over her chest. Weaponizing the book, she smacked him on what barely qualified as a bicep. "No, my parents would probably stage an intervention if I brought another chapbook home."

Peter rubbed his assaulted arm. "They must have been proud about the Beckwith scholarship. That's a big deal."

"Eh, they were whatever about it. They see it as a way to get scholarship money, but they worry my interest in it runs too deep, that I'll morph into a starving artist."

"How do you see it? It's your life. People might tell you how you should run it, hell, they will tell you. You have to keep your head down and remember that you have the final say."

"The truth is, I'm not sure what I want to do. I'm sick of the interrogations and suggestions from my parents, from my college counselor. It's too much pressure, you know? I'll turn up on campus come fall, undeclared, and figure it out like everyone else. Which reminds me ..."

She produced an envelope from her purse, extending it to him and then immediately retracting it. "I don't want to keep anything from you, and if we're going to hang out or whatever it is that we're doing, this is something you should know about."

Ryleigh transferred the document to his waiting hand. The mustard 'M' hit him like an uppercut while he scanned the acceptance letter. Everything blurred together after the first few lines, brain checking out once the significance had been gleaned. By the fall, she would be gone.

He returned the paper, bearing no indication of the numbness sheathing his every muscle. "University of Michigan? That's incredible."

"I thought you had a right to know after the Hemlock drama. Enough about me, let's discuss the reason we're here. You owe me an explanation for this fake girlfriend business."

Peter knew this avenue of discussion could not be avoided forever, and yet he had put it off like a cumbersome article hours before deadline. He leaned against the bookshelf, confident he would not knock it over and create a domino effect throughout the store.

"I thought introducing you as my girlfriend would get my dad off my back, at least while they were in town. Of course, it didn't make much of a difference. I shouldn't have involved you."

"Is he always like that?"

He flashed a broken smile. "More or less."

"I don't know how familiar you are with the formalities of dating, but it's not okay to introduce someone as your girlfriend - especially to your parents - if you haven't even consulted with the girl in question."

"I wasn't sure if you would go along with it." His arms felt impossibly heavy. The imagined weight pulled his shoulders low.

Her cheeks adopted a rich hue that would have made the most dazzling garnet gems envious. She freed the strands of hair that were tucked behind her ear. They cascaded to disguise her reddening face. "The fact that you think I wouldn't play along with being your fake girlfriend is hilarious."

"Why's that?"

When she looked at Peter, her usual cheerfulness was gone. "I'll let you mull it over."

"Open your eyes."

Ryleigh's heart skipped a beat. Harris glowed against the bleak backdrop of the night. Streetlamps, windows, and traffic lights twinkled like a thousand fireflies. Even the suburbs emitted a distant gleam, houses decked out with Christmas displays competing to be seen from outer space. It was ironic, a Californian showing her the beauty of this sleepy Connecticut town where she had spent her entire life.

"This is normally when I'd take you for a drink. Obviously, that's out of the question so I had to brainstorm an alternative." Peter wriggled out of his peacoat and held it open. "Here, put this on. You need it more than I do."

His heat transferred to her as she plunged into the fabric that had been nestled against him all evening. The coat swallowed Ryleigh, but, surrounded by his warmth and his scent, she did not care. "Is this where you come to air your complaints toward humanity?"

"Something like that. When I started working for the paper, I'd come up here and chain-smoke a concerning number of cigarettes before deadline."

"What made you quit?"

He planted his forearms on the building's ledge, hands cupping the crooks of his elbows. "Cappuccinos. I was 23 when I had my first sip, and we've been in a loving relationship ever since."

"Relationship. There's an unfamiliar term."

Ryleigh gripped the lapels of the coat. She wondered if the admission acted as a gateway for him to see through her tough girl facade. Did he connect the dots of her pathetic existence: that she had never been on a date, never had a boyfriend, never had sex? Whatever conclusions he may have drawn, he kept them to himself.

"Are the guys at your school morons, or what? No one's ever asked you out? Actually, I believe it. You're pretty intimidating for someone of such diminutive stature."

"I like older guys."

"Oh, yeah? I had no clue." Peter smirked. His fingertips skimmed along his jawline. "For what it's worth, if you weren't in high school, I'd ask you out in a heartbeat."

"You could ask me out now, if you weren't wigged-out by societal backlash. Who cares what everyone else thinks?"

"Excuse me for having morals."

Peter's morals would be the death of her. Though they stood a handful of inches apart, his standoffishness made it unnavigable. Because this was not a date, she was just his kid barista cashing in on an IOU. The breath she pulled in failed to vanquish the hollowness invading her chest. She concentrated on her boots, feeling small and helpless in the reflection of the patent leather. "What happened with you and Kendall?"

"I suppose if I don't tell you, you'll get it from her?"

Ryleigh nodded.

"I'll give you the PG-13 version, not because I don't think you can handle it, but I'd like to spare myself some embarrassment. I'd also like to preface this by saying she and I were pretty good friends leading up to this." Peter thrust his hands into his pockets, arms tucked at his sides. He cast his gaze at the concrete. "We went out one night for drinks, and afterward, we ended up at her apartment. Things escalated. It had been a long time since I'd been physical with some-one, and combined with the alcohol, let's say it was a recipe for disaster."

"I don't get it. You guys didn't hook up?"

She knew exactly what he meant, but torturing him brought her immense pleasure.

"We were heading in that direction. Jesus, you really don't get it?" He seemed to be on the verge of vomiting. "I came all over her skirt."

Biting her tongue hardly dampened her maniacal grin. Buckling to her knees, she quaked with soundless laughter. Red waves of humilia-tion crashed over Peter's face.

"You're a sadistic girl, Ryleigh Branson."

16

JUST SOME KID

Peter leaned against the hood of his car. Dainty snowflakes flurried around them, melting instantly upon contact. Scattered water droplets clung to Ryleigh's waves, making it look as though someone had sprinkled silver glitter in her hair. She tipped her head toward the sky and the tiny crystals delivered a shower of kisses unto her face. For an irrational moment, Peter envied those snowflakes. He too wished to melt into her skin and cease to exist.

"Tonight was almost perfect." His coat still hung around her shoulders while the sleeves lay vacant.

"Enlighten me. What did I miss?"

He knew the answer long before asking the question. He had seen it in her crestfallen glances on the roof, in the way she had simultaneously held her breath and his hand. Peter saw it presently, in her slow smile and that glossed-over gaze which refused to let him go.

His fingers tangling in her hair spurned a mild pain in his chest. Not a day had gone by where he did not reflect on the transcendence of their first kiss. She had made him feel whole, if only for a minute. Peter needed to feel that again.

The tips of their noses brushed as he leaned into her. "Keep your tongue to yourself, this time."

"Oh, of course. We wouldn't want you feeling morally compromised."

Languidness laced his acquisition of her silken lips. This contact was something to be savored, to bottle and revisit throughout a lifetime. Their mouths tangled and untangled, creating their own brand of intimacy despite their stoppered lips. His pulse waxed percussive, resonating like a lone, thundering drum amid the stillness of the street. Her teeth skimmed his bottom lip, as if considering to defy the boundary he had set. Ryleigh never crossed the line.

In fact, she was the one to pull away.

"That bad, huh?"

Shaking her head, she removed and returned his coat. She crossed her arms. "No, it's not you. It's me, I felt … guilty."

Guilty? Why should she feel guilty? I'm the one sullying her youth via my selfish inability to cut her out of my life.

"For what?"

"For wanting something you're so unwilling to give."

The phrase feasted on his nerve endings like a hoard of ravenous termites. *That can't be how she sees it.* He rose from the hood of the car. They were both quiet for a beat as they headed up the paved path toward the Bransons' home.

Manic energy rose in Peter, squeezing a response past his tight lips. "It's not that I'm unwilling to give it. It's a lot more complicated than that."

"Because I'm in high school, right? Because to you, I'm just some kid who makes your coffee."

"I don't see you that way. That's what bothers me."

A broad-shouldered man sporting plaid pajamas and glasses emerged from the shadows of the unlit porch. As Peter pieced together who this must have been, every bit of breath whooshed out of his lungs.

"Peter, isn't it?" he demanded coolly.

"Dad, stop."

Ryleigh's weak interjection made little difference. Mr. Branson joined them on the walkway, daring to enter Peter's personal space.

Rage illustrated itself across his features like a cartoon character, skin reddened and neck corded.

Her father was out for blood.

"This is the guy who's been texting and calling you, is that right? Your mother's convinced of it. And do you know what she said when I asked her why on Earth she let our daughter drive away with a grown man? Your mother said, 'I didn't think she would lie to our faces, Dex.'"

The ruthless reprimanding broke Ryleigh. She turned to Peter and soundlessly sobbed into the wool of his coat. He made the fatal mistake of wrapping an arm around her shoulders.

"Take your vile hands off my daughter, you pervert."

A glinting gold wedding band was all he saw before her father's fist met his unsuspecting face. The punch landed on his cheekbone with a grotesque crunch—either from Mr. Branson's knuckles or Peter's defenseless zygomatic—and skidded to graze his left eye. A vertigo of suffering danced in his dizzied head. Fire, ice, pain, numbness. He stumbled backward from the impact, collapsing on the snow-dotted lawn after a series of unsteady footsteps.

"And you. Get inside the house, young lady. Move it."

The Bransons' front door slammed shut.

Peter could have cried out countless expletives, could have pushed to his feet and booked it out of the neighborhood. But the source of his strength was locked away in her house.

He lay defeated on the dead grass and let the snowflakes nurse his searing face.

"What do you have to say for yourself?"

Ryleigh's tongue was caught in a paper shredder, mangled and incapable of speech. Her lips pressed together to form a thin line as she searched for an explanation. She was not quick enough to prevent her father's tirade.

"Tell me, Ryleigh Collette, what business do you think you have prancing around with a grown man? Your mother agreed to letting you go out with someone college-aged, not someone old enough to be a tenured professor."

Too ashamed to meet her father's glare, she focused on the rug in the middle of the sitting room. The saliva she swallowed felt like an immovable boulder lodged in her tender throat. It took all her strength to hold back the stinging hot tears that clouded her vision.

In her peripheral, a glimpse of her mother's shadow danced along the wall. Charlotte rounded the staircase, clothed in a fuzzy pink bathrobe and hair secured in a ballerina bun.

"You're in high school, for God's sake." Dexter clung to the edge of a wingback chair. His eyes widened, giving the whites more real estate. "What do you suppose this guy wants from someone your age? One thing and one thing alone."

Her pitiful levy broke. Tears flowed over her waterline and streamed across her cheeks. "If you'd give him a chance, you wouldn't say such foul things. You don't know anything about him!"

"Apparently, I don't know anything about my own daughter." His booming baritone ricocheted off the walls.

Dexter said nothing to his wife as he swept out of the room. Seconds later, a door banged upstairs.

Trembling, Ryleigh sank to the floor, crumpling in a defeated mess on the rug. Her thoughts spun like the needle of a compass. Tonight felt like a reconciliation between Peter and herself. A fresh start. That second chance was gone, courtesy of the lie that sponsored her fantastical evening.

One night of bliss and you've wrecked this to hell.

Charlotte knelt beside her weeping daughter on the carpet, rubbing her convulsing back.

"I've never been very good at this." Her mother's forehead creased to reveal its faint wrinkles. "I knew your father would be upset when I told him, but I had no idea he'd react so conversely."

"Conversely? Dad punched him in the face."

"You have to think about it from his perspective. Suppose you have a daughter one day, and one night, she brings home a guy who's old enough to be her father."

"Peter is *not* old enough to—"

She's right. People have kids when they're in high school.

Her chest tightened as the potential ramifications of her mistake set in. What would this lie cost? Would she be forbidden from seeing him? The notion left her nerves raw.

Rug fibers scratched her face, but the irksome sensation dulled in comparison to the relentless knifing wreaking havoc on her heart.

"We've decided to take your phone away for a few months." No matter how carefully Charlotte chose her words, they failed to mask her disappointment. "Why didn't you tell me that day, at Murphy's? Whatever happened to transparency? You used to tell me everything."

"I'm friends with a 35-year-old guy. I don't think transparency would've aided my case."

"35? My God," she mumbled under her breath. Her mother extended an open palm. "Phone."

Ryleigh surrendered the device and cupped her hand over Charlotte's, pleading at her with glassy eyes. "Read our messages, mom. He's a good guy."

"You two are just friends?"

She thought of their kiss, and how it somehow eclipsed their first. Things had always been confusing between them. Tonight's sliver of clarification perhaps meant nothing after the drama with her parents.

"Maybe we've entered a gray area."

"I'll look over the messages. I may not like this, or understand it, but I'm willing to try. For you. I'd like to know who you're spending time with, even if I disagree with the age difference. Your father, on the other hand, I can't promise he'll come around."

Ryleigh struggled to nod her head in response. She felt undeserving of this olive branch. Was this one of those parental maneuvers steeped in reverse psychology? 'We'll let her think she has the upper hand …'

She swallowed heavily as her mother bounded upstairs, leaving her to rot beside the crackling fireplace with nothing but her guilt-laden conscious for company.

Pink, swollen flesh stared back at Peter in the bathroom mirror. There were no cuts, no scrapes, only red splotches that would be replaced with unsightly blueish-purple bruising in the days ahead. He had tried to do the right thing with Ryleigh, to kiss her in a chaste way, and how did the universe retaliate? A perturbed father's fist in his face.

"You did this to yourself."

They were the same words Mr. Roberts had spoken to a then 22-year-old Peter the first and only time he missed deadline. The throbbing in his cheek intensified when he stopped to think about how much of his life had gone to waste over this career he had become submissive to.

Leaning on the sink's ledge, he buried his face in his hands. Broken, unsteady breaths escaped. A tornado of clashing emotions raged in his heart, fighting one another for dominance of his mood.

The scholarship article had been his first strike, the punch a clear second. One more lick of karmic retribution and he was out.

"I need a drink," he murmured, whisking into the kitchen. Peter spied the three bottles of red wine atop the refrigerator with immediate disinterest.

Liquor had never been a big deal to him, but he kept a supply on hand. He should have displayed it in a glass box proclaiming, 'Break in case of romantic folly.'

It certainly would have made it easier to find.

He rummaged through several cabinets, fighting hard to recall where he hid the long-forgotten bottle of whiskey, until he located the dusty vessel. Deciding that a cup was unnecessary, Peter threw back a swig of the aged liquid. He welcomed the burning sensation that trickled over his lips and along his throat. It dulled the stinging in his cheek, righted the weakness in his legs.

He retreated to the living room and flung himself on the sofa, placing the whiskey on the floor within arm's reach.

You put your neck out on the line, knowing things would end this way. You knew it wouldn't work with her, that there were too many complications.

"Why couldn't you just ignore her when you met? What's so charming about her?"

It was an inane inquiry. He had been at Ryleigh's mercy ever since she whispered 'antithesis' in his ear at the football game. Maybe his obsession with her predated that; maybe it could be traced back to the first time she looked at him, blue irises popping against her overly lined eyes like a clear sky bordering a thunderstorm.

His ankle twisted as an unwanted sensation built inside of him. Unadulterated urgency flooded his veins, a triple dog dare from his dangerously low serotonin to take another drink.

"Every time things go south with a girl you end up with a bottle of liquor, how's that?"

Heather. *Drink.* Kendall. *Drink.* Ryleigh. *Drink.*

And what's the common denominator? You.

He lay perfectly still on the couch, riding out the intense but familiar paralysis of anxiety. Peter caught his breath as the initial panic and fear disbanded.

Worry made a terrifying comeback when he remembered the last time he had been rendered this hopeless. But this would not be like last time. He had a low stock of whiskey. He had left the pain medicine in the bathroom where it belonged.

'Don't you ever scare me like that again,' his mother had said when he woke up in the hospital seven years earlier.

Peter had brushed lips with death once and he was in no hurry for an encore. No, he would begrudgingly remain on Earth and carry out his life sentence of wallowing in the confounding misery of human existence. He just needed to drink enough to forget the memories swirling in his head.

Heather's lies. Kendall's thighs. Ryleigh's eyes.

"This is all that'll ever come of your pathetic life, capping off the night with a stiff drink and all your problems," he whispered, losing consciousness.

Peter kicked himself for being eight minutes late as he sprinted through the hallway to his office. He flipped on the lights as the fire in his lungs subsided from running most of the way to the newspaper building. Blinding fluorescence flooded the room, further agitating the migraine rattling around in his skull.

While the outdated desktop computer started up, he made use of the time by checking the voicemails on the clunky landline. The red, flashing number on the device indicated five new messages.

"Hey, Peter, this is Brad from the Audubon Society. I got your message about scheduling an interview and wanted to follow up. If Wednesday works for you, I'm ..."

Fuck Brad. Fuck birds. Fuck Harris.

Peter wanted to crawl between his sheets and sleep the next decade away. He clutched his stomach as a crippling siege of nausea overpowered him.

"Oh, God."

Looking around in a frenzy, he snatched the mesh wastebasket beneath his desk. A waterfall of vomit flowed into the trash can, oozing through the metal cross hatching. He cursed the uselessness of the mesh material as his spell of sickness tapered off.

"Rosenfeld, would you mind ..." Mr. Roberts materialized in the doorway.

Self-consciousness threatened to further wreck Peter's immune system as his boss studied the unsightly pool seeping out of the wastebasket and onto the carpet.

Mr. Roberts removed his gold-wired glasses and examined his sickly employee; thick hair in disarray, an unshaven face, dark circles framing his bloodshot eyes, slacks wrinkled beyond repair.

"Go home, Rosenfeld."

TWO MONTHS LATER

17

FINE, FINE

he many illuminated windows of *The Harris Chronicle* acted as a dim spotlight inside the darkened coffee shop. The Roast was deader than dead for a weeknight.

Peter had not been avoiding the cafe, though he made it a point to avoid Ryleigh. Whenever she dwelled on it, the world seemed to slow down. If she could sustain that state, maybe he could catch up to her, maybe he could digest the sticky predicament in which they found themselves.

"I ended things with Colin." Andrea stirred her iced macchiato, white swirls of milk blending into the espresso.

Ryleigh should have gauged the breakup by the two inches missing from Andy's caramel tresses.

"Everyone who splits this time of the year always gets back together by prom. Come April, your Prince Charming will be on your arm, escorting you into the exhibition center."

She frowned and ceased the compulsive stirring. "Are you even listening to me? I broke up with *him*."

"Sorry, I—"

"You have a lot on your mind, right? I've heard that line from you during our last trillion conversations. Your dad punched paperboy and now he's ghosting you. I refuse to sit here and let you spend the rest of our senior year as a lovelorn zombie."

"He's not ghosting me. My dad's held my phone hostage for two months."

Her father had returned her phone that morning, attached with a jaw-dropping offer. Seizing her recyclable cup, Ryleigh zeroed in on the newspaper building.

Within thirty minutes, she would be knocking on Peter's office door. Would he slam it in her face? Turn her away?

She swallowed the lukewarm remnants of her latte along with her concerns.

"Well, seeing as I'm single and you've been ditched by your fossilized boyfriend, I guess we have no choice but to be each other's prom dates. Better than going stag."

Ryleigh bit the inside of her cheek. "One, Peter's not a fossil. Two, he is *not* my boyfriend. Three, I'm not going to prom. Forget it."

"I smell boy trouble." Kendall squatted by the display case, boxing up the unsold pastries. "You need to straighten out whatever's brewing between you and the coffee purist. He's making my shifts unbearable."

"She'd need a miracle to work that one out. Her dad punched him in the face," Andrea volunteered.

Kendall held her chin high. "I knew he was lying. When I asked about his shiner he said he hit his face fixing something under his sink. There's no pipe in existence that could've caused that much damage. Seriously, though? I can't picture him in a fight."

"Peter told me what happened between you guys." Ryleigh's face felt impossibly hot. She restrained her focus to the tabletop, unwilling to meet her co-worker's gaze after such an intimate revelation.

"That was my favorite skirt. I bet he left out the part where he offered to pay my dry-cleaning bill. He's a trip, huh?"

Andrea stilled before slipping into a pained expression. Rising from her chair, she said, "I'll leave you two alone to discuss your X-rated filth." She aimed a french tip at Ryleigh. "I'm not dropping this prom thing. You. Me. Dresses. Memories. Magic. We're going."

"You're not going, are you?" Kendall asked once the front door swung shut.

"Not a chance." Ryleigh joined her at the case. She assembled one of the mini, white pastry boxes. "Do you mind if I take some of these?"

"Be my guest. My boyfriend's thoroughly annoyed with the hoard of treats I bring home every night. I've started to pawn them off on family members." Kendall's movements slowed. She placed croissants in the larger box with great deliberation. "Peter talks about you, you know."

"Yeah, right. Like what?"

"Like he should've been more careful because you're the best thing he's ever had. Lovesick stuff."

Not even a twinge of jealousy edged her tone. And why should Kendall be jealous? Peter was nothing more than a hilarious anecdote in her life.

"Lovesick?" Her stomach contorted at the adjective.

"Believe what you will, but I haven't seen him this despondent since I accidentally put peppermint syrup in his cappuccino a few Christmases ago. He's got it bad for you."

How could he possibly 'have it bad for her' when he had erected a steel wall of resistance? Were they talking about the same Peter Rosenfeld? The emotionally unavailable guy who never seemed to relax enough to have one iota of fun? The guy who had demoted her to closed-mouthed kisses?

Yeah, because nothing screams attraction like retracting established physical boundaries.

And though it had been annoyingly innocent, the memory of their snowy kiss at the end of her driveway refused to fade. Not that she wanted to forget the gloriously gentle pressure of his mouth, or the invasive bite of his cologne, or the heat of his thumb blazing a trail across her icy cheek.

She had a feeling there was a slim chance of reliving such a delight upon turning up at his office, and that all-too-real notion busted her heart's flotation device, letting it sink to the bottom of her soul.

To dull the searing ache in her chest, Ryleigh grabbed pieces of bakery tissue and retrieved slices of banana bread and a couple of plain bagels, his favorites. She would need him in an agreeable mood, and carbs were the way to Peter's caged heart, after all.

"What do you know about his ex?" The question ran a hundred warm-up laps in her mind, and she still felt unprepared when it slipped out.

Nosiness was not something she prided herself on, not like Andrea, who wore the quality like a badge of honor.

Kendall halted her pastry selection. She dropped her voice to a fraction of a decibel, as if Peter could hear them from across the street. "Heather? Not much. Except that she's the reason he left Cali. So, I'd guess whatever she did had him pretty fucked up to abandon his friends and family on a whim."

Everything within Ryleigh splintered, creating small cracks for his hurt to seep into her fissured tissue. A rising tide of saliva goaded her violent nausea, but she found herself unable to swallow and banish the boiling sickness.

She almost rattled off an affectless laugh at her body's involuntary reaction for the sheer irrationality of hurting for a man who refused to let her get close to him.

But, perhaps this jagged piece of his past explained away some of that detachment.

Pushing to her feet, Ryleigh glanced at the entrance to *The Chronicle's* office and her pulse tripled its normal beats per minute. Facing Peter after months apart would have been awkward enough without this newly acquired information about his failed relationship.

Focused on the bit of floor between them, she pleaded, "Could you, uh, could you not mention this to him? That I asked?"

Kendall mustered a quick, unconvincing smile. "Don't worry about it."

Three hundred words of a draft detailing a college student-led renewable energy rally stared back at Peter. A few more sentences and it would be done, submitted and out of his life, much like the women who had come and gone.

He had no tenacity.

If he had remained silent and ignored Heather's wrongdoing, would they have still been together? If he had continued to pursue Kendall after their intimate mishap, would she have still been interested? If he had never read the scholarship article, would he and Ryleigh have gone out?

Five hours remained until deadline, and his final article of the evening neared completion. Peter had not acquired a superhuman ability to compose at an unthinkable pace, but he had come in four hours earlier than everyone else.

As soon as he woke up, he went to the office. Being at home was too much to handle under the torment of this crushing duress which bore no expiration date.

The silence. The emptiness. The loneliness.

His glowing phone screen vied for attention out of the corner of his eye. It faded momentarily, reviving its luminance to reveal a new voicemail from his mother.

"Honey, you haven't returned my calls in weeks and, well, I'm a little more than concerned. I know you're old enough to take care of yourself, and maybe I shouldn't worry so much, but I can't help it. I hope you know, whatever's going on, I'm always a phone call away."

Peter siphoned a stinging breath and looked toward the paneled ceiling. Disappointment surfaced when those square tiles failed to provide answers to any of his innumerable problems. He made a bid to return to his work as if he had never received the message, but his mother's desperate speech rendered him unable to concentrate.

He bit his tongue while the dial tone purred.

"Hey, sweetheart." She spewed motherliness. Her giddy demeanor belied the concern-drenched voicemail. "It's about time you rang me back. How are you?"

"Fine, fine. How've you guys been?" Peter returned the question out of respect rather than genuine curiosity.

"You know us, same old thing. And you are not 'fine, fine,' mister. If that were the case, you wouldn't dodge my calls for weeks on end."

"Seriously, mom, I'm fine."

"Listen, Peter Zayn, I've been your mother for 35 long years. I know you don't like to talk about these things, I just …" Her tearful voice pleaded with him. "For Christ's sake, let me help you before you wind up in the hospital with another tube down your throat. I can't watch you go through that again."

The color drained from his face, a tango of dizziness following in its wake. He had fought hard to forget the details of his 48-hour stint in Dominican Hospital. The events preceding his stay, however, refused to detach from his memory.

"Who's on the phone?" Gideon shouted, trying to join the conversation from another part of the house. "Not that cable company again, is it?"

"It's our son." The reply dissolved any interest Gideon harbored toward the call.

"Dad can't hear, can he?"

"No," Janet sniffed. "He's in the study."

The familiar screech of his mother sliding back their ancient glass door and stepping onto the patio filled his ear. A loud snap indicated a cigarette being lit in preparation for anything he may throw at her.

"Ryleigh's parents didn't know we were hanging out. They weren't exactly keen on our friendship. Her father, in particular, wasn't pleased, to put it lightly."

"I'd imagine that came as quite a shock for them. You need to understand that as parents they're in a tough spot. You're *much* older than her, honey. Some people aren't going to accept that right away, or at all. These things take time. I'm sure they'll change their mind once they get to know you."

"If I'm even afforded the chance." Pessimism dripped from the tip of his tongue. "I have a story I need to finish up. I'll call you tomorrow, alright?"

"You better keep your word, or I'll fly out to Connecticut to lecture you in person. I love you, Peter."

A soft knock sounded on the door.

"It's open." He muted the call for a fraction of a second, unmuting it only to deliver the parting, "Love you, too, mom."

Peter did not greet whoever had entered the room. He cowered behind preoccupancy, responding to a time-sensitive e-mail. After skimming over what he wrote, he sent the message and switched tabs to the renewable energy story.

"What do you need?" he asked, refusing to divert his attention from the computer screen.

The visitor's shoes shuffled on the cheap, scratchy carpet as they approached. A ghostly hand with chipped red nail polish extended to his right, slipping a white box onto the desk. Peter squared his jaw at The Roast's familiar, stamped black logo.

He spun around in the swivel chair and caught Ryleigh by the wrist, mid-exit. "What would your dad say if he knew you were dropping by my office?"

But Peter did not give a damn about Mr. Branson. There Ryleigh stood, held in place by his charged grasp, smelling almost as tantalizing as the pastries.

"That's why I'm here." She shook her wrist from his death grip. Even under the plight of irritation, her beauty was unjust. "My parents want you to come to dinner on Saturday."

18

APPROPRIATELY AGED

Peter quaked on the Bransons' doormat, cradling his oldest bottle of shiraz and failing to pull himself together. The neighborhood's noises amplified his trepidation: the ominous roaring of a lawnmower, creaking trampoline springs, an incessantly yapping lapdog.

It had been all of two days since Ryleigh delivered the news about the paramount dinner, and he had processed the monumental invitation no sooner than the evening had arrived. What was he to do, cancel at the last minute?

Nonsense. So, there he stood, a quiet mess on the porch, overdressed and underprepared.

Straightening his belt, Peter rang the doorbell. He observed the oddity of his battered sedan parked all too near the family's luxurious vehicles. It served as a visual reminder that he was an unwelcome visitor in the hell that was suburban Harris.

His pulse flittered in his throat when Ryleigh—and not one of her parents—answered the door in a rust turtleneck and skinny jeans that hugged her hips.

She scanned him from head to toe. "Hey, you made it."

"I'd like to come inside, if you're done ogling me."

Her foot shot out to block the door from opening. "A few things before you come in. This dinner was my mom's idea. She's the more liberal one. My dad," she licked her lips, "he's going to need way more convincing. You need to be on your best behavior."

His inhibitions went down the drain. He angled to kiss her cheek, whispering, "I've been on my best behavior the last six months."

Stunned to silence, she moved aside and granted him entrance. It opened into a formal sitting room, so meticulously decorated one would think it was staged for a magazine photoshoot. Peter's grip tightened on the wine as he studied the sumptuous fixtures and finishes, trailing behind Ryleigh through the narrow hallway.

Inadequacy constricted his veins. He had to wonder if, somehow, their undefinable attachment had been a joke to her, if he had been nothing more than an amusing, urbanite puppet in a game of rebellion against her parents.

Ryleigh whipped around, halted palm pressed to his stomach. Her soft voice soothed his self-contained illogical diatribe. "Relax, alright? If disaster strikes, we'll recalculate."

"Okay."

When they reached the kitchen, she branched off to help her mother transfer prepared dishes to the dining room, leaving him alone with a man he now feared.

Dexter wiped his hands on a dish towel. He was intimidating even with his back turned; not because he appeared threatening by nature, but because Peter had firsthand experience with his ire.

"I'd prepared one of those classic dad lines like, 'Hope you didn't have any trouble finding the place,' and then I thought, gee that's silly, he's been here before. Either way, I'd hope this is your first time inside." He rounded the island and extended a hand toward his daughter's potential suitor. "I don't believe I introduced myself during our initial meeting. Dexter Branson."

The informality with which he spoke about the violent outburst made him seem like a megalomaniac.

Something familiar rang out in that name, in that face.

They had met once, more than a decade prior. Peter had his suspicions when Ryleigh mentioned his line of work at the ugly sweater gathering, but now, looking him in the eye, he was one hundred percent certain.

Peter shook the outstretched hand. "Rosenfeld."

Ryleigh coiled her ankles around the legs of the dining chair. Tension was a horrendous misappropriation of what hung in the room. These stakes were nuclear.

She stole sips from her bubbling flute of root beer while the adults indulged in the full-bodied wine. Cyanide would have been a more apt beverage to survive this near hostage get together.

"Rosenfeld," Dexter said, twirling his fork in a pile of garlic whipped potatoes. "Where do I know that name?"

Peter had no intention of bringing the actual reason for the name's familiarity to the forefront of his memory. In fact, the night would go much more smoothly if Dexter had somehow forgotten why 'Rosenfeld' rang out in his mind as if he had been branded by a red hot poker.

He played coy. "Read the paper?"

"Ah, you're a journalist," Dexter gathered. His mouth became taut, walnut brows stiffening.

"My father says the stuff I put to print is a far cry from journalism. But, technically, that's my official job title."

Ryleigh ached at Peter's discomfort. His eyes shifted, never lingering on anyone for more than a few seconds.

Nudging his loafer, she gave him a smile so slight, it went undetected by the others. Her adventurous toes grazed the skin just inside the cuff of his dress pants. He directed a piercing glance at her through the stemless glass as he downed the rest of its contents, a silent but certain 'knock it off.'

"You wrote that piece about my practice when it opened, isn't that right?" Dexter blinked in slow waves, a forged front of calmness. He peered at Peter over the top of his spectacles. "The one that said, 'A pediatric dentist office without child-friendly decorations is terrifying. Parents may as well take their kids to a haunted house?' You honestly thought that was a winning quote to include in your article?"

Peter grimaced as the damning line was recited.

"I give members of this community a chance to voice their point of view. Who am I to suppress their opinions?" Ryleigh kicked his knobby ankle, inciting a wince from its receiver. "I apologize that I, no doubt, offended you. I hadn't been with the paper long, and I was still feeling out my voice. What made you go into pediatrics?"

"I'll be asking the questions tonight."

Ten minutes into dinner and they're at each other's throats. Ryleigh hung her head low, peeking at Peter through her mascara-coated lashes.

Charlotte, aided by a gratuitous gulp of red, tried to keep the dinner from careening off its track. "Ryleigh tells us you're from California. Which part?"

"Santa Cruz. It's about an hour from San Francisco. I've been here since 2005."

"And was that after high school or college?" Dexter asked, hijacking the polite turn in conversation. Amicability was not on the menu tonight.

"College."

"And you have what, a bachelor's, a master's?"

"Bachelor's."

"And how many families' dinner tables have you sat around convincing parents that you aren't a threat to their teenage daughter?"

Oh my God. This is a nightmare.

Cold sparks of shock hit Ryleigh's core as a heaviness burrowed in her stomach. Peter stared at his plate as if it were an exquisite work of art, while Charlotte cast a nasty glare in her husband's direction.

"This wine is fantastic, by the way. And it's appropriately aged." Dexter shoveled a piece of broccoli into his mouth and presented their guest with a hard look. "Would you mind going up to your room, pumpkin? I'd like to speak with Peter, alone."

"I don't know what you think you're doing with my daughter, but I intend to find out." An unsightly vein throbbed in a grotesque manner on Dexter's temple. "I'm permitting you this chance solely because Ryleigh doesn't have a habit of making poor decisions, and quite frankly I'm mystified by all of this."

The men remained at the dinner table, seated opposite one another. Peter likened the situation to a suspect being taken to a police station for questioning.

Did chasing happiness qualify as a crime?

Ryleigh had gone to her bedroom, as ordered by her father; a princess locked away in a tower. He had a sinking feeling his rescue efforts would fall short.

"Your concerns are valid. Believe me, I realize the circumstances are unusual."

This was his chance, his one chance to prove his worth to Dexter, and the outlook for the remainder of the evening was grim.

He scoffed, flaring his nostrils like a fire-breathing dragon. "That's certainly one way to put it."

Why did you think this was a good idea? Why did you agree to this? Can't you see his mind is made up? Peter placed an elbow on the table and rested his cheek against his outstretched hand, formulating a response.

"Look, Mr. Branson, I'm not here to bullshit you. I'm not going to fabricate anything for the sake of getting on your good side. What I will tell you is that I'm an honest guy, and I hold Ryleigh in high regard. You should know, she and I are just friends."

He ignored Peter's ad-libbed but heartfelt speech.

"Just friends? Well that smoothes everything over, doesn't it? That makes all of this alright in your book? Justification. There's a word you need to familiarize yourself with. How did this even happen?"

"It was a mutual thing," Peter stated without any frivolous extrapolation.

So much for 'honest guy.' Ryleigh had pined for their togetherness, or their ever fluctuating lack thereof. But he could not divulge to her father of all people that she had been the instigator.

"Mutual," he repeated, rubbing his arm, perhaps staving off the temptation to pulverize the other half of his face. The imagined threat made Peter flinch. Dexter stood and brushed off his slacks. "I've had all I can handle for one evening, I'm afraid. You can show yourself out."

An unsettling chill snuck into the home as he departed through a door on the other side of the room.

Trudging through the hallway, Peter felt foolish for showing up. Perspiration ran amuck beneath the trappings of his dress shirt. Two hours earlier, he had questioned Ryleigh's importance to him. Now, he grew hysterical over the prospect of her disappearing from his life. His brain conjured every possible defense to block out the thoughts that were trying to penetrate the delicately constructed fortress.

Chill until you get home, you can make it.

"Nice seeing you again, Peter," Charlotte called from the kitchen as he passed in the hall.

"You too, Mrs. Branson."

He did not give in to the voice in his head urging him to stop and ask Charlotte why she had thought it wise to bound herself in holy matrimony to a raving lunatic.

Nearing the staircase in the living room, he froze upon encountering a pair of small, arched feet sticking out from the bottom step. Peter inched forward, revealing himself to the eavesdropper. He shot his thumb backward, "How much of that did you hear?"

"Enough." Abandoning her spot on the steps, Ryleigh joined him at ground level. "Can I walk you out, at least?"

"Yeah, but we should make a break for it before your dad comes shuffling through to kick my ass—again." Peter laughed despite the pain radiating in his chest.

His distraught dream girl led them out to the porch. Night swallowed the neighborhood, putting the evening's noises to rest. A half moon hung in the sky and cast silvery light on Ryleigh's perturbance.

"It's safe to say your dad wasn't too impressed with me. I can't believe he remembered that godforsaken article. That didn't help."

She regarded him as if he had uttered the most imperceptible thing in the world.

Ryleigh gestured between their bodies. "Peter, what are we? I mean, what is this? Because I overheard your distinction of 'just friends' and I'm not cool with that. I've waited patiently in your friendzone long enough."

He could not refute the truth. Cue the excuses.

"You're leaving in August."

"Why can't we have until then? What's stopping us from making the most of the next seven months?"

"I'll tell you why. I can't give myself to you knowing that before fall hits, you'll be gone. In a few weeks, I'll be 36 and I've been in one serious relationship. *One.*" He flashed a finger. "I can't even kiss you without carrying around the guilt of someone serving a life sentence."

It had all become too much. Their feelings, their families, their fate. His cynical obstinacy and her naive fragility. The cosmos had pulled out all its stops to drive a wedge between them. Yet, they were still fighting for this, each in their own way.

"You can try. We can make it work"

"Try? What more do you want from me?" His temperature rose to match his agitation, a matchstick burn striking the base of his neck. "I came here to work things out with your parents and I sat, politely might I add, through your dad's ridiculous interrogation."

Her eyes glassed over, filling with tears as her lips trembled. She stared at him with a blankness that suggested she was at a loss for words.

Once her emotions caught up, Peter stood no chance.

"I want *you*, you idiot," Ryleigh enunciated through gritted teeth. "All of you. I want to be yours."

19

YES, DADDY

*P*eter despised covering The Bridal Expo, yet he wound up with the assignment every year. It was coordinated by boutique dress shop owners and middle-aged mothers, the latter inviting their daughters to participate in the show and crossing their fingers that it may bring them good fortune to tie the knot. As much as he would have loved to dive into that load of superstitious nonsense, he had been sent to extract an economic angle.

There were but two bridal shops in Harris, rendering them natural-born rivals. They may have been in the business of love, but at the end of the day, they were both in the business of making money.

Knotted owner Angelica Hughes monopolized the left side of the room. The other side showcased offerings from *The One,* owned by Theresa Dawson. Rows upon rows of white and off-white dresses occupied rolling racks. The stuffy, itchy garments showed off their beads, glitter, pearls, and sequins, begging to be purchased. Peter tried his best to avoid looking at any of the prominently exposed price tags. One year, he nearly fainted upon discovering an innocent looking gown was comparable in value to a month of his salary.

Models stood on circular platforms at each boutique's display, giving them the appearance of fragile dolls. Each woman wore a different style of dress, its name on a sign at the model's feet, making it easy for the shop owners to provide visual examples for the expo's attendees.

Peter approached Mrs. Hughes, pulling out his recorder and taking a sip of the now cold cappuccino he carried.

"I'm Peter Rosenfeld, with the *Chronicle*." He flashed his credentials. "Would it be alright if I ask you a few questions about your involvement with the expo?"

"You've been covering us for what, 10 years or something?" Mrs. Hughes shook her head, waving a hand in dismissal. She twisted the stack of gold bracelets on her wrist. "I know who you are, sweetheart. No need for formalities."

"Sorry. Second nature." He launched into interview autopilot with the click of the record button. "What can you offer attendees of the expo that they can't get at your boutique, *Knotted*?"

"I run a 15% discount on all of my gowns for this event. It might not seem like a lot, but 15% savings starts to add up when you're making a large purchase like this."

Out of the corner of his eye, he spied a diminutive model with skin as colorless as her dress climbing onto one of the round platforms. She whirled around to face the crowd, petrified like a deer in headlights. Biting down on his curiosity, he pressed onward, "Last year, did you notice that your participation in this show led to higher sales?"

"It's hard to say. I do most of my business in the fall, and that stays pretty consistent." Mrs. Hughes retraced Peter's gaze to the awkward model. "My, my, she's gorgeous in that gown."

He terminated the recording. "Excuse me for a moment. I think I know that mermaid."

Ryleigh relinquished a $5 bill from her wristlet in exchange for a shiny plastic button marked 'Harris Bridal Expo 2019.' Feminine energy stifled the room. The civic center bustled with groups of women of every age and relation, all diamond rings and designer handbags. She felt out of place in her ripped jeans and dirty sneakers.

Finding Peter amid the herd of women should have been a non-issue. Still, a superpower to detect testosterone would have proven useful.

"She's perfect." A woman with big hair and pearl earrings pointed at Ryleigh, assessing her features. A second woman, donning an awful leopard sweater, stood by her side.

"Perfect for what?" Ryleigh glanced around to ensure she was the one to whom they were referring.

The pair of older women took the polite inquiry as an indication of interest. They each grabbed one of Ryleigh's arms and guided her toward the rear of the building.

"One of our girls couldn't make it; she has horrible food poisoning," Leopard explained as they ushered her through a set of black double doors.

Women in their 20's and 30's squeezed and shimmied into the confines of wedding gowns in the hidden room. Some were getting their hair and makeup done; most of them acted as if they would rather be somewhere else. She did not blame them; hitting up a bridal event was the last way she wanted to spend her Sunday, but she was here for the greater good, to reiterate her romantic convictions to an oblivious journalist before her longing and his denying drove them mad.

"It's good of you to step in," Pearl added.

Not like you gave me a choice.

A dress was thrown over her head and her waves were glazed with a shameful amount of hairspray, sparing Ryleigh no time to formulate an argument as to why she could not volunteer to be a glorified mannequin for the afternoon. She fanned a hand in front of her face to dispel the cloud of aerosol fumes, coughing while being tugged along yet again by the two older women.

Leopard swiveled Ryleigh's shoulders to face the proper direction. "Your platform is the one marked 'mermaid' for *The One*'s display."

Keeping the flared bottom of the dress off the floor as she trudged toward the display, she was at least thankful they had left her ratty sneakers on; anytime she wore even the smallest of heels, Ryleigh made a fool of herself. The dress pinched her hips as she stepped onto the platform, causing her to squinch.

"This is ridiculous," she murmured, smoothing out the prickly lace material.

Her throat went dry when she turned to face the crowd, spotting Peter at the other boutique's display. She considered escaping through the exit in the far corner of the room, anything to prevent him from seeing her in this get-up.

But it was too late.

"Are you out of your mind?" Peter demanded. A camera with a faded leather strap hung around his neck. He noticed her eyeing it and tacked on, "Short-staffed. And thank God I'm the one taking pictures, or you'd be plastered all over the paper with the other girls. Imagine if your parents saw that we were at a *bridal* expo together. I'm sure that would go over real well."

"I wanted to see you," Ryleigh said, the five words begging him to forgive her unexpected presence. The benign phrase softened him, relaxing his posture.

The platform she stood on almost brought them to eye level. Peter picked up on details within her face he had previously overlooked: the feathery quality of her brows and a tiny, heart-shaped birthmark on the bridge of her nose.

"How did you know I was here?"

"Ms. Walters told me you were covering the expo, and I thought you wouldn't mind if—"

Peter threw his hands in the air. "So now you're best friends with the receptionist? I don't believe this."

"You'd be surprised what kind of information I can coax out of people with a half dozen Long Johns and my luminous smile."

"Were you at the same dinner? I didn't exactly earn your dad's seal of approval. Unless your goal is to see me gutted and hung up in the town square, I think you should go."

The speech required unbelievable strength. Peter did not want her to leave, but he knew it was for the best. He would have loved nothing more than for her to remain, to steal glances at her in that beautiful gown while carrying out his interviews, enamored by Ryleigh's radiance from afar.

A crowd formed near the pair, drawn in by their public love quarrel. Among them were the two boutique owners.

Mrs. Hughes chimed in, "It's about time you settled down, Peter. Is this the lucky girl?"

"I'd be a dead man before her father let that happen."

Several gasps erupted from the onlookers.

"I don't care what he thinks." Ryleigh squared her bare shoulders. "I'm not going to cut you out of my life just because my dad has a problem with us."

Us. Had he made such an impression on her to warrant the use of this intimate personal pronoun? The answer was a resounding yes. Each flitter of her shadowed lids inaudibly beckoned for a proclamation of commitment. Perhaps the wedding dress had gotten to both of their heads.

"You know how you asked me what we were that night? What we're doing?" Peter inched toward her to generate some separation from the gathering gaggle of people infringing on their private moment.

Every curve and minor imperfection of Ryleigh's face had him moonstruck. He could not be held responsible for whatever tumbled from his mouth.

"I can't give you an answer, because I don't know. All I know is that, if I don't at least give whatever this is a chance, I'll regret it for the rest of my life." Peter dropped to one knee, holding onto her hands. "Ryleigh Branson, will you do me the incredible honor of saving myself from eating copious amounts of Chinese food out of paper boxes on my birthday, and join me for dinner?"

Her lips quivered, accentuating the slight dip in the center of her chin. "You know I will, you dork."

Ryleigh sat at the table alongside her parents, who were unaware that this morning's meal would be served with a heaping side of satisfaction. She drank her orange juice and fought to contain a smug smile as her father flipped through that day's edition of the *Chronicle*.

Unease filled the breakfast scene, any plausible avenues of conversation dashed before they could be vocalized. The fallout of the dinner party had left her relationship with her parents tense and fractured. Peter was worth the brief period of familial dysfunction.

"Ryleigh Colette Branson." Dexter gripped the newspaper and crumpled its edges. *Bingo.*

She feigned ignorance, discharging her lividity on the toast she buttered. "Yes, daddy?"

"What's this?"

He slid the paper across the table. Ryleigh did not spare a glance at the picture, she had a copy of it saved to her camera roll, along with some candids she and Peter had taken together after the expo. Charlotte glimpsed at the page long enough to gleen why her husband was upset.

The headline of the article in question read, 'Love Abounds at 2019 Bridal Expo.' Ryleigh's picture accompanied the piece, with the incriminating 'photo by Peter Rosenfeld' clinging to its edge.

"A bridal event? What, do you think this is funny? Have I not made myself clear? I don't want you associating with this creep. Period."

"Peter's a great photographer, don't you think? He's an even better kisser."

Dexter snatched the paper. "That's it, no phone. Hand it over."

"I thought you might say that, so I signed up for my own plan, which I'm paying for with my *own* money that I earn from *my* job." Ryleigh rose from the table, yanking her backpack from the chair's post. She paused in the doorway that led out to the garage. "Peter's a great guy, and he respects me. There's no reason for you to keep bitching about him."

Her parents flinched as the door slammed.

"Did she say, 'bitching?'" Dexter pinched the skin at his throat. "What are we going to do about this, Charlotte?"

She thumbed the picture. "Look at her face, Dex. Maybe it's love."

"Love? Please, she's just a kid. Why'd you let her get on birth control, for God's sake? You don't think that's emboldened her to pursue something like this?"

Charlotte shrugged, gathering the empty plates from the table. "At least if she finds herself in that situation, she'll be prepared."

"How are you not infuriated over this?"

"I'm not over the moon about it. I've accepted it for what it is. Ryleigh won't be living under this roof forever. After the summer, she'll be off at school. Do you want to spend her last few months at home fighting over some guy?"

"What are you suggesting? That I turn a blind eye?"

"You need to look at this from a more logical angle. She'll be states away from him. What are the odds of this fling surviving? He's a passing phase."

Dexter cogitated on this for an extended period, finally dissenting, "I still don't like it."

"I'm not asking you to like it. I'm asking you to give her some space to make her own choices. She'll never know what it's like to fall if we're always there to catch her."

20

CHEAP WAY OUT

P: Should be heading out in 20. I'm going to swing by my place and change.

R: can't wait! i'll hit up your guest parking and we can walk to dinner.

nbeknownst to Peter, Ryleigh had already been in his condo for an hour, thanks to the glorious stupidity of a spare key he kept under his doormat. Vanilla extract and peanut butter permeated every square inch of the home as cookies baked away in the oven. She had enough foresight to bring the ingredients from home, premeasured. And thank God she had. His pantry was the textbook definition of barren.

Being alone in his place stirred something unfamiliar within her. The air of unease made the passages in her history book blend together to create an abstract display of incomprehensible proportions.

Three glasses of water and restless legs proved to be a miserable combination for sustaining the study charade. She wandered through the narrow hallway to the bathroom, but her bladder's insistence waned upon noticing the adjacent, half-open door.

His bedroom.

You can't go in there. Don't be ridiculous.

Sweat broke out on the soles of her feet in a bid of physiological dissuasion. Ryleigh knew she would be better off returning to the dining nook, checking on the cookies, getting a jump on her history paper—anything but entering that room. But her stubborn feet vetoed any movement. They remained glued to the spot, cementing her mere inches from the devilishly enticing cracked door.

It did not creak as she pushed it, but rather it swung silently to rest against the doorjamb. Standing there in Peter's bedroom, Ryleigh felt as if someone had taken a rolling pin and made quick work of her insides.

She surveyed the space in a singular sweeping glance, convinced that he would be none too thrilled to come home to a surprise guest rifling through his things.

Disappointment struck when she eyed the pristinely made bed; she had expected unmade and inviting. Her fingertips glided over the wrinkle-free comforter on the way to the nightstand. It played host to items which were innocent enough: a weathered paperback with a receipt in place of a bookmark, a bottle of water, a digital alarm clock.

The picture Peter had taken of her at the bridal expo peeked out from underneath the book, edges jagged from being ripped straight off the page. Her chest fluttered with longing when she made the connection to its dubious placement.

A white-capped shaker of prescription pills stationed on the corner demanded her acknowledgement. Prying into something so personal was verboten. Curiosity funded her reluctant pivot, gravitating toward the tangerine bottle instead of the door.

Fluoxetine.

Tempting as it were, she refrained from conducting a quick internet search on the medication. Reading the label had unleashed a

Pandora's box of guilt, set off by the invisible, undefined line Ryleigh had crossed upon seizing the pills.

The bottle tumbled out of her hands as the oven emitted a repetitive trio of beeps. "Shit."

She replaced the medication on the nightstand, exactly as Peter had left it, and shut the door precisely halfway.

Her heart raced at a record-setting trillion beats per minute when he unlocked the front door. Ryleigh held steadfast to her curled up position on the corner of the couch, monstrous textbook nesting on her knees.

"You really shouldn't keep a spare key under your mat. What if I had been a serial killer?"

"Jesus." Peter dropped his keys and work bag. Terror painted itself across his sharp face. *Damn, even scared Peter is hot.* "Congratulations. You're the first girl to burglarize her way into my place to stage a birthday surprise. I'm not sure if I should be flattered or freaked out."

"Happy birthday, handsome. I'd like to take this opportunity to point out, you're exactly twice my age now."

"Don't remind me." He claimed the opposite end of the couch and unlaced his loafers. Nodding at the plastic-wrapped red blooms on the coffee table, he said, "I'm messing up already. I should be the one giving you roses."

"Men can get flowers without feeling emasculated."

Setting her textbook aside, she snagged a cookie from the foil-covered plate. Ryleigh buried her cowardice and straddled his lap like it was nothing. His muscles stiffened as she settled in, arms limp at his sides in a silent protest of uncertainty toward the arrangement.

Her excessive readjustments were more a means of torturing him than seeking personal comfort.

Peter managed to squeak a comment past his comatose veneer. "Surely you have better things to do leading up to a date than baking cookies for a crotchety, old reporter. I'm genuinely concerned for your social life."

She edged the treat into his mouth.

"My social life is bordering on nonexistent. Save your concern. And you're not old."

"I'm on the wrong side of 30. You don't have to stroke my ego. But I guess I appreciate your valiant effort. FYI, this is infinitely better than what my ex unwittingly gifted me for my 21st."

"Which was?"

He presented a crooked grin. "Syphilis."

She loved the way his teeth came together to form neat rows, combined with the juxtaposition of their uneven bottom edges. Her pulse had to think twice before continuing its steady rhythm.

"You're so disgusting, it's almost sweet. I can't tell if you're joking."

"Guess you'll never know." Peter laid a hand on her yoga pant sheathed leg. His palm parked on her thigh, transfusing heat to her through the thin cotton barrier. Ryleigh reined in all of her focus so as not to let her eyes roll into the back of her skull. "Are you wearing these to dinner?"

"News flash, takeout is on the way as we speak, courtesy of my one-day modeling career. I didn't think we'd make it to dinner."

"How'd you figure that?"

She spoke while unfastening the first few buttons on his gingham shirt. "Because this is the first time we've been alone since you've given in to my girlish charm. And it's your birthday, so we should celebrate."

Lust pooled in her abdomen at the pronounced tightness of Peter's khakis. Heat flooded her cheeks as she sat perfectly still atop him, his desire pressed into her through their combined layers of damnable fabric.

Ryleigh had next to no exploits with guys, but some sort of foreign, sexual wisdom came to light around Peter. It was as if his reluctance brandished her with confidence. She caught his earlobe between her teeth and swore he sighed.

His eyes opened, honey drizzled on stone.

"Come on. We shouldn't be doing this."

"Did you or did you not proclaim in the middle of a crowded room that you would give us a chance?" Ryleigh eyed the wispy, sable hair on his partially exposed chest. "I didn't know *this* was hiding under your dress shirts."

He laughed. "Why do you think I keep my shirts snapped up to the collar? I can't risk repulsing the general population."

"Or attracting freaks like me, apparently."

"You're not repulsed?"

She released a hot breath against his neck, nose grazing the inflamed skin. "No, I don't think 'repulsed' is an accurate portrayal of what's happening in my underwear."

That electric utterance was the only encouragement he needed. His tongue swept into her mouth, every movement interwoven with the confidence of someone who had time and experience on his side.

A current of pleasure ripped through Ryleigh as his thumbs massaged the inside of her thighs. He was dangerously close to where she wanted him to be. His fingers trailed over the topside of her leg, traveling to her backside. Every hair on her body raised when Peter's hand slid beneath the band of her yoga pants to ensnare one of her bare cheeks.

"I thought you said you were wearing underwear?"

"It's a thong, moron. They're a must if you wear a lot of yoga pants. No panty lines."

"Thanks for the visual," he mumbled between kisses. "I've spent an unhealthy amount of time wondering what kind of panties you wear."

"God. Hearing you say 'panties' is way hotter than it should be." Ryleigh leaned back and bit her lip. "Is that what you think about when you're getting off to my picture on your nightstand?"

His head dropped to the top of the couch, directing his embarrassment at the ceiling. "In an ideal world, you wouldn't have seen that. You were in my bedroom?"

"For a minute." She worked on the rest of his buttons, each release of the plastic hardware dousing gasoline on the fire between her legs.

"You know, if you wanted nudes for your birthday, all you had to do was ask."

"I haven't slept with anyone in five years. Do you think I possess the courage necessary to make such a demanding request?"

"Five years is better than not at all."

"You're a virgin?" Peter's rough voice went quiet. He enunciated the assumption as if her sexual status was a betrayal.

"Is that so shocking?"

"No. I don't know. I didn't … I didn't expect it."

"Why's that?"

"You're comfortable with yourself, confident."

Ryleigh traced the trail of hair that disappeared below his beltline. "It's because you make me feel comfortable and confident. Inside, I'm as terrified as you are about all of this. I think I'm putting pressure on myself to make a lasting impression on you since I'm leaving in a few months."

"Trust me, I'm in no danger of ever forgetting you."

He grabbed her hips, but instead of pulling her in for another round of kisses, he airlifted her off his lap. She dropped her shoulders to shield her shrinking heart.

"Where are you going?" Ryleigh asked when he migrated toward the hall. Her fingertips grazed the space where their bodies had sealed together like the inseparable Lovers of Valdaro.

"To take a cold shower."

A sinful assortment of street tacos arrived while Peter was showering. She deposited the brown, stapled bag on the dinner table and resumed her perusal of his extensive CD collection.

Most of the albums predated the 2000s, and though she listened to her fair share of old music, she only recognized a fraction of the artists housed on those melamine shelves.

Dropping to her knees, Ryleigh retrieved several cases, admiring the bizarre artwork on their covers. There was something enigmatic about the disarray of the library. Perhaps some strange legion of order existed among those shelves, but she did not know Peter well enough to discern any subtle categorization.

Not even the sound of the bathroom door opening pulled her from her merciless snooping.

"I know you've probably never heard of these little discs," Peter said, grabbing one for emphasis, "but these are CDs. A long time ago in a world not so different from our own, this was *the* way to listen to music." He crouched beside her, donned in a t-shirt and sweatpants. She kicked herself for staring at his forearms. "Hard to believe, I know, but trust me: this was it."

"Oh, fuck off." Ryleigh snatched the case from him. "Is it awful that I find your sarcasm attractive?"

"Is it awful that I find your inaugural use of 'fuck' attractive? Since when do suburban princesses use such foul language?"

"It must be your bad influence."

"Bad influence? I suppose I've earned that label. Speaking of, where do your parents think you are?"

"I didn't exactly tell them I was leaving." No doubt her parents would be furious whenever she returned home. *Like I need a reminder.* She utilized an imaginary tamper to banish the harsh truth from the undercurrent of her thoughts. "If they go poking around for leads on my whereabouts, my best friend will vouch for me. She's a solid alibi."

His mouth hid behind his hand, speaking through his fingers. "Does it bother you? Lying? Sneaking around?"

"It's a trade-off. Seeing you makes it worthwhile."

"I couldn't have gotten anything past my mom in high school if I tried. She was the school nurse, and she had her two fingers on the pulse of gossip as much as on her patients. We've always been unnaturally close, though."

"Yeah, my mom and I were close until I started working at the shop." *Factor in our tight, conflicting schedules and add a middle-aged man to the equation and that basically sealed the decline of our relationship.* Ryleigh, desperate for a subject change, performed a sweeping gesture over the CD shelves. "I must know, which is your favorite?"

"No competition there." Peter rose to his full height, ascertaining the prized disc in an instant. The mustard yellow artwork featured nothing more than a man clad in head to toe denim rocking a bucket hat—the pre-Y2K accessory alone tipped her off that it was a '90s relic.

"New Radicals. Never heard of them."

"You're breaking my heart." He clutched his chest in faux discomfort. After a moment of hesitation, he added with a slight shrug, "I'll loan it to you."

Ryleigh nodded, fingers trailing over the spine of the case. The medicine bottle tossed pebbles at the window to her subconscious, vying for further reflection. She had invaded a private sector of his life. A very private sector, judging by a reluctant internet search she had vowed not to conduct. Peter cupped his face, gloomy eyes trained on her. Meeting his gaze made her stomach carry out olympic-grade somersaults.

Those dismaying gymnastics bullied her to submission. "Peter, are you alright?"

"Excuse me?"

"Earlier, when I went into your bedroom, I-I saw your medicine." The breath Ryleigh drew in failed to satisfy her greedy lungs. "I realize I'm completely overstepping a boundary here. I shouldn't have infringed on your personal space."

A pitiful, strained smile tugged at his lips.

"At first I wasn't going to look it up, because I felt guilty, but I caved. I had to know. When I found out what it was for, well, I felt even worse. I had no idea that you were—" She exhaled, body crumpling. "Please, don't think I expect an explanation. It must be off-putting just hearing—"

He formed an 'X' with his arms, a nonverbal command for her to halt the incessant jabbering. Peter employed an emotionless stare, stuffing his hands in his pockets.

"I was searching for a cheap way out of an unpleasant situation, and I sought help afterward."

The oversimplification left her gaping like a codfish.

"Did you just casually imply that you tried to ..." She did not vocalize the words, for then they would become true.

"So, what's for dinner?" Peter questioned as if they had not been discussing attempted suicide seconds ago.

His dismissal made her blood run cold.

"Tacos."

Ryleigh kept careful watch over him as he unpacked the brown takeout bag like the disturbing yet vague conversation had not taken place. He must have perfected his mask of apathy over the years; Peter wore his signature look of indifference all too well.

Her insides shattered. That expression she had often beheld with adoration suddenly struck her in a much different way, for now she knew it was a front.

21

HELLMOUTH

Ryleigh had fallen asleep during their third movie. Waking her up and sending her home would have been a wiser choice. It would have been the 'adult' thing to do. Peter could not bring himself to disturb the peaceful sight of her slumbering in the crook of his arm.

Tiptoeing through the hall, he peered into the living room to see if his company still lurked in the catacombs of dreamland. He edged closer, matching his steps with the subtle rise and fall of the blanket animating each of her passing breaths. Peter perched on the arm of the couch, captivated by the girl who had thrown his existence out of whack.

Her balled-up fists clutched the blanket, its gathered soft fabric resting under her chin. Tousled waves splayed atop the pillow; the effects of her hair gel waned, resulting in slight frizziness. Traces of black liner clung to her lash line, fading to gray from overextending its wear. Night's rejuvenation plumped her already full lips, flooding them with a pink a few shades darker than their natural color.

How could someone be this gorgeous with day-old makeup clinging to their skin and yesterday's clothes on their back?

She shifted, presumably to lay on her side, but misjudged the margin of clearance and tumbled off the furniture. Ryleigh's eyes sprung open like shutters that had been pulled too tight upon making contact with the floor. Peter let out a low, steady laugh as she tried to untangle herself from the sea of blankets which had swallowed her whole. A muffled groan resonated amid the mound of cotton.

"Good afternoon, sleeping beauty."

He nearly died when she emerged armed with narrowed, bleary eyes. Peter had become a sadist for those blue daggers. She scrubbed a hand across her face and pushed to a sitting position. His mouth went dry as she discarded an inaudible yawn, regenerating like a Disney princess. Baby birds may as well have chirped and circled her head during her delicate stretches.

"What do you find beautiful about drool-crusted lips and ratty hair? Please elaborate." Ryleigh found her footing and folded the wrinkled comforter. She halted on the fourth fold. "Did you say afternoon?"

"It's 1 o'clock. That's p.m., unless you have an alternate definition of afternoon."

Kneeling by the coffee table, she flipped her phone over and muttered under her breath at the one and two zeros on the lock screen. "Why didn't you wake me up sooner?"

"I haven't been up long."

"What kind of lunatic sleeps until the afternoon?"

"Someone who works 50 hours a week, and gets home after midnight." Peter slid to the floor, keeping enough distance between them not to spy on her cellular activity.

Rather than angle the phone away from him, Ryleigh turned to nestle into his side. Traces of fruity perfume lingered on her clothes. "Is that why you don't date? You're one of those guys who's married to his job?"

"Work is the only way I stay sane."

"You could stand to have some fun every now and then." She tipped her head and he seized the opportunity to steal a quick kiss. Her thumb zigzagged in a series of movements on the phone's display to pull up an e-mail. "Can you believe this?" Ryleigh gestured to the maximum brightness screen. *Why doesn't she just stand outside and stare at the sun?* "Housing e-mails in March? I haven't even graduated."

Leave it to an ill-timed University of Michigan e-mail to diffuse his post-birthday euphoria.

"Any wisdom you'd care to dole out on dorm life?"

Peter anchored an arm around her midsection. "Nope. I lived at home all four years of college. Wear shower shoes and employ your common sense, you'll turn out alright."

"Solid advice."

"Are you working today?" He stroked her waves like they had been in a relationship for years, one in which these types of gestures were performed out of subconscious regularity.

Even in this moment of tenderness, Peter knew she was not his to have. Not forever. Ryleigh was nothing more than a roadblock on the miserable, winding path of his terminally single life.

She corralled the study paraphernalia crowding the coffee table and stowed them in her backpack. "No. Actually, I'm supposed to be meeting a friend later. We're going shopping for prom dresses. Nauseating, right?"

"Prom, huh? I bet half the student body is in competition to be your date."

"Do I detect jealousy? That's cute." Her hands cupped either side of his face. "I'd rather slit my throat than attend a formal dance with an idiotic, 18-year-old boy for company."

Was he jealous? Is that why his stomach burned at the idea of her with another guy? Jealousy could not plant its invasive roots. It was a gateway emotion to love and attachment, two things he could never connect to Ryleigh.

She had shimmied halfway into her backpack straps before swinging the bag around to unzip the main compartment and retrieve something from its depths.

A sheepish smile formed while she fiddled with a strand of her hair. "I almost forgot to give you your birthday present."

Peter accepted the gift, shredding the paper as he spoke. "You've already given me more than I deserve. You didn't have to go through the trouble of—" His gaze darted between Ryleigh and the small, unwrapped box. "A Tascam? I can't accept this. It's too much."

"The guy at Best Buy convinced me that it's the tour de force of recorders. Do you love it?"

"Of course, I love it. It makes my old recorder look like a piece of shit. Well, it is. I've had it since college and it's a miracle it's held up this long." He scanned the specs on the packaging, feeling like an ecstatic child on Christmas. "This is the nicest thing anyone's ever given me."

"Maybe it was a selfish gift. I wanted you to have something tangible to remember me by."

A noxious cloud of fictitious pressure smothered him, neurotic smoke rings of needless analysis. The phantasmic fumes insisted he needed to reciprocate the gesture.

"Let me see your keys." He curled his fingers several times as if to say 'hand them over.' Eyebrows furrowing, she edged toward him and surrendered the coveted item. Peter looped his spare key onto her ring. "Now you don't have to break into my place."

Ryleigh raced to the second floor in a mad dash effort to escape her father's megaphone of doom projecting from downstairs. *You are so dead.* But as she climbed the final stairs, her heart flitted in assertion.

One night with Peter was well worth any consequences that were to be hurled at her.

Once in the safety of her bedroom, she popped the borrowed New Radicals CD into the disc drive of her laptop. An upbeat tempo kicked off the opening track. She regarded the gleaming new addition to her key ring, a shining symbol of defiance. A harsh rapping on the door punctuated the lead singer's melancholic wailing.

The thin slab of oak shielding her from an onslaught of unhinged parental rage swung inward and bounced off the doorjamb. *Showtime.*

She spun around in the computer chair to face her father, crossing her legs to exude a casual vibe. Though, she gathered that the 'I have nothing to hide' act would not get her far judging by his police take-down of the door.

"Why'd you even knock if you were planning on coming in anyways?"

"Don't talk to me like that, young lady," Dexter cautioned. His expression shifted between fury and disappointment faster than she could blink.

"Young lady? How old am I, 12?"

Ryleigh fought to maintain a calm exterior as she internally succumbed to a sinkhole of panic. Defying her parents was not in her wheelhouse, but in this situation, resorting to the extreme seemed to be the only option.

"I'd suggest you watch your tone. And where exactly were you all this time?"

"With Andy."

"Oh, is that so? Because I rang up the Fuentes' late last night, and Andrea told me you weren't at her house, that you hadn't even stopped by her house for a moment. You were with *him*, were you not?"

She broke her focus on the plush rug and dared a quick glance at her disenchanted father. The accusation had deflated her forged tough-girl attitude beyond repair.

"You wouldn't even give him a chance. You'll never understand," Ryleigh complained, voice tremulous as her courage abated.

"Do you realize I cancelled all of my appointments at the practice today to make sure you made it home, in one piece? I want to protect you, not punish you." He snatched her twinkling key ring, shaking it like a mad man. "What's this? You've got a key to his place now? You're going to end up pregnant before graduation at this rate."

No, he made it clear he doesn't plan on sleeping with me.

"It's not like that." Ryleigh vaulted out of the computer chair. "You have no faith in me. Do you think I would be that irresponsible? *You* raised me. I've done everything you and mom have wanted me to do, my whole life. When is it time to start living for me?"

She swiped her wristlet off the desk, snatching the key ring from her father. Their arms brushed as she moved past him out of the room.

Dexter trailed her down the staircase. "Have you lost your mind? Where are you going?"

Expedient footfalls pummeled the wood in tandem.

Clack. Clack. Clack.

"I'm meeting Andy. We have plans."

"You honestly think you can just waltz out of this house after everything that's transpired? I have news for you, sweetheart, you're not an adult yet. You can't come and go as you please. There are rules, and you broke all of them with your little sleepover."

"If your rules revolve around keeping me from the one thing that makes me happy, I won't be adhering to them."

"Take a good, hard look in the mirror and see if you like who you're becoming. You said I raised you. Well, this sure as hell isn't the daughter I raised."

"Whatever." Indifference elbowed her already weakened chest. "I'm going to be late."

The stuffy but expansive junior formal section in Nordstrom had Ryleigh mortified at what the monumental event signified.

Graduation approached without mercy. Summer rode her heels, nipping at her ankles, bearing an aching reminder that this fraily constructed fairytale with Peter would soon crumble, reduced to a woeful pile of ash.

"I asked Zeth Katsaros to prom," Andrea announced, sifting through an ombre collection of orange dresses at an alarming speed.

"Katsaros," Ryleigh repeated. Her hand froze, fingers spread on a glittery halter. "Wait a minute, isn't he on the soccer team? You didn't."

While she had no intention of attending prom, Andrea's blatant sabotage of their girls' night out ignited a quiet storm in her mind's harbor. Andy had betrayed their sacred vow of friendship on the phone with her dad, and now *this*?

She freed one of her infamous, earsplitting shrieks and beamed on the other side of the rack, smoothing her flat-ironed locks to command some calm. "Oh yes, I did. And he said yes."

"I'm sure Colin will be thrilled you're going to prom with his teammate. I thought we were going to be each other's dates? You could've alerted me to our change of plans."

Ryleigh plastered on a smile so fake, it felt as though her cheeks had been ripped apart.

"I didn't think you'd care since you'll probably spend the night sulking in the corner, given your displeasure for teenage-infested social gatherings." Andrea pulled several dresses—delicate apricots and peaches—draping them over her arm. "I'm surprised you showed up today. I haven't heard from you outside of school in weeks."

Playing Barbie doll dress-up with her perfect, preppy best friend lost all of its appeal as agitation bubbled from the tips of her toes to the roots of her bedhead.

Inhaling a deep, controlled breath that would pave the path toward vengeance, she laid the foundational layer of bedrock. "I stayed overnight at Peter's place."

This kind of tidbit usually kept Andrea's scandal tank on an unbudging 'full' for a week. But she shied away from her gossip queen title, downcast lashes and halo of nonchalance earning her a gold medal in indifference. "Did you sleep with him?"

Ryleigh's eyes capsized in her skull. "Why does everyone think we're sleeping together?"

"When two people love each other very much—"

"Shove it, Andy."

"Who else mentioned it?" Despite her considerable stack of gowns, Andrea remained unflinching in pursuit of fully browsing the boundless selection.

No dressing room attendant in their right mind would have let her through the door with an entire runway in tow. Perhaps guilt had taken over the dress shopping in light of the obvious confrontation barreling toward her.

"My dad." Those words rivaled the speed and damage of a lightning bolt, out of one's mouth and into the other's ears tinged with an accusatory malice. "Thanks for ratting me out."

Andy's frantic hanger flipping stilled.

"I didn't rat you out, I just told him the truth: you weren't at my house."

"God, I can't believe you. What happened to our figurative blood oath? We're supposed to be in this high school survival thing together."

"We were. Until you decided some 40-year-old guy who has absolutely nothing going for himself was more important than me."

Invisible cinder blocks tied themselves around her ankles. Had she been that neglectful of their friendship?

"That's not true."

"Of course you'd say that. You can't see anything past the animated hearts dangling in front of your eyes."

Oh, how this day had devolved from the high note on which it had begun. She had awoken on Peter's couch, wrapped in ephemeral bliss, only to be eaten alive by a hellmouth of social and familial problems.

Her chest hitched as if someone pinched the layers of skin sheathing her sternum. "Why are you being such a bitch?"

"Gee, I don't know, Ry. Maybe because when I told you I broke up with my boyfriend you gave me a spacey comment for consolation. Maybe because you've ditched our Saturday movie night ritual for a month. Maybe because prom is the last big thing we're doing together, and you don't seem to be the least bit excited about it."

"I'm not going to prom."

The sun burned out in her golden complexion, giving way to uncomely sallowness. She replaced the dresses on the rack, each painstaking return of the carefully selected garments sparking greater indignation. "Then why are you even here?"

"To support you. I know I've been absent lately, and I'm sorry. I want to make things right between us."

Andrea averted her iridescent copper eyelids as she turned on her heel in parting. "I think we're past that point."

22

COMPLICIT

*P*eter waited on the side of the exhibition center, as per Ryleigh's instructions. He made sure not to stray from the appointed post. If Dexter happened to see him, their carefully constructed cover would be blown.

Chatter ascended at the front of the building as students arrived. His nerves grew in conjunction with the steady uptick in volume. He and Ryleigh were embarking on an honest to God date.

A *real* date, where they dressed up and flaunted their not-quite-togetherness to the world.

The Bransons' sleek, black SUV swung into the parking lot at eight past seven, joining the long line of cars crowding the designated drop-off zone.

He toyed with the keys in his pocket, sweat slicking his palm. Nausea asserted itself from the pit of his being, forcing him to rely on the wall for support. His introspection superseded the cement mixer he now had for a stomach; could they pull off the evening without a hitch?

Peter's systems leveled out to homeostasis when Ryleigh rounded the corner, dressed to kill.

She ambled toward him in low heels, charcoal dress bouncing at her ankles, its billowing hem teasing but never touching the concrete. "Hope I didn't keep you waiting too long."

"Not at all." He cleared his throat. Though he fought hard to concentrate on her face, his traitorous gaze wandered to the chiffon clinging to her curves. His heart did not skip a beat, it skipped three or four. Ten, perhaps. "Ryleigh, you look—"

Eyes tumbling toward the heavens, she offered mocking guesses. "Nice? Ready to seduce the flu?"

"Ah, no." Rubbing the back of his neck, he dared, "You look beautiful. You *are* beautiful."

She licked her lips to conceal a grin.

"Don't make me cry, Rosenfeld. We haven't even left the parking lot. I'll kick your ass if you ruin my makeup." Ryleigh performed circular gestures in front of her face. "I know your inherent masculinity precludes you from appreciating it, but this took an hour. 60 minutes. It's basically the Mona Lisa of my cosmetic-wearing career."

They fell into step as they crossed the lot to his car. He wanted to hold her hand but thought it unwise given the sheer number of people hanging around the entrance, some of whom were faculty of Victory Hills. People he may have very well been acquainted with through interviews.

Anxiety-inducing headlines rattled off his mind's paranoia-powered printing press: 'Local journalist seen snatching innocent girl from prom.' 'Cradle-robbing reporter can't stay away from H.S. senior.'

The melodic clicking of Ryleigh's heels on the asphalt soothed his overzealous concerns.

He unlocked the car and yanked open the driver's side door, preparing to duck inside until he noticed Ryleigh staring with gathered eyebrows across the parking lot at a newly arrived couple. The girl wore an apricot dress and her date had coordinated his tie.

Oh, no. Do you see that look? She's already regretting her decision to leave with you. You can fix this. Convince her to stay.

Peter deduced the girl must have been Andrea precisely as she said, "I *told* her they'd be back together by prom."

"Do you want to go say hey? I can hang here."

"No. No, I'm not ready for that."

He got in the car and she followed his lead. But Ryleigh dove into the backseat rather than the passenger side. "You guys still aren't talking?"

"Not since our fight in the middle of Nordstrom. During which, by the way, she said that you have absolutely nothing going for yourself."

"That's a relatively accurate assumption."

The shrill whining of a zipper being pulled filled the cabin, followed by the chiffon scratching against itself, pooling in layers as she peeled it off her body. "I don't really want to talk about Andy."

Peter trained his eyes on the car parked in front of them, then the lamp posts lining the sidewalk, the temperature gauge. Anywhere but the rearview mirror, where he may have caught a glimpse of her sans the extravagant gown.

Incongruous emotions fenced one another amid the internal deliberation. He despised himself for wanting to look, yet found that he craved more of her with the passing of time.

Each second, Peter gained a greater understanding of her beautiful mind. On each occasion she bared her soul, he was tempted to lower the barriers enlisted by his ever-present worry and dissuasion.

Neuroticism had become his ultimate cockblock.

A rustling grocery bag, signaling the retrieval of her non-prom clothes, broke him out of his reverie.

"I think it's adorable that you're obviously trying to not look back here, but I don't care if you watch me change."

Five-alarm heat set his sunken cheeks ablaze. "I'd like to preserve whatever modicum of decency I have left."

"Would it kill you to be indecent for an evening?" She imprinted a kiss on his cheek as she climbed over the console in a backless dress and dirty sneakers before collapsing into the passenger seat.

His fingertips ghosted over the smokey lipstick stain, pulse poised to combust in his tight throat. The plum pigment smeared on the pads of his fingers. Peter marveled at those smudges, the physical evidence of affection.

"Let's go, paperboy."

Ryleigh birthed a grin that set his soul on fire—because the magnificent display of joy was at the prospect of going out with *him*.

Peter made a questioning face at Ryleigh's half-completed canvas. "Your palm tree looks like an overstuffed blunt."

He embodied the casual but simultaneously cocky nonchalance of an artist, daring to paint in office wear, sleeves cuffed at his elbows.

The top button of his lavender dress shirt was undone, a comfortable middleground of emphasizing his pronounced collarbone while shielding the subject of self-consciousness that lay beyond the other buttons.

How Ryleigh craved to see, smell, and touch that part of him again. The cursed track lighting in the studio only further elevated his heart-throb status.

They perched on rickety metal stools donned in smocks. Ryleigh had taken off her shoes to create a free-spirited painting experience, and the instructor grimaced whenever he passed by, giving her naked feet a distasteful side eye.

The mustachioed gentleman avoided their station altogether when Peter joined in on the shoeless adventure.

"Thanks for the astute observation, Bob Ross. Your halfway decent art skills are ruining all the fun. Where'd you learn to paint?"

Dipping her brush into the emerald pool of paint on the plastic tray, Ryleigh tried to rectify the horrendously executed tree which should have gotten her permanently banned from any paint and sip establishment in New England.

If she had any forewarning of the venue for their outing, she would have cautioned Peter that nary an artistic bone resided in her body.

"Set design. I was a drama geek in high school, and before you slingshot a smart remark, I joined out of desperation, not genuine interest. There was this girl I liked, Sadie. I thought she'd be into me if I hung around her fellow thespians. Didn't work out. At least I can paint a palm tree that doesn't resemble something you'd find in Seth Rogen's couch cushions."

"Kendall was right, you are a dick." A resigned sigh escaped from Ryleigh as she stared in defeat at the hopeless palm tree. She plucked up a fresh, fine brush and dotted dark brown speckles amid the sand. "So, I'm guessing you didn't take Sadie to either of your proms, then?"

He had taken her to dinner ahead of their instructor-led class at the paint studio. And while technically they were not together, the properness of the date gave them some semblance of a real couple, a *normal* couple.

Though that thin illusion shattered each time Peter sipped from his merlot along with everyone else, while Ryleigh nursed a can of green tea and licked her wounds over having her faux adult status revoked.

"Prom is another thing that never worked out. I asked my lab partner senior year, and she agreed but then she stood me up the night of. I spent what would have been my prom drinking rum in a rented tux on my bedroom floor. And dare I say, that pathetic anecdote just about sums up my lackluster existence."

"What do you mean?" Ryleigh laughed.

"I mean, whenever I ask a girl out, something always goes wrong. It's like a curse. My mother must have pissed off one of those palm-reading, love and relationship crackpots before I was born."

"That's a wildly unrealistic theory. And, in case it escaped your notice, we're out on a date now. What's happened?"

His hand came to rest on her bare thigh, blessing the flesh with a deliciously gentle squeeze that sent a shiver up her spine. A half-smile tugged at his thin lips. "The night is young, sweetheart."

The abject sarcasm may have cancelled out the swoon-worthy usage of 'sweetheart' to anyone else's ears, but Ryleigh had learned to take what she could get.

Their instructor commanded the room's attention, demonstrating how to achieve the look of glistening water, but she tuned out his nasally self-important speech and turned inward. Plus, her painting had been rendered unsalvageable.

Sparkling water would not distract from the tropical horror she had splattered on this innocent canvas.

Her butt ached from sitting on the metal stool for nearly two hours. As she sat there, spaced out and rubbing her foot on the stool's inner ring while the elitist instructor babbled on, it occurred to her that during their many talks, Peter gave no present-day insights, no mentions of current hobbies or hint of a social life.

Everything he mentioned lurked in the past. It was an odd thing to process, realizing she knew so little about this person who she felt she had known her entire life.

Ryleigh eyed him, appreciating the comical sight of someone his stature perching on one of the studio's short stools. His face hovered close to the wet canvas while he applied white strokes to his sea of blue with the utmost precision.

"Peter, what do you do for fun?"

"I go to work, I come home, I sleep—and I do my best not to think about the time in between."

"Don't you get bored? Don't you want a hobby?"

He retired the brush and turned to her, elbows resting on his knees. "What? Like you with your poetry? I don't need to sit around and read revered verses from long-deceased men to infuse some arbitrary meaning in my life."

"Well, what do you need?"

"Nothing. See, that's my point. The details of our lives, what we choose to do with our free time, or if we choose to do nothing … none of it matters. We're all going to end up six-feet-under. You know that saying, 'Get busy living or get busy dying?' I've gone with the latter, and I've made my peace with it."

That dark part of his soul had crept out and manifested itself as the uninvited third-wheel. The part she had first brushed with when he vaguely alluded to his suicide attempt.

Normally, Ryleigh was enamored with his cynical tirades, but she failed to pick anything attractive out of the latest bleak monologue.

"God, I didn't know you were such a nihilist. Wish I had known that before I swiped right on Tinder and arranged this artsy but now seriously depressing date."

"Sorry to disappoint. I don't have a Christian Slater-esque comeback for that."

"Who's Christian Slater?"

"Nevermind." He smiled to himself, finger tracing the wine glass' stem. "Some of the things that tumble out of your sassy mouth make it easy to forget your age."

Here we go with the age business.

"Is that something you dwell on? My age?"

Peter dipped a detail brush into a shrinking puddle of white paint, filling in the final touches on his passable scenery piece. Damn him and his semi-decentness at painting.

"I try not to. Things between us would be a lot less complicated if I could ignore it entirely. I'm not wired that way. I fixate on something until I'm physically ill." His expression softened, the scratchy quality of his voice lessening. "You calm some of that, when I'm with you, anyway."

"What's something you obsess over?"

"With you? Numbers, lately. I push them around in my head, willing them to make sense but they never do. You and I are numbers that never add up, no matter how you arrange us. Like our ages, they're obscene next to each other. Then I project, you know, in the future. When you're 40, I'll be 57, and that doesn't sound as egregious but the deficit is the same. Always."

The irony of him discussing a potential future together while he rejected anything more than making out was not lost on Ryleigh. This man was an enigma.

And despite the conjectural nature of it all, a light-hearted feeling settled over her. "We could do long-distance. Tons of people do it."

"Those are the other numbers I've been crunching. Ann Arbor is

700 miles from here. My car's unreliable in town. I doubt it would survive a 10 and a half hour trip."

"So, all of these scenarios you're exploring ... I can read between the lines but I won't let myself believe it. I need to hear it from you. You're going to miss me?"

"Of course I will. I never expected to feel this way about you. Really, I *shouldn't* feel this way about you." He glanced in her direction, speaking where only she could hear. "You're so fucking young. It's absurd."

Couples began packing up, returning empty wine glasses to the bar area and carrying their masterpieces out the door, wrapped in the magic of a night out without any complications, soon to be wrapped up in each other.

Those lucky bastards.

"I've been thinking lately. I got accepted everywhere I applied, including UConn. I know it's a 40-minute drive but that's doable. I'll come home on the weekends and we can be together."

Sober, sensible Peter made a comeback as the merlot buzz waned. Balsam and citrus notes playing off his cologne enraptured Ryleigh as he bent forward, leaning into her with feverish eyes.

"I want you to understand right now, in this moment, that I care for you. Very much." She cringed when his paint-stained hands cupped her face, feeling the green and blue acrylic sullying the foundation she had blended out to perfection.

With twitching fingers, he seized her hands, transferring more paint to her porcelain skin. In the span of this conversation, she had become his art project.

"I'm not going to be complicit in this hypothetical plan you just laid out that will, inevitably, wreck your future." His pained stare burrowed inside her until it bottomed out at her core, so invasive she had the urge to look away. "You have the world in your pocket, opportunities waiting down every avenue. I've already figured myself out; I have a career, I own a home. We're not on level ground here. You're going to Michigan, because you and I are an impermanent part of each other's lives."

Impermanent? Ryleigh was convinced liquid pessimism ran through his veins in lieu of blood.

An ache radiated in her jaw due to the longstanding rigor of its clench. "Because, according to you, we're a bunch of numbers that don't add up. Right?"

"I didn't mean to upset you." He pinched the bridge of his aquiline nose, mumbling, "I shouldn't have had that wine."

Peter was an expert marksman, never failing to shoot down her expectations when they flew too close to the sun.

Her neck grew hot as her mind raced, searching for explanations to questions she feared were unanswerable.

What were they even doing? Peter refused to concede to a relationship, wanted nothing to do with her once she was gone, and continuously rejected her cloying physical advances since her damned virginity had come to his attention.

"Forget about it." She untied her smock and draped it on the stool. Swiping her wristlet off the station, Ryleigh crossed her arms, gaze trained on the glossy floor. "Could you drop me off in North Woods?"

Ryleigh scooped a small handful of white rocks from the Fuentes' flowerbeds. The first one she flung missed its target, bouncing off the brick house and disappearing into the thick grass. A fire surged in her arm, a byproduct of the amateur, underhand pitch. *I need to go to the gym.*

She infused every ounce of her frustration toward Peter into an overhand attempt, which struck the bottom right pane of Andrea's window. Ryleigh launched another. And another.

Blue light from the television danced through the glass. If she was inside, she would certainly register the unmistakable clicking of the pebbles.

"Come on, Andy. It's freezing out here."

A mini dress and no jacket had been a poor choice as she fell prey to the capricious Connecticut night. Goosebumps sprouted on her arms and legs, nipples puckered to the point of unfathomable hurt.

She had resigned to head to the subdivision's entrance and order an Uber when a window screeched behind her.

"Halstock, you have *some* nerve showing your face after—" A waterfall of extensions cascaded over the window's outer ledge as Andrea's face materialized. "Oh, thank God it's you." She slumped against the open frame. "I had a shitty night."

All it took to mend a broken friendship was a collectively miserable night and boy/man problems.

Who knew.

"That makes two of us."

Andrea appeared to squint into the yard at her friend, who was in danger of becoming an ice sculpture.

"Ryleigh Branson, are you wearing bodycon on prom night? This has to be your worst fashion offense of the school year. You look like you're trying out for a *Pretty Woman* reboot."

"I'd love to give you some context on my alleged fashion crime and swap stories from our respective evenings, but if you don't let me inside, I'm going to lose my pitiful boobs to spring frostbite."

Holding up a finger, she shut the window. Ryleigh jogged in place while on standby for her savior. Her hopeful bout of exercise did little to alleviate the marrow-deep chill which had frozen her bones from the inside out.

The salmon-colored door swung inward just enough for Andrea to shimmy outside. She tread with ginger steps through the grass, cringing at the lack of protection her flats provided against the damp blades.

Pajamas had replaced her prom dress but the regal hairstyle and professionally made up face remained intact.

A stately aura surrounded her as she examined Ryleigh's alley rat attire, paying particularly scrutinizing attention to her jawline. "Is that … paint, on your face?"

"Yeah. Long story."

Standing there felt like being naked in a room full of strangers rather than the formerly comfortable company of the girl with whom she had been friends since elementary school.

Ryleigh tucked a strand of hair behind her ear. "I saw you and Colin going into prom, looking like you walked off the pages of a fairytale pop-up book. How did he manage to mess things up in the span of three hours?"

"You saw us? I didn't see you inside. And trust me, I wouldn't have missed you in that outfit."

Enough about my clothes, woman.

"No, I didn't go in. Peter picked me up, which is the origin of my long story." A knot in her stomach willed her to adopt a bent posture. "Andy, I'm sorry I haven't been here for you lately. I've been spending too much time with someone who's an impermanent part of my life, and too little time with someone who I know will always be around."

"Jesus, what, did you two break up?"

"You have to be together to break up."

"I should apologize, too, for calling your ... well, I guess he's not your boyfriend. I'm sorry I basically called your whatever-he-is a loser. Just because he drives a junkyard on wheels and reports news in a dead-end town doesn't make him a loser. And he makes you happy, so he must be pretty alright."

Every bit of tension rushed from Ryleigh's body, relief overshadowing her subzero state. She nodded to the flashing window. "What's on?"

"*The Lumberjack Who Loved Me.*" Andrea buried shameful laughter in her hands. Rocking back and forth on her heels, she asked, "Do you want to come up and watch the rest?"

"Most definitely. It *is* movie night, after all." Ryleigh grinned and leaned into Andrea, hooking their arms together as they headed up the cobblestone path. "Give me the damage: what's the flannel count so far?"

23

ANN ARBOR

"2%, 180 for our favorite grumpy journalist." Oscar slid the steaming cappuccino across the pick-up counter. He backed away, fists balled up to mimic a crybaby.

The frightening disregard with which baristas flung drinks across cafe counters should have been outlawed. Witnessing that hair-raising journey unfold brought Peter one step closer to an aneurysm.

He seized the cup. "Yet you wonder why I don't tip."

"Don't harass my underlings, Rosenfeld." Kendall emerged from the storeroom with a cocked brow, a subdued smirk and an armful of precariously balanced Torani bottles.

"Underlings?" Slipping his phone out of his pocket, Peter consulted the time and claimed a seat at the vacant espresso bar. He had a few minutes to kill.

She pointed to the line below 'Kendall' on her nametag, which normally said 'coffee expert.'

It now read 'manager.'

"Oh, shit."

"'Oh shit' is exactly right. You better watch your smart comments and limit your beverage remaking requests. There's a new sheriff in town."

"Seriously, Ken, I'm happy for you. You deserve it."

Kendall ripped plastic seals off the line of syrup bottles, replacing the caps with pumps. "The timing was weird. I've been thinking about leaving and then this happened. Life's funny like that."

The first sip of coffee trickling along his throat mirrored the curative properties of an IV drip. He was wholly reliant on the waking powers of espresso on this particular morning. *Morning*, a word that had almost been entirely eradicated from Peter's vernacular. Yet there he sat in The Roast at a spry 8:30 on a Saturday, press badge and sling camera bag in tow.

"Leaving, what?" He put his elbows on the bar, A/C exposed vinyl icing his forearms. "The shop?"

"The shop. Connecticut. Jake has a steady thing with that gallery in Boston, you know? He comes home most weekends, but damn if I don't miss him. The last few months with him coming and going … it's awful. You get used to having someone around, and then it's weird when, suddenly, they aren't there."

His activity stilled: breath halting, heartbeat slowing. Soon, he would become painfully aware of that very feeling.

Finger running along the recycled sleeve, he shrugged, "Boston's only two hours away."

"It's viable, for now." She gathered the collection of caps and dumped them in the trash. Sighing, she mimicked Peter's posture on her side of the counter. Her shimmering umber eyes locked onto his cup. "It won't work forever. Not like this. Something has to give."

Hearing Kendall doubting the endurance of a committed relationship in the face of a 120-mile barrier eased his guilt over ruling against long distance with Ryleigh.

Eyeing the camera case, she perked up, losing herself in someone else's business to silence her own misery. "What did they pin you with today? I thought you were allergic to photo assignments."

"Graduation coverage. I volunteered."

"You mean Ryleigh's graduation?"

Tail between his legs, he uttered a soft and slightly ashamed, "Yeah."

She tapped one of her neon pink plugs. "Do you know what you're doing to that poor girl? You're breaking her heart a little more every day and she's still head over heels in love with your dumbass."

Peter downed the remnants of the cappuccino and dismounted the bar stool, slinging the camera case onto his shoulder. He tilted the empty to-go cup toward her in an accusatory manner as he backpedaled to the side exit. "She is *not* in love with me."

"Yeah, alright. Keep living in your neurotic fantasyland where people don't catch feelings."

Cameras flashed interminably throughout the arena as proud parents captured their child's monumental achievement. The seniors of Victory Hills seated on the main floor paid no attention to the bright lights, acting like celebrities running errands while disregarding the paparazzi.

Everything about graduation coverage set Peter off. The unnerving noise when the crowd dispersed to locate their graduates. The sweltering heat hanging in the arena thanks to the thousands of bodies it housed. The inescapable hounding from parents to feature their summa cum laude daughter or son who was snubbed the honor of valedictorian.

But he refused to fall victim to those standard irritants. Work had taken a backseat. He had come to support Ryleigh.

Teens followed one behind the other in a constantly sweeping curtain of black Jostens, accepting their diplomas as the remaining names were called.

On the stage, the principal rambled on and showed no signs of stopping, much to the chagrin of the impatient seniors. *Click.* Peter snapped a picture of the ancient man delivering the farewell speech. He lurked off to the side, midway through the student seating area, a non-intrusive location for photos.

Not that any angle in the entire arena would have miraculously refined his lousy photography skills.

"It is my great honor to dismiss the class of 2019, for the final time," the principal croaked, hunched over the podium as though he were ready to divulge a secret to the crowd. "Graduates, please rise and move your tassels to the left of your caps. It has been a privilege to know each and every one of you, and I wish you all luck as you transition into this next phase of life. Thank you."

Pure chaos ensued once the students were formally dismissed. Parents flooded the main floor in a riptide of prideful zeal, abandoning their seats and belongings. Screams and sporadic bursts of applause erupted around the room, mingling with the perturbing discordance of no less than a thousand voices.

Okay, the aforementioned irritants still bothered him.

Ducking into a secluded alcove, Peter studied his subpar shots, a third of which were under-exposed.

Awful. Even worse. Usable.

He glanced up from the tiny screen displaying his failures, surveying the celebratory scene as much as he was searching for the lone black-robed student who mattered.

The logical route to locating her would have been a text, but the school had dissuaded the students from bringing cell phones into the ceremony.

And for whatever reason, Ryleigh had decided to abide by the rules on this one occasion.

"Oh em gee, are you here with the paper?" came a breathy exclamation, honing the essence of a fangirl.

Ryleigh had ditched her baggy robe and did not seem to be the least bit concerned with the whereabouts of its lank corpse. Fuzziness blanketed his brain as she twirled around in the required white dress, which he had accompanied her to every department store in the greater Harris area to find. She wore strange shoes with miniature clear heels, raspberry-inked toes peeking out beneath the transparent vinyl bands.

"Oh, please, take my picture, Mr. Reporter."

"You're going to give me a heart attack on the job. That dress is lethal." Peter cradled the camera in his hands to spare his aching neck, but the relief was short-lived when he remembered what hid in the sling bag. Tugging on the zipper, he produced a shy smile, "I have something for you."

His heart cartwheeled as she clawed at the brown tissue paper, revealing the hardbound journal he had purchased weeks earlier. A Blink-182 rabbit sticker clung to the top right corner, the same one that had adorned her previous journal.

He clutched the camera strap for support when her awestruck eyes landed on the Langston Hughes poem he had printed out and adhered to the inside cover.

A wide smile lit up Ryleigh's face and served as a spotlight in their dim, sequestered hideout.

"*Dreams*, definitely apropos for a graduation. Good work, sir." Her fingers traced those familiar words, stilling when they arrived at his handwritten inscription.

Ryleigh,

I'm sure you're well-acquainted with these words, but I found them most fitting for the occasion. Even though you say poetry is just a hobby, you should know that you have a real knack for it. No matter what you choose to do in life, I hope you continue to write.

I only knew you for a short period of time, and yet you've had a greater impact on my outlook than my psychiatrist has in seven years. You've (mostly) shaken me from my cynical torpor and reintroduced me to the beauty of life, and taught me to appreciate the little things.

It's disgusting how much I'll miss you, but I'll eventually find solace knowing that you're off doing wonderful things and basking in the freedom of young adulthood (which, by the way, enjoy it while it lasts because it's crippling college loan debt and a web of other unpleasant financial obligations the minute you leave that campus).

Take care of yourself out there. And remember, pressure is imaginary. No one is in control of your life except you.

So, grab the helm and steer, darling.

Hand shooting to her mouth, she turned away slightly while a series of jerky shoulder contractions left her shaking. She clutched the journal to her chest, facing him with shining eyes and a trembling chin. "I love it."

Ryleigh strained on her tip-toes and embraced him, movements trailed by the debilitating redolence he had come to associate with her hugs. She clasped her hands around his neck and brought the tips of their noses together.

Did she detect the clamorous banging of his heart?

"Congratulations," Peter whispered, pulling her flush against his lanky frame. He stroked her tumbling waves and branded a publicly respectable trio of kisses onto her lips. Stars littered the backdrop of Ryleigh's irises when he begrudgingly surrendered her mouth. "What are you doing tonight?"

Her thumb dipped within his pants and his lungs became as useless as a busted airbag. Grinning, she circled the hook and bar closure. "You, if I'm lucky."

"Always with the extreme." He laughed off his unease. The intimate atmosphere of the alcove paired with her teasing touch had Peter so punch-drunk, he was tempted to indulge her of the request. "You're going to get kicked out of your own graduation."

She extracted the indecorous thumb in an instant as a familiar voice approached.

"There you are. We've been looking all over for—" Charlotte's relieved mother front fell to pieces upon locking eyes with him. Adjusting her purse strap, she extended a collected, "Hello, Peter."

Lips parting, his mind stalled in computing a response and malfunctioned entirely when her husband joined them.

What do you say to the parents whose teenager daughter you've been sneaking around and stealing kisses with?

Together, they formed a terribly awkward quartet in the cramped alcove, all the space surrounding them greedily consumed by tension and disparaging, unaired thoughts. Peter almost would have rather them said something, anything to punctuate the piercing silence grating his eardrums.

He had to question his sanity for willingly attending any function where Dexter Branson would be present, the man who had been out for his blood since the year's first snowfall.

But his reason for attending stood tucked under his arm, and she did not budge as the four of them bathed in the stifling reality that dominated the scene in which they were suspended, staring helplessly at one another and much too fearful to let any words slip, lest any of them prove regrettable.

Dexter's hands briefly clenched before slipping into his pockets. Mustering cordiality, he acknowledged, "Peter."

"Mr. Branson."

He offered a tentative nod. "Dexter will do."

Adrenaline coursed through Peter. Was her father offering some kind of truce? The next inquiry, though extended with a degree of resignation, gave him further reason to ponder the unprecedented civility.

"Would you care to join us for brunch?"

Unbelievable. Those few excruciating moments standing in their presence were tortuous enough; he did not feel like journeying through the nine circles of hell via sacrificing himself to an entire brunch.

At least his Beatrice would be at his side.

Charlotte patted her ponytail, chiming in, "We insist."

He winced as Ryleigh pinched his wrist, a quiet though violent plea to accept. No amount of covert sleeve tugging or lip biting on her part would have driven him to comply.

"I wouldn't want to impose." Peter rapped on the NENPA badge clipped to the pocket of his dress shirt. "Plus, I have a story to wrap up. It'll probably be another half-hour."

"Maybe some other time, then," her mother said. "These weeks are flying by. I can hardly believe it. Pretty soon, we'll be in Michigan."

A breath caught in his chest. "We?"

"Didn't Ryleigh tell you? We're going to Ann Arbor at the start of July."

He almost abandoned the family in favor of continuing his assignment, thinking that if he excused himself from the conversation, the revelation would hold no weight; even though, beneath that illogical layer of his brain, it was already crushing him, twisting his veins and compressing his organs.

And while it was not Heather-level betrayal, the blatant omittance made him wonder if he could trust Ryleigh.

Peter's eyes flitted to her. "No, she didn't mention it."

"They're flying out to tour the campus. Unfortunately, I won't be able to join them. But you're more than welcome to swing by my practice while the girls are away." Dexter removed his glasses and used the untucked hem of his pinstriped shirt as a makeshift cloth. "I'll give you a cleaning, on the house."

Calling him by his first name, extending brunch invitations and doling out free dental exams?

He's priming you for slaughter.

"I'll take you up on that." Disgruntlement flattened his tone. Turning to Ryleigh, he directed the next question to her and her alone. "How long will you be gone?"

"Four days, maybe five. I don't remember. We've had it booked for a few months." She stared at her raspberry toes.

"A few months? And you didn't think to mention it?" Though their argument was only warming up, Peter forgot her parents stood three feet away, petrified in their upper crust garb. "Would you mind if I steal her for a few minutes?"

"Of course not. We'll meet you at the car, honey." Charlotte blew a kiss to her daughter before hooking arms with a grimacing Dexter, who no doubt gave her an earful of protest once they rounded the corner.

He pressed his hands to the wall on either side of Ryleigh, hanging his head to bring them closer to eye level. She shifted on her feet within his arms' prison. The room spun in and out of focus around them, and while she was the source of his disorientation, she was also the one thing grounding him.

"What the hell is going on here? Since when do you keep stuff like this from me?"

"I'm not your girlfriend. Do I really owe you an explanation?" She gave a half-hearted shrug, tossing her head back. "Why does it matter so much to you that I'm leaving in a few weeks when I'm leaving for good in a few months?"

"It shouldn't matter, but I wish you had told me. I don't like being blindsided."

"You're so confusing."

Ryleigh avoided his tense features by examining the fire extinguisher cased within the wall.

"And why's that, exactly?"

Arms pinned to her stomach, she snapped, "You've made it abundantly clear we have until I leave and then nothing more will come of us. So, why are you frustrated that I neglected to mention a brief trip?"

He sank to a squatting position, muscles tensing as he scrubbed a hand across his heated face.

"Why? Because I was expecting to spend every spare minute with you until August 27th and now you're dropping this shit on me. Out of nowhere. And you weren't even the one to tell me, you dumped that task on your *mother*. Do you expect me to be cool with the fact that, suddenly, I have 100 less hours to spend with you?" More to himself, he mumbled, "I need a fucking cigarette for this."

"Tell me I mean something to you, something more than you let on, and I'll believe what you just said."

Ryleigh stared at him, eyes turning glassy from a brewing storm of tears. Even in the face of his grand irritation, she did not falter in her gaze.

Coals backlit the darkness of her pupils. That soul-searching, unending stare edged with yearning said more than any poem she might have written or filibuster persuasion she might have spewed.

And then he understood.

He felt those three deadly words as if Ryleigh had delivered them in the form of a telekinetic message, transported between two ordinary people.

But she had not said it aloud, and until that fateful moment, if it ever were to arrive, Peter would ignore what was presently written all over her hauntingly beautiful face.

24

LETTING GO

Ryleigh had been gone all of 48 hours, and Peter could hardly stomach the absence. The moment they said their temporary goodbyes, a piece of his heart had broken off and gone with her, unwilling to remain intact in protest of the departure.

Two days, and he bordered on falling apart.

"Are you here to make an appointment for your child, sir?" the buoyant receptionist asked as he entered Harris Pediatric Dentistry. "We actually just closed a few minutes ago, but I don't mind helping you schedule a visit. What's the name of the child?"

While he originally had no intention of taking Dexter up on the offer extended at graduation, he had already watched *Steel Magnolias* four times and the next item on his solitary to-do list would have been jerking off until he rendered himself catatonic.

Better to get out of the house.

"I don't have any children." Peter surveyed the waiting area's lack of childish decorations; not even a fish tank or a bead maze resided in the sterile space. "I'm a friend of Dexter's."

"His friend?" The woman, whose silver-plated name tag read 'Sara,' replaced several large black binders on the shelves lining the far wall.

"I may have fibbed a bit on that one. I'm sort of dating his daughter, and he invited me to swing by for a cleaning."

Tucking one of the binders to her chest, Sara pinned him with an incredulous stare. "Oh? I didn't know Ryleigh had an older sister."

Peter was in no mood for a judgment call from a stranger; he was grieving the temporary loss of his not-quite-lover for crying out loud.

"She doesn't. I know, I'm 36, she's 18. Yadda, yadda. We've heard it all before, so spare me the sideshow look on your face, alright?"

He relished in the uncomfortable expression the receptionist wore as she reluctantly disappeared to go fetch her boss. No sooner than Sara had left, she rounded the corner and ushered him through the archway.

"Third door on the left," she said, breezing past Peter.

His scalp prickled as he mentally prepared himself to face Dexter while shuffling through the narrow hallway. How would he act without his wife and daughter around?

Though, he was never a shining example of amiability in their presence, either.

Stomach quivering, he reached to open the examination room's door, but was halted by his buzzing phone. Wondering if it might have been Ryleigh, his fingers inched into his pocket before snapping back to the door handle. *Just call her back after.* Clicking a button to cease the device's vibration, he stepped into the space where Ryleigh's father waited, where he may have very well been cleaning a heavy duty hunting bow rather than a saliva ejector.

Peter produced a half-smile for the man in the white coat. "Shouldn't this place have a dinosaur out front? Something to ease the kids about their impending mouth torture. I thought my article would make a difference around here."

He could see Ryleigh in her father at that moment, and it made his heart clench; the same ocean eyes, the same dip in their chin. Maybe the masturbatory coma had not been the worst idea.

"Oh, it did. We used to have one at the entrance, if you can believe it, but it scared some of the kids so I had to get rid of it." Despite channeling humor, an underlying edge of fatherly stringency always laced his tone. Dexter assessed Peter's black joggers and faded UC Santa Cruz shirt. "Off work today?"

"Yeah, though I'd rather be there, truthfully. I'm not a big fan of weekends, and I usually take some assignments home with me when I *am* off."

Brightly colored posters decorated the walls, ranging in theme from proper flossing etiquette to water conservation while brushing. Just what every kid wanted to look at while being poked and prodded with horrifying dental tools.

"Your boss must love you." Dexter unwrapped and arranged various disposable dental instruments on a tray. He jerked his head in the direction of the examination chair, which was clearly designed for children and not a 6'2" adult. "You can go ahead and have a seat. I'm just setting up."

Peter cringed at the desperate squeaks that escaped as his weight settled against the chair's frame. His legs hung over the sides, shoes planted on the floor. The armrests cut off at his elbows and thus made for a comfortless arrangement. He felt like a giraffe lying on a longboard.

And probably looked like one, too.

"Let's see what we're working with." Retrieving a mouth mirror and a sickle probe from the tray, Dexter set to the task. "You're not a smoker. That's a relief. I was under the impression that was a common habit among journalists."

"Harris is hardly large enough to have its own paper. It's not the stress-inducing environment that breeds smokers," he attempted to say despite his tongue being held aside by the cold metal mirror. "I smoked in college, but I gave it up after I'd been here for a couple of years."

"Glad to hear you kicked that. It's a nasty habit." The concentration on Dexter's face was unbreakable, forehead creased in a series of deep, weathered lines. "You don't floss much, do you?"

"Who does?"

"I do," he stated with a bit too much conviction.

"You have to; your reputation depends on it. It's like if I didn't read the newspaper, people would question my authority." The conjecture sounded less than eloquent with a mouthful of metal.

"Fair point," Dexter concurred. "If I'm going to get any work done, I'm afraid you'll have to keep the talking to a minimum."

Softening his hold on the armrests, Peter tried his best to relax in the chair. Dental examinations had always made him skittish and this was no exception.

It did not help to ease his anxiety that the man handling the instruments happened to be Ryleigh's father.

"The campus is absolutely gorgeous," Charlotte commented, fluffing her cobb salad with a fork. "I bet it's breathtaking in the fall with all of the trees. You'll have a great view walking to class."

"Yeah. Everything's amazing."

Ryleigh sampled a nibble of the steaming pesto panini on her plate. Cheese strung from the bread to her mouth, connecting them as one. Her finger snapped the threads of vegan mozzarella with a swift, slicing motion.

This was the most delectably stringy vegan cheese she had yet to encounter, and her roiling stomach refused to be excited about it.

"Where's your mind, honey?"

"Somewhere it shouldn't be." She shied away from her mother's concern, peering out the large glass window beside them, instantly regretting that she had opened herself up to the parade of affection that lay outside Le Croûton.

Several couples passed by on the sidewalk, holding hands and laughing. Some of them carried coffees, while others tugged on dog leashes, but all of them were unapologetically smitten. Her heart crumbled at the unyielding display of infatuation. *If I stay in Connecticut, that could be us.*

Charlotte patted the back of her daughter's hand.

"I know it's difficult to think of leaving Peter behind. But let's not forget you've worked your entire life to get to this point. There will be other boys—men, I promise."

A mother's intuition never failed to amaze her.

"But there won't be anyone like *him*. I don't know if I could ever move on, or if I even want to try. I think I'm in ..." She tapered off.

"Hanging onto these feelings for him will only cause you more pain. You have to be realistic about this." A sympathetic smile played at her lips, but it did not reach her eyes. "If the two of you have agreed to end things once you leave, then you have to be receptive to the idea of letting him go."

Ryleigh sniffled, tears dripping onto her barely eaten panini. "What if I'm not ready to let go? What if I'm not ready to say goodbye?"

Throughout the duration of the trip, she had lost her appetite. Being away from Peter resulted in her disinterest of basic human functions; showering, sleeping, and eating had all been neglected since she had arrived in Ann Arbor.

She suspected it would be no different when she returned in August. Sure, the campus was crawling with single, willing guys; but they were her age and their fingers were far from grazing their ceiling of maturity.

A gap year was appealing. But what good would it do? Any choice they might make would just postpone their seemingly inevitable fate.

Their clock had started ticking when they met.

Charlotte twisted one of her pearl earrings, glancing out the window and then back to her daughter.

"Your father and I are going on a trip for our anniversary next month. He wants you to stay at the Fuentes's but I told him you'd be okay at the house." The mischievous sparkle in her hazel eyes gave away her otherwise solid poker face. It was her tell, a code. "What do you think?"

Ryleigh's chest expanded with possibilities, like someone had pumped it full of helium and she would float out of the chair at any second.

"I'm almost 19. I can handle being alone for a weekend."

"Since the day Ryleigh was born, I dreaded the thought of her dating. The past few years I realized that day wasn't far around the corner. I tried to prepare myself for whatever was to come. Though, I'll admit, I really wasn't expecting *this*," Dexter unloaded as he examined Peter's teeth and gums.

He was trapped, forced to endure everything that came out of Dexter's mouth, whether it was pleasant or otherwise. The exam turned therapy session justified a fifth viewing of *Steel Magnolias* to calm his shot nerves.

"I thought it over and I decided we were lucky she brought you home." He paused to clean off one of his tools. "She could've walked through the door with some teenage delinquent. But instead, she brought you home. I can't say that I'm completely comfortable with the age difference, but realize I handled it poorly upon our first meeting. I'm usually not so narrow-minded. When your only child is involved ... well, if you have a daughter one day, you'll understand."

"It's unorthodox, I know. When I met Ryleigh, I assumed she was in college. You can imagine my surprise when I found out that wasn't the case," Peter said once the mirror and probe were removed for the final time.

Dexter placed all of the instruments back on the tray, disposing of his blue gloves and facial mask. Crossing his legs, he let out a subdued laugh.

"She's always been a little ahead of the curve regarding maturity. It makes sense that she would be better suited for a relationship with someone older. I suppose, in the future, I need to remind myself to form my opinions of the guys she brings home based on their character rather than their birth date."

The words struck Peter like a stinging slap across the cheek. *What was he trying to say, exactly? That we could never be long-term? You already knew that.*

He knew that his non-relationship with Ryleigh neared its expiration date, and Dexter was simply acknowledging that obvious fact. Why did his words feel like an attack, like a challenge to his integrity?

"I appreciate you not indulging her in the recent scheme of staying here for college. Truthfully, I'd be crushed if she went anywhere other than my alma mater, and Ryleigh's worked far too hard to give this up."

Dexter went to UMich?

"I couldn't agree more," Peter lied.

In dissuading Ryleigh out of her UConn scheme, he felt like Jackson deciding to pull the plug on Shelby. And he hated himself for not agonizing over the decision as much as Jackson had.

On the way out of Dexter's practice, Peter immediately dialed his mother back upon discovering she had been the culprit behind the dismissed call. Anytime he missed a call from either of his parents, he feared the worst-case scenario.

"Hello?" Janet answered.

No despair. No worry. Relief flushed through him. She had only wanted to talk.

"Hey, sorry I missed your call earlier. I was at the dentist. Well, technically I'm still here, in the parking lot. I'm rambling. How are you?"

"Since when do you go to the dentist?"

"Answering my question with a question, how very mom-like of you." Peter plucked at his t-shirt. He had been outside for all of two minutes, and the Connecticut summer had left its mark, the humidity birthing beads of sweat on his sticky skin. "Ryleigh's dad offered a free exam and I was just trying to be nice, so I went along with it. I don't want him to think I'm some schmuck, you know?"

Janet employed her not so subtle detective skills.

"I'm glad to hear that you two are trying to get along. Is he warming up to you at all?"

Sara exited the office, a massive bag slung over her shoulder and the handle of a water bottle precariously dangling from two fingers. She nodded in Peter's general direction and then kept her head down on the remainder of the walk to her car across the lot. It was not a friendly nod but rather one of concession for outdoing her at their front desk showdown.

"We're on a first-name basis, that pretty much tells me all I need to know. I guess it doesn't much matter what he thinks of me at this point, though."

"Why's that, sweetheart? Is something wrong?" Concern wormed its way into her tone.

"I thought I told you? Maybe not." Peter scratched his neck. On how many occasions would he be forced to rehash this topic? The universe continued to find ways to make him reconcile with the fact that he was losing the best thing he had ever had. "Ryleigh's moving in August, to Michigan."

"That's awfully far away," his mother considered. "Why is she leaving all of a sudden?"

Muscles tensed, he leaned against the hood of his car, bracing himself to deliver the jarring revelation he had been hiding since first announcing their faux relationship to his parents.

"It's not so random." He dripped in false bravado all the while hoping he did not faint on the scalding pavement. "She's going to college there."

Janet maintained an extended silence, and Peter wondered if she had hung up. Though, he would not have blamed her.

"The graduation you covered in May, was that her graduation, then?" A shriek pitched her voice to an unpleasant, though not quite, deafening volume.

Peter moved a hair away from the speaker, flinching at the potential matriarchal disapproval despite the thousands of miles of safety separating them.

His mother was not a judgmental person, and he reasoned that she was simply experiencing some initial shock.

Well, he hoped that was the case.

"Come on down and claim your prize," he quipped, biting his tongue as it slipped out. "Sorry."

"I'm used to your smartass remarks by now. In fact, I'd be worried if you stopped with them." Janet stifled a laugh, and a lightness settled over him at having avoided a red-hot tongue-lashing. "Goodness, Peter, this certainly sheds more light on why her father was so angry with you. When you told me she was 18, I assumed she was a freshman in college."

"I know it's an unusual circumstance, but she means everything to me. And if I could do it over, I'd make the same choices." *Those words just came out of* your *mouth. Do you hear how pathetic you sound? You sound like a desperate D.A. who knows they got stuck with a losing case.*

But in this closing statement, everything about his ties to Ryleigh became solidified. Peter understood that, given the chance to go back to the start, he would not have changed anything. They would be met with the same obstacles and, ultimately, the same fate.

He found a sort of odd comfort in this realization.

2 5

HARDBALL

$\mathcal{R}$yleigh idled by her bedroom window, cell phone pressed against her bare shoulder. It was a wonder the device did not clatter to the floor amid her trembling and near hyperventilation.

Tonight was *the* night—or so she hoped.

"He's on the way over as we speak."

"So, your parents just left you home alone for the weekend even though they know you're romping around with Walter Cronkite?" Andrea's incredulity pushed itself through the receiver.

Some of her stress dissipated at the humorously inaccurate comparison, and she was glad she had phoned Andy for moral support.

"Cronkite was in broadcasting."

"Whatever, you knew what I meant," she scoffed, only to have her inflection inflated by scandal. "I have to ask, does he know you're a virgin?"

"Unfortunately, yes, he's aware." She zeroed in on the brown bag from the drugstore she had precariously placed on her nightstand, stomach flip-flopping at the thought of christening its contents. Intimate was a lofty cry from where their physical relationship stood. She was primed for the kill, thoroughly fed up with Peter's lack of

184

romantic motivation. After his birthday, he had been all too chaste in his handling of her, hands never again venturing beneath her clothes. This was Ryleigh's shot to make him see her as a viable sexual companion, rather than just some younger girl whom he only seemed to view as a confusing, and perhaps troubling, friend. *Desperate times, desperate measures.* "I'm kind of freaking out."

"I'm sure he's been around the block. Plus, it'll be a great primer for your undergrad professor bang marathon. Don't worry, it'll be great."

Easy for her to say. Andrea had much more experience in the guy department.

Disjointed rumbling sounded in the driveway, signaling either Peter's arrival or the unsuspected landing of a commercial aircraft. She peered through the curtains and her chest swelled with an excess of oxygen and overwrought anticipation upon spying the familiar silver sedan parked outside. "He's here. I gotta go."

"Oh my gosh. You better call me and tell me ev—"

Click.

Ryleigh, though jelly-legged, descended the steps in pairs, reaching the first floor landing in record time. A heavy knock echoed throughout the empty home as she dashed toward the foyer.

Stopping short of the door, she regarded her cartoonish avocado tank and shorts with a mix of horror and humiliation.

Oh yeah, he's bound to take you seriously in this.

She pulled the door open and fought the urge to hide her dreadfully juvenile loungewear behind it—and she wished she had hidden, because his gray eyes instantly dropped to her pajamas, though he said nothing.

"Hey, you," Ryleigh said, greeting Peter with the same phrase he had used the night of their non-date.

Did he remember those words? Did he know how often she recounted things he had said to her, fearing she may forget them in the fall when she would be bogged down with lectures and papers?

He pressed a kiss to her forehead before moving past her and toeing off his loafers. Peter looked at her pajamas again as a smirk slowly built on his tired face. "Isn't it past your bedtime, little girl?"

Asshole. But her traitorous body was aroused instead of enraged. Swallowing, Ryleigh locked her gaze onto him.

"Don't talk to me like that unless you're willing to handle the consequences."

"I don't want to be a buzzkill, but it *is* one a.m." He produced a bout of uncomfortable laughter, an incriminating hue of pink tingeing his cheeks. "Where should I put my bag?"

She studied every square inch of Peter from where she idled by the stair's railing, snapping mental pictures and filing them away for her impending departure. Unbearable pressure lodged in the rear of her throat while considering that, soon, her only remnants of him would be carefully preserved memories.

Peter's hand waving in front of her face dispelled the unintentional impassiveness. "You alright?"

Was he that blind to the feelings boiling inside her, ready to overflow, the feelings that had been steadily building since he berated Ryleigh for not deducing his bagel choice?

"Yeah." Her eyes flitted to the staircase. She climbed the first few steps before turning to him, "You can put your stuff in my room."

"You could open a library with all these books." Peter gestured to the cramped corner-hugging shelves, adorned with cliché fairy lights, which she had plugged in along with the lamp on her nightstand. Combined, they provided the perfect wash of light. Light that somehow made Peter even more irresistible as he sat in her desk chair, sporting lounge clothes with his mile-long legs outstretched and feet propped on the edge of the mattress. "I've gotten rid of so many over the years. If I had kept them all, I'd probably be renting a storage unit by now."

They were alone in her bedroom and he wanted to talk about books. *Books.*

"There's no way I can haul all of them off to my dorm, as much as I'd like to. Maybe you can take some of them off my hands."

"Hard pass. I spy one too many sparkly vampire romances from here. There's no telling what other literary disasters lie dormant on those shelves."

She rolled her eyes. "They're not as bad as you think."

Tugging at the elastic band securing her braid, Ryleigh ran her fingers through it, unthreading the mass of wavy hair. She leaned back on the heels of palms to accentuate her chest, cursing the fact that smiling avocados were printed all over her breasts.

"Let me ask you something," Peter said, elbows resting on his knees. *Why no, I'm most certainly not wearing a bra. Thanks for noticing.* The anticipation drained from her veins when he pointed to the blue and maize pennant pinned above the doorframe. "Is Michigan your dream or your parents'? Because a little birdie told me it's your dad's alma mater."

If he was going to hardball her, he could at least do it on her terms. Ryleigh patted the comforter, watching with bated breath as Peter returned the squeaky chair to the desk and joined her on the bed. And while he put an annoyingly respectable distance between them, it felt like a step in the right direction.

"Go on," he prompted.

"It's a mix. I've always wanted to go, and regardless, he pushed me in that direction. I'll admit that, yes, my attendance there means a lot to him."

Words tumbled from his mouth but the loose, rundown collar of Peter's t-shirt affording a teasing glimpse of hair captured any shred of focus she had to spare. The sinful view charged her fingertips with an electric need that begged Ryleigh to re-explore the erotic wonder-ment of his chest, his stomach, to retrace the trail of hair that disap-peared into whatever paradise resided below his beltline.

He caressed the arch of her foot, dismantling her fantasy. An amused grin tugged at the corners of his lips, and they parted to expose the two rows of semi-imperfect teeth that fried Ryleigh's brain like a cracked egg on summer pavement.

"You didn't hear any of that, did you?"

Bringing her knees to her chest, she squeaked, "Sorry."

"There's no way in hell I'm repeating that epic monologue. Just make sure you're doing it for yourself. We talked about this, remember?"

Doing it? Does he mean ...

No, you idiot, he's talking about school.

She migrated to his saintly post on the edge of the bed and kissed his stubble-coated cheek, taking delight in his theatrical swallow. The day-old bristles attacked her skin like tiny knives. Ryleigh let her lips glide along the needlelike hair, "You think you're so old and wise."

Lids shut, Peter tipped his head toward the ceiling. She clenched her thighs and wondered if what had plagued her mind for months had finally made a bid for his attention.

"I'm at least one of those things, so maybe you should risk the gamble and heed my advice."

"Peter?" His lids flew open, eyes on her in an instant. Heat crept up Ryleigh's neck at the stormier gray invading his irises, dark enough to obscure their usual flakes of honey. "Will you stay up here? With me?"

The few seconds of silence that slipped by felt like an eternity to her tell-tale heart, which was ready to burst through the floorboards of her compromised sternum.

Palpable agony weighed down her light voice, an agony for which he felt entirely responsible. He had pushed Ryleigh away one too many times, and now she believed he did not want her when in fact he had never wanted anything more.

Shifting to face her, his thumb stroked her cheek, inciting memories of their first kiss. "Did I give you any indication otherwise?"

"I figured you'd try to sleep on the couch or some other B.S." Ryleigh rubbed her forearms. "You always seem to have an excuse not to get too close to me. Why is that?"

"Self-preservation?"

His heart stung as she removed his hand and crawled to the head of the bed. Once snug under the sheets, she stared him down, awaiting a genuine response.

Peter's brain stalled in determining a suitable answer while he joined her beneath the covers. The problem was that nothing disputable lay within her statement. Only the searing clarity of truth.

He owed Ryleigh the same.

Emboldened on the brink of confession, he let his hand trail under the hem of her flowy tank. "You really want to know why?"

His palm slid against her hot skin, resting a twitch away from the waistband of her shorts. Ryleigh's muscles clenched beneath the stationary touch.

Desire burned blue flames in her eyes. "Tell me."

"I'm afraid if I get too close, I won't be able to let you go."

Her makeupless lashes fluttered, conjuring fresh tears. Lips brushing his, she whispered, "Then don't."

Everything broken within Peter was mended, once again made whole, with the slow kiss he bestowed upon her. Her tongue was quick to part his lips but she did not betray their agonizingly languid tempo. Chills ran up his spine despite the fire roaring in the pit of his abdomen.

He forgot about their ages. He forgot about Michigan. This moment existed independent of that universe.

Peter's pulse became more erratic the longer their restless tongues entwined, past the point where he usually broke away, and decidedly further when Ryleigh's shorts vanished. His formerly courageous hand did not stray from her stomach, branding him a coward in the league of her daring touches.

She pulled one of his curls taut and gazed at him through half-hooded lids. "You can touch me, Peter. I'm not made of glass."

Peter dropped his forehead to hers. "Then why am I so afraid of breaking you?"

"Break me? Rosenfeld, you're the only thing keeping me together." He shut his eyes as her tongue outlined his earlobe, flaying his skin like the tip of a lighter. "Do you even have a clue how you make me feel? Every time I'm around you, it feels like my body's over-heating."

Though his chest was seconds away from an irreparable implosion, Peter grazed her silky underwear, eliciting an immediate sigh from the woman sidled up to him. The fluid leaking onto his boxers felt more pathetic than sexy, but he ignored that inner voice of insecurity, seeking refuge in Ryleigh's neck where he planted kisses on her burning skin.

He slipped two fingers within the material, and her breath hitched as he skimmed the lake of her arousal.

"Christ," he muttered.

Hatred slithered through the cracks of this new pleasure. Why had he set so many boundaries? What, if anything, was perverse about this melting and mingling of their bodies and souls?

Peter could hardly believe his long withstood guard toward her affections had been completely lowered.

And yet, they were a tangle of limbs and fervid kisses, peeling clothes off each other with reckless abandon.

He appraised the tantalizing canvas beneath him, fingertips winding along the delicate curvature of her breasts and coasting across her concave stomach.

"That first day in the shop, when you looked up at me with those big, blue eyes, I knew I was fucked," Peter admitted between kisses while hooking a thumb in the side of her underwear. "I may have been too stubborn to do anything about it, but I knew."

Ryleigh caught him by the wrist and the halting action sent him into a spiral.

Did I fuck this up? Did she not want to go this far?

Throat constricting, he laced his fingers in hers, mumbling, "We don't have to take this anywhere you don't want to go, alright?" He pressed a kiss to the back of her hand. "The last thing I want is to make you uncomfortable. I'd never forgive myself."

"Everything's fine." She shook her head, teeth scraping her bottom lip. "I just want you to know, I'm glad this is happening with you and not some random fraternity asshole." Ryleigh propped up on her elbows, hovering in front of his face. "I trust you."

All Peter needed to snap back to reality was her intimate warning label. The advisory lifted the lustful haze that had clouded his judgement since agreeing to stay in her bedroom.

But, God, how he wanted her. And it was not until then Peter registered he could never have her, at least not completely; he was twice her age and, in a few weeks, they would return to being strangers.

No, he could not do this. Not to her.

Peter broke away and yanked on his boxers.

"We can't do this."

Ryleigh was left dumbfounded in the middle of the mattress, clutching the sheets to her bare torso. Bewilderment trumped her devastation. One minute his hands were roaming all over her and the next he was on the edge of the bed, face buried in his hands. Pain radiated in her jaw as she tried to understand why he would not allow her this bliss, why he would get *that* close to her, only to back out.

"Why do you get to call all the shots? I'm as much a part of this ... whatever we are, as you."

"You don't know what sex does to a relationship. It changes everything." Peter utilized that certain grown-up, 'I'm older, I'm wiser' tone she deemed condescending.

She despised when he resorted to this voice.

"So, what? We're not in a relationship." She strived to keep tears at bay, tears that were testing her waterline's levy. "Why are you treating me like a child?"

"Because, Ryleigh, I care about you and I don't want you to make a mistake. You're leaving. I'll become a footnote in your past, a faded memory of the old life you left behind. I'm not the person who should be responsible for taking something so precious away from you, something you can never get back." As he spoke, she studied the shape of his spine, easily observable in the hunched-over position he had taken.

"It's my body. Don't you think I should be the one to decide who takes what from me? And clearly you don't care, but I wanted it to be you," Ryleigh spat out.

Peter turned toward her, an animalistic edge animating his visage, and yelled in an eardrum-bursting octave. "Why are you being so stubborn about this? I told you, I can't do it. I *won't* do that to you. I know you'll regret it."

Each one of his poisonous words skewered her already sluggish heart. She could not confine the tears any longer. They cascaded down her cheeks at an unthinkable pace, an endless stream of saltwater.

"I won't regret it, that's what you don't understand." Ryleigh's insistence faltered through the sobbing.

Launching to his feet, he paced around the bedroom.

"Oh, no? I'm sure your freshman year you'll meet some guy and fall in love. You'll wish you had saved yourself for him. Then what? How will you feel then, knowing you lost a piece of yourself here you can never reclaim?"

"How can you not see that person is you? That I'm in love with *you*, dammit," she wailed, fists clenching the sheets while her kiss-swollen lips quivered.

Her eyes widened upon realizing what she had said.

"You're 18, what the hell do you know about being in love?" he demanded, ignoring the confession as if it was not monumental.

This was not how Ryleigh had envisioned professing her love to him: nearly naked and crying amid her rumpled bedsheets, mid-argument.

But their entanglement had long been marred by inconvenience, and this instance was no exception.

"All I know is that I've never felt this way about anyone. I didn't think it was possible to feel this way. When I'm away from you, I feel sick. I get lightheaded whenever I see you. My stomach knots up and I can't breathe." Her voice crumbled. "You're all I think about."

2 6

HEATHER

*T*his time she said it.

The vocalization could not have been clearer. The weight of the phrase hit him like a pile of bricks in slow motion, the enunciation of each syllable striking with devastating impact.

What was he to say in retort? That his tongue tripped on itself whenever they spoke? That she made his knees quake and his heart soar?

It sounded exceedingly cheesy in his head, and he doubted it would sound much better vibrating over his gravelly vocal chords, which presently ached from their torrid shouting match.

Peter slumped to the floor. He primed himself to deliver unto her his ultimate truth, the tiresome verity that had weighed his body down the bulk of adulthood. "Someone else said that to me, once. I found out too late she didn't mean it."

"Is that why you hate relationships? Because you got your heart broken?"

Ryleigh seemed to have offered herself an explanation rather than posing a legitimate question. Sliding on her tank top, she moved from the bed and sat across from him on the floor.

His jaw shut like a padlock, unwilling to respond. Peter's heartbeat thrashed in his ears as he bore all of his focus on the wall.

For years, he had banished the humiliation, pain, and choler associated with the dreaded past relationship, keeping it well-guarded from others but from himself most of all. But there was no way out of the conversation at this point, especially after disbanding their almost-lovemaking.

"Her name was Heather." The two dangerous syllables sharpened his husky tone and harpooned his aching chest, clawing at layers of scar tissue surrounding his bitter heart that had never fully healed.

"Is she the reason you tried to … why you're on your medicine?" Even in this arena of vulnerability they had entered, Ryleigh did not utter a word about the horrible act he had been driven to commit.

Nodding, he remained quiet as he collected the courage necessary to proceed with the story that had been hidden away for so many years. The story that was not in the headlines he diligently composed week after week, but rather one he had tossed into his filing cabinet, hoping it would never again see the light of day.

Tonight, it made the front page.

"Our junior year of college, she asked me out. I was sort of starstruck by her audacity. She was the first girl who'd ever shown any interest in me. I was crazy about her, and even though it came back to bite me in the ass, I trusted her. So, I gave her something I could never get back."

Peter's speech deliberately mirrored their previous conversation while his eyes pleaded forgiveness.

Chin trembling, tears flowed from Ryleigh for the second time that night. A bolt of grief struck her, punishment for how she had treated him in the wake of their interrupted intimacy.

All this time, he had wanted to protect her, to shield her heart from what had shattered his.

"In the middle of senior year, I found out she was cheating on me.

With my best friend. I was angry, confused. I didn't understand how she could claim to love me, but then have the nerve to do something that demonstrated the total opposite. I was completely destroyed. It's a miracle I graduated on time." An eerily reminiscent smile punctuated his intensity. "That's how I ended up here, a Californian in Connecticut. I wanted to get as far away from her as the country would allow."

"I can't believe your girlfriend betrayed you like that, but your best friend, too? That's awful. I can't even imagine how you felt."

Her sliver of consolation, while heartfelt, was fruitless, evident by the harrowing hollowness of his glare.

"It was terrible, but that's not when ..." Peter trailed off, sighing. "Fast forward: I've been working at the paper for a while and my career is steady. The rest of my life? A fucking mess. I hadn't dated anyone since. I tried, but nothing worked out. I wasn't clicking with anyone and, even though she'd hurt me, I couldn't keep her off my mind. Because that's what attachment does, it keeps you blind and loyal to shitty people."

"I thought I was ready to settle down. You know, all the things people think they want when they're heading into their 30s." He released a dark laugh. "So, I looked her up online. We reconnected. I told her I'd be going out to California soon to visit my parents. It was a lie, of course. I hadn't planned a trip. I only wanted to see her."

Ryleigh's shoulders hunched, envious of this deep, obsessive love Peter had for this woman, and perhaps not for her. She feared this Californian harlot had ruined him forever, that he was no longer capable of love.

"I flew out, and we met up for lunch one day. When she walked into the restaurant, it was like the first time I saw her, across the lawn of our college campus." Something in Peter's eyes suggested that he was in a far-off place, submersed by the ghost of his own memories.

"We caught up, and I thought everything was going fine, until I pushed the idea of being a more permanent part of her life. That proposition triggered the seven-headed beast. She wasn't interested. But instead of politely excusing herself, she stayed to humiliate me.

She said I was a 'nice boy' and that's why she'd asked me out in the first place, because she thought she needed a change from her usual taste in guys." Peter lowered his head, muttering, "Can you believe that? She reduced me to a fucking social experiment."

"We got into a fight, right there in the middle of the restaurant, at the height of which she admitted to cheating on me the entire time we were together, not just toward the end with my best friend."

"When I got back to my parents' house, I sort of … spiraled. The pain was overwhelming. I had to get rid of it, make it stop." His vacant gaze fixated on his lap, unbudging as he gathered the strength to proceed.

"The next thing I remember is waking up in the hospital with a tube down my throat and a million IVs in my arms. My mom was there, waiting. She found me lying on the floor when she came home from work. I wouldn't wake up; I couldn't wake up. I thought I'd done myself in. It was the most irrational decision I've ever made: trying to end my life over a girl who viewed me as a way to pass the time. But it made sense in the moment, and gave my emotions permission to defy rationality."

"The day I woke up, I remember the doctor stopping by my room. He told me I wouldn't have made it if my mom found me any later. She saved my life." Peter's body shook, tears falling from their reservoir. Watching him cry destroyed Ryleigh. She felt helpless, like there was nothing she could ever do to fix him. "I was embarrassed that she'd seen me in such a pathetic state of self-loathing, but mostly I felt indebted to her for what she'd done."

Peter was her battered and jumbled Rubik's Cube whose colors she had at last aligned, each uniform face highlighting all that was beautiful and flawed within his soul.

"I know you think I'm young, and that I don't know what I'm doing or what I want; but I meant what I said earlier. I love you, Peter." A nonhomogeneous cocktail of hurt and devotion swirled in her gut. She swiped the back of her hand across her puffy eyelids. "Nothing you just told me changes that."

Ryleigh tossed and turned all night. Having Peter here was supposed to be comforting, but not when the uncomfortable weight of his secret shared the bed with them.

Her heavy lids fluttered open and shut, like a drained butterfly struggling to flap its wings. She fumbled to click the lock screen on her phone upon each occasion, fatigued eyes hardly registering the numbers.

5 o'clock. 6 o'clock. At 7, Ryleigh gave up the gun.

As she crept from the clutches of the memory foam mattress, her slumbering companion did not stir. Peter slept on his stomach, wiry arms buried beneath the pillow, comforter halting mid-back. His deep exhalations were audible, though she was pleased to note they were a far cry from snores.

The sight of his long, lithe form tangled in her marigold sheets was something she could have gotten used to.

But it was only hers to behold one more morning.

A brick lodged itself in her stomach. Ryleigh did not want to think of losing him, not with his demons clinging to every inch of her psyche, not with last night's passion and raw sincerity tarrying on her skin.

She swiped a t-shirt from her dresser and bemoaned the less than stellar underwear selection. In hindsight, postponing laundry day had not been the brightest idea what with Peter spending the weekend at her place. Snatching the least embarrassing pair, patterned to the nines with corgis, she went next door to the bathroom.

While the water heated in the shower, she removed her invisible retainer and rinsed it under the faucet before retiring it to its case.

The hot streams pelted Ryleigh awake, serving as a welcome precursor to the overindulgent amount of coffee she planned to drink. That comfort eased her tired mind, inviting more pleasant thoughts to take root—particularly, thoughts of what went down in her bed some six odd hours prior.

How long she had awaited a moment like that with Peter, and how quickly the splendid ordeal had ended.

Ryleigh tried to recreate the experience, hands wandering to every coordinate he had caressed. He handled her body with such care, almost like he was afraid to touch her. Or perhaps, he had forgotten the mechanics of intimacy during his years of abstinence. She wanted to believe the former: that he was a gentle lover.

If Peter had things his way, she would never find out.

Once out of the shower, she knotted the t-shirt at her waistline and brushed through her dripping hair. She stole a glance inside her bedroom, where Peter was still very much out for the count, and then headed downstairs.

Her heart ached prancing around the house without him. Ryleigh craved his company, every second of it he could spare. The hourglass of their semi-relationship mercilessly consumed their precious grains of time.

Soon, they would be left with nothing.

Pre-heating the coffeepot was second nature when Ryleigh swept into the kitchen each morning. She scooped grounds into the forever filter as the temperamental appliance took its sweet time warming up. If one thing would summon Peter, it was coffee.

But, she did not expect it to work its magic pre-brew.

"Cute panties." His scratchy voice resonated at her rear. The mocking overtone was so obvious, it may as well have reverberated off the walls. "What do you think a corgi would make of you plastering their heart-shaped butts all over your adorably flat backside?"

Flat? Ugh. She did have a flat butt, but let the record reflect, it was grabbable; and Peter had grabbed it on plenty of occasions without airing a single complaint.

"Shut up. And good morning to you, too." Ryleigh rolled her eyes, clamping the fresh lock on the bag of ground coffee. "I didn't know you were capable of waking up this early."

"It's weird, before I opened my eyes, I swear, I knew you weren't there." He clutched something in his left hand as he headed to the sink and turned on the faucet. Peter cupped the empty hand, letting water pool in it.

A small collection of pills vanished into his system—but these were noticeably different than his other medication. He must have detected the stifled look of curiosity on Ryleigh's face.

Flexing his hands, he said, "Arthritis."

She snagged some creamer out of the fridge and cut off the coffeemaker as it delivered an obnoxious beep signaling the completion of a brew cycle. "I thought people didn't get arthritis until they were a million years old."

Peter came up behind her, arms wrapping around her waist. Those sinewy limbs enveloped her, ushering in his maddening non-showered essence: repugnant VOC-laden ink from the newsroom clashing with soft and spicy sandalwood deodorant. The tender gesture almost reduced her to tears.

What if this is the last time he holds me like this?

Though he was hellbent on Ryleigh having a 'normal college experience,' she feared—and understood now more than ever, tethered to his warm, lean body—a normal life could not be led in Peter's absence.

His breath tickled the top of her head. "A depressed recluse with joint problems. Looks like you've hit the boyfriend lottery."

Peter identified his critical mistake the second she spun around in his arms. The jerking motion cast tiny water droplets off Ryleigh's swishing wet strands.

Her eyes narrowed as she searched his features. "Boyfriend? When did we unban those terms from our *situation*ship?"

While he had no idea what 'situationship' meant, the connotation seemed negative. It hurt to hear her refer to them in such a way.

"I put you through it last night. You've earned the right to a temporary title." Of course this beautiful cappuccino-making poetess was a temporary installment in his life. He had been foolish to believe otherwise, to distort glimmers of hope into rays of truth. Their truth existed, though hidden, in the fabric of this painfully delusional conversation. "B.F.N.—boyfriend for now."

"Being able to call you my 'boyfriend for now' for a few weeks is my greatest romantic accomplishment to date." Ryleigh strained on her tiptoes to steal a kiss and the sweet, knee-buckling scent of coconut shampoo emanating off her water-logged tresses swarmed him. She peeked at him while pouring creamer into what he hoped was her mug. "Do you want yours black?"

For once, coffee was not his number one priority. Something more pressing vied for that coveted spot on his agenda. Peter yearned to hoist her onto the kitchen island and finish what they had come agonizingly close to actualizing the night prior. But that desire was lethal, poised with the ability to hurt them both. He could not, in good conscience, send her off to UMich a fragile mess because he had been too weak to suppress some carnal urge.

Who was he kidding? He would be the fragile, inconsolable mess, likely falling into another five-year dry spell.

"I don't want your sugary, vegan creamer," he teased, planting his palms on the cool countertop. "You guys don't keep milk around? Don't tell me your parents are dairy-free, too."

Ryleigh offered him the mug of black coffee. "Here's the thing: there *is* milk in the fridge, but it's unopened. My dad's going to go all CSI on my ass if they come back and there's milk missing."

"I've certainly pissed off your dad enough for one lifetime." Peter added a splash of the questionable creamer to his coffee. He brought the mug to his lips, eyes cutting to Ryleigh amid the tentative first sip. "If the world's supply of milk bottomed out, I might drink this. That's a hefty might."

She hoisted herself onto the counter, and he irrationally wondered if she had eavesdropped on his filthy thoughts. "Someone woke up on the wrong side of the bed."

"Someone woke up alone in an unfamiliar bed, is more like it."

Ryleigh plucked at her ratty t-shirt, shrugging, "I couldn't sleep."

He dared to ask a question he already knew the answer to. "Would this have anything to do with what happened last night?"

"It's a combination of things, I guess."

Peter dropped his voice, hand covering her thigh. "You can be honest with me, Ry. We can discuss this like adults."

"Right, but—"

Ryleigh swallowed hard, fingertips twitching. It pained him to see her this way; the last thing he wanted was for her to think her emotions were invalid.

She sighed before biting the center of her lip.

"It's just, and I don't mean to be harsh, but what's the point? Why should we hash these things out if we aren't building a foundation?"

She's right, you know. Her timid truth bomb struck with the impact of a cannonball.

A few weeks. That was all they had.

Peter did not wish to withdraw interest of any kind from her, because that voluntary surrender signified the imminent end of their involvement. His stubborn, lovesick brain refused to acknowledge the concept of letting Ryleigh go.

Part of him worried that in doing so, he would lose himself. He had no intention to revisit that treacherous low.

"You're right." The two words knocked the air from his lungs, a sucker punch of bad karma for betraying his frail heart.

27

DYING FLAME

"My dorm mate's going to hate me right off the bat. I packed three giant suitcases," Andrea joked. She was rooted in the same spot on the floor that Peter had occupied when he shared the gruesome tale still haunting Ryleigh's dreams. "You're more of a minimalist. This shouldn't be hard for you."

Fretting over what to pack was the least of her concerns. In three days, she would be on a plane moving out of state, leaving behind a man she now knew to be suicidal.

That sobering detail dulled the excitement of narrowing down which jeans she should bring along to her dorm.

With trembling hands, Ryleigh folded an indigo sweater and placed it in the open suitcase atop her bed. She gave it a second look before tossing it into the designated donation pile on the floor. "I'm surprised you're over here. I thought you'd be clinging to Colin until the second he left for Indiana."

"We decided it would be best to go ahead and break up, or 'say our goodbyes' as he put it." Andrea flashed air quotes. "It wouldn't have made sense for us to keep this going. We'll be too far apart. Don't get me wrong, I'll miss him, but it is what it is, you know?"

Ryleigh marveled over her fashionista friend's sudden onslaught of wisdom. "Careful, you're starting to sound like our mothers."

What did everyone in her life have against long-distance relationships? They had worked for plenty of couples.

Sure, maybe there was a degree of selfishness involved: staying in a situation and making it work was far less emotionally taxing than letting go of someone for whom you harbored undetachable feelings.

"What about you and paperboy?" Andrea winked. "Is he tagging along to the airport or anything?"

"No. We both agreed that would be a nightmare. I'm stopping by his place later to return a few things and say goodbye." Her ribs compressed, an excruciating sensation that had been gaining momentum all week.

The second she boarded the plane, any semblance of her and Peter's togetherness would shatter. They had lost.

"You seem pretty bummed. Are you sure you're good with this?"

"Honestly, no, I'm not. I feel like my whole life is on the verge of falling apart." Ryleigh buried her face in one of the many throw pillows littering the unmade bed. It brought her decidedly less comfort upon realizing she could not remain in that solace of linen forever. Peeking from behind the pillow's corner, she whispered, "I told Peter I loved him."

"Shut up, you didn't." Her friend sprang into motion, channeling the urgency of an emergency responder. Well, hot goss qualified as an emergency in Andrea's book. In a flurry, she was at her side, ready to pry for details. "What did he say?"

Ryleigh licked her lips, shoving her arms beneath the pillow. "He didn't exactly reciprocate. It's complicated."

"Complicated how?"

"As in he has baggage. And I don't mean to shut you out, but if we keep talking about this, I might lose it because I'm still processing that night."

"At least you told him how you feel, Ry. The fact that he hasn't said it back doesn't mean he doesn't feel the same way."

A stupidly hopeful flutter brushed against Ryleigh's heart. *If that's true, if he loves me ...* But it did not matter much. Not now. They were an exponential number of ifs away from figuring this out.

And they were out of time.

Her cell phone vibrated on the dresser. After rubbing her face into the pillow, she padded over and checked the message.

"You know what they say, speak of the devil," Andrea smirked.

Ryleigh penned a quick response and brought up a music streaming app before retiring her phone to the tired piece of furniture. The first few piano key strokes of *Crying Like a Church on Monday* filled the room with its gloomy brilliance.

"It's not Peter. It was Kendall. They're throwing me a little going away party tomorrow night at the shop once they close. Do you want to come?"

Fanning herself, she said, "Definitely. It'll give me an excuse to finally chat up that hot male barista I've been eyeing since you started working there."

"Jeez. I guess Colin is yesterday's news. And I hope you're not referring to Oscar because he's an asshole."

"Yeah, but he's a *hot* asshole."

"God, which part of the brain is responsible for making women lust after guys who will inevitably treat them like shit?" Ryleigh balled up a pair of sweater tights and tossed them at Andrea.

"Probably the same part that drives young girls to date guys who are old enough to be their daddy." Her highlight-dusted nose wrinkled. "Oh my god, you don't call him that in bed, do you?"

She concentrated on folding a stack of cardigans, fighting hard to ignore the heat enveloping her ears. "We've only been in bed together once. If I had to guess, I'd say kinky nicknames aren't really his thing."

Pondering Peter's preferred bedroom salutations when she was on the brink of losing him was a great idea. Totally.

"Did you run out of skips or something? This sounds like reject funeral music."

One of the knit cardigans fell from Ryleigh's hands. She aimed a finger at Andrea. "Gregg is a lyrical genius. How dare you insult the beautiful music he's gifted the world."

"Beautiful? Are you nuts? *This* is a song somebody throws on in the background when they're getting ready to off themself."

"Andy."

Quietly, in the darkest recess of her mind, she wondered if Peter had played the seductively depressing album when he had his pill and alcohol sponsored foray into death.

With each passing hour, Peter's chest became tighter, greeting him with an ache of infinite depth. He studied the clock in an obsessive manner through his bleary eyes, willing the ticking hands to cease their sluggish movement.

Peter's normal routines had fallen to the wayside. His condo appeared to have been invaded by a group of unruly teenagers; an endless parade of unwashed clothes and dirty dishes cluttered the space.

The fluoxetine bottle on his nightstand had been empty going on a week, but he did not see the point in going to the pharmacy to get it refilled.

He would have suffered with or without the medication.

Things felt far from complete with Ryleigh, and yet he had resigned himself to saying goodbye. It was, of course, the logical thing to do. She was a charismatic stranger who had somehow drifted into his tranquil tide, but now the current was ripping them in different directions.

Because fate was a tease who never put out.

A key twisted in the lock, jolting Peter out of his comatose state; as he got his wits about him, he realized he had not the faintest clue how long he had been lying on the living room floor. He compelled himself to sit up and straighten his clothes. Surely, the forged effort to appear put together did little to conceal the devastation annihilating every cell in his body.

"Oh, dear." Ryleigh froze as the door shut behind her, clutching Peter's decrepit student newspaper sweatshirt and New Radicals CD. Had his been intact, the image would have broken his heart. Instead, it grounded him in reality, forcing him to acknowledge that she was leaving.

Leaving Harris. Leaving Connecticut. Leaving him.

"Why didn't you just burn everything?"

Setting the items on the coffee table, she crouched beside him. The familiar rings of liner circled her eyes. Those bewitching eyes he looked into for close to a year, the ones he was minutes away from never seeing again.

"Because I love you, and I value your possessions, silly man." Ryleigh ruffled his tousled curls. Their weight exacerbated the messiness. "You could use a haircut."

A subtle redness capped the tip of her nose. Though, her immaculate cosmetic mask discredited the notion that she had recently wept.

"I thought I'd grow it out like that thing from The Addams Family after you leave."

She plopped onto the couch—oh, the couch. How could he ever sit on that thrifted beast once she left? Memories of them were ingrained in its weathered fabric, preserving every kiss, every embrace.

Too bad it was inanimate and therefore incapable of receiving the memo that he did not wish to remember such things.

A smile coiled onto her lips. "You mean It."

"What?"

"You said 'Like that thing,' but Thing is the severed hand. You were thinking of It, cousin It."

He joined her on the couch and their hands converged, fingers intertwining perfectly, as if they had been molded for each other. The touch, however subtle, sent much-needed waves of comfort throughout Peter's wrecked systems.

"You're spending our last evening together lecturing me on The Addams Family tree? Shouldn't we be discussing more pressing matters like, I don't know, say for instance, who's going to make my coffee with you gone?"

"You don't have to worry about that. Just ask for a pump of vanilla when you go to the shop."

"Dammit, girl, I knew you were poisoning me. Why'd you do it? Confess." He pulled her into his side, thumb stroking her shoulder.

The coconut fragrance of her shampoo wafted up to him, making his stomach roll. It smelled like a tropical vacation from hell; she was preparing to jump on a flight and leave him stranded on a deserted island.

"I thought I'd put your coffee purist notoriety to the test when we met. Vanilla's the most neutral syrup we have, so I went with that. I totally expected you to storm the shop and yell at me that first day, but you didn't notice the flavor. And when you showed up the next day and told me how much you liked it, I kept adding it."

"That's beyond fucked up."

She gazed up at him. "You should be thanking me for upping your cappuccino game."

"I'll thank you in five years when I contract heart disease or type 2 diabetes, you sadistic brat," Peter mumbled.

Ryleigh stretched her neck to meet his lips, but when they connected, it felt like someone had cracked open his sternum and ripped out his barely beating heart. The pain transfused in their kiss far outweighed what Heather had dealt him. And perhaps a bit of fury hid behind the torment, because while he had no control over what Heather did to him all those years ago, he had a choice on that couch.

But he chose to say nothing.

Instead, Peter savored the kiss he knew would be their last while his heart clenched, knowing that no one else would ever be able to kiss him in that earth-tipping, breath-ceasing way again.

When the pressure expanding in his chest became too much, he pulled away and slipped into his patented indifference. He buried his head in his hands to collect himself before straightening and fixing her with a no-nonsense look.

"You should major in prolonging, you have a real knack for this. Seriously, though, it's probably for the best, for both of us, if you go ahead and go."

"Alright." Ryleigh swiped at her eyes. The dampened hand moved to cup his cheek as she conjured a perfunctory smile. "Promise me you'll take care of yourself. Take your medicine, and *stop* eating microwave meals."

He leaned in to steal one last kiss, muttering against her mouth, "I don't make promises I can't keep."

Peter refrained from lacing his hand in hers as they made the short trek to the front door. Shoulder pressed to the wall, he stared down at her sullen face, and his organs knotted like a scout master had done a number on his insides. He knew he should have said something, but there seemed to be no words for a moment like this, entrenched in the bitterness of preliminary separation.

"Can I call you sometime?"

"I don't think that's a good idea. No calls, no texts, no e-mails, no tweets, no whatever it is you Gen-Z kids do."

Nodding, a laugh ripped through her hushed hysterics. Her fingertips brushed across the doorknob as she turned to look at him over her shoulder, "A part of me will always love you, Rosenfeld."

It took everything within him to manufacture the two words that would give her the impetus to walk out the door.

"Goodbye, Ryleigh."

Peter was the furthest thing from present when he returned to the office the next evening. He had not touched anything resembling work, nor had he even bothered to turn on his computer.

The previous day's edition lay on his keyboard, marked with a sticky note which read, 'One for the history books.'

Asher's first front page piece.

And while his chest should have swelled with faux fatherly pride, any capability of experiencing joy, even if on behalf of others, had been stripped from his limbic system.

Head on his desk, he looped the cursed New Radicals album on his phone. This music used to foster productivity; the despondent, impassioned melodies carried him throughout the day. Now, the songs he had listened to for years sprouted new meaning.

Upon hitting shuffle and hearing Gregg Alexander's wailing vocals, Peter knew he could never 'just listen' to these tracks again. The melancholic tunes had been imbued with the effervescent spirit of one Ryleigh Branson.

Hands trembling in his lap, he recalled how she had sung along to every meandering word of *I Hope I Didn't Just Give Away the Ending* on the drive to their paint and sip date.

With each note came a memory of her, flickering in his mind like the faintness of a dying flame.

It was only a matter of time before she burned out.

The music reduced to a low volume as a text came through. His knee bounced, breath accelerating while wondering if Ryleigh might have been the sender. He had given her no-contact rules, and it was no secret the girl had a penchant for rebellion.

A heaviness weighed on his weak frame upon opening it and seeing that it was not from his suburban princess. *She's not yours anymore. Never was, technically.*

K: Get your mopey self down here and grab a cappuccino. On the house.

P: Unless it's laced with formaldehyde, I'm not interested. But thanks, Ken.

"Pete," a barbaric voice sounded, coinciding with a knock on the doorframe. *Mike.* What did that bastard want? "Boss wants to see you."

Any scathing response escaped him.

With each step toward Mr. Roberts' office, he regretted departing from the solitary haven of his own. His throat felt like it had been mangled by a wood chipper after a sleepless night of hysterical sobbing. A Visine bottle jostled in his pocket as he went, patiently waiting to douse his bloody eyes every six hours on the dot. He was in no condition, mental or otherwise, to socialize. But Cliff cut his paychecks so he thought it best to comply with the unexpected summoning.

Stopping short of the ominous door, Peter drew in a sharp breath before entering.

"You wanted to see me?" he asked, shutting the door.

"Take a load off, kid." Mr. Roberts signaled to the leather armchair in front of the grandiose mahogany desk. He had called Peter 'kid' when he first started working at the *Chronicle*. The bizarre resurrection of the nickname had him wondering if a new wave of layoffs was being doled out. "I don't like nosing around in people's business, but I noticed you've been a little off lately."

"That's putting it mildly."

He folded his hands atop the desk like a seasoned mafia boss. "Would this have something to do with that girl in the picture on your desk?"

It begins and ends with 'that girl in the picture.'

Peter had planned on being polite, not vulnerable, while in his boss' presence. Both had been ushered out the window with the provocatory question.

"What? You think you're Sherlock Holmes for making such a profound connection?" Sinking in the chair, he decided to indulge the older gentleman if it meant he could soon return to the pity party of sulking at his desk. "She's moving to Michigan."

"That's rough. I'm sorry to hear it." Mr. Roberts manufactured a heavy nod. "I've never seen you so enthusiastic about your work as you have been the last year. I can't help but think she contributed to that. And your slightly cheerier demeanor has been a nice perk."

Peter rose from the visitor's chair. Heat coursed through his body, urging him to tug at the collar of his shirt for relief. Firing a finger at the ground, he said, "Did you invite me in here for a pep talk or to make me feel like shit? Because I'm getting mixed vibes here."

Mr. Roberts' unruly white eyebrows drew together. "Kid, I asked you to come in here because I have something rather important I'd like to bring to your attention."

"Losing my girlfriend wasn't enough of a blow? Now I'm getting laid off, too?" *She was never your girlfriend. You made sure of that.* "Do you know how much student debt I have hanging over my head? Actually, nevermind the student debt, do you know how much I'm still paying off in medical bills? Our insurance here is shit, Cliff."

"Son, I didn't call you in here to lay you off. And, yes, I agree with you on the insurance. We're looking into some new options." Chuckling softly, he steepled his fingers and leaned forward. "Listen, Peter, I want to make you editor-in-chief."

The hair rose on Peter's forearms and bumps sprouted on his skin, breeding a sweeping, tingling sensation.

A promotion? He had no idea how much Gloria made, but it must have been pretty decent since she drove around in something considerably nicer than his piece of junk SL2.

The thought alone of rubbing the elite position in his father's face dulled his aching, pseudo-breakup hangover.

"What about Gloria?"

"She's leaving. That new husband of hers is PCSing to Texas. You're the natural choice to replace her. You have the seniority, anyway, so I don't anticipate any pushback around the office if you take the position. So, kid, what do you say?"

Jaw clenched, he hovered in the doorway. Any other day, Peter would have jumped out of his skin at the offer—and his acceptance should have been a no-brainer. He had worked his rear end off at this paper for the last 14 years.

Was it what he wanted: to further engage himself in a nocturnal, 50 plus hour a week career which kept friendships and any chance of a love life at bay?

But Ryleigh had infiltrated the formerly impenetrable walls of his hectic life, and perhaps, eventually, someone else would come along and do the same.

Peter squeezed his eyes shut as a knot twisted itself in his stomach at the fleeting thought of her; the young woman who had made him feel like he was living, truly living, in a world in which he had previously only existed.

The one he had been too foolish to keep.

When he opened his bloodshot eyes, a storm surge of tears clouded his vision. Tears he did not dare let fall.

"I don't know."

28

MICHIGAN

The job offer distracted from his pathetic state of self-loathing for about four minutes. *Four* minutes.

That was all it took for the emptiness to reclaim his chest and a fresh wave of tears to build behind his eyes.

Tongue wedged between his teeth, Peter keyed in commands on the outdated copy machine, punching in the wrong code three times. Keeping Ryleigh out of his thoughts long enough to concentrate on the simplest tasks proved impossible.

A searing ache ripped through him, its intensity suggesting she had died rather than was moving away.

How could Cliff spring a promotion on him at a time like this, when he was grieving the loss of his still very alive ex-not-quite-girl-friend? Had he no compassion?

Nausea clawed its way up his throat, and Peter regretted not taking the night off. Hell, he should have taken the entire week off to mourn Ryleigh's absence.

The repetitive whirring of the copier led his delirious mind astray. So what if he took the job? He would still work for the same small paper, with the same hours and the same shitty insurance in the same, sleepy Connecticut town in which he had squandered his adulthood.

Peter had enough money to get by, and while it would have been nice to pay off his student loans at a more expedient pace, and perhaps acquire a reliable car, he found that financial freedom was no longer his most earnest desire.

What would he have been working toward, exactly? Why should he rush to pay off the mortgage to a home he would, undoubtedly, share with no one?

Because the one person he could envision living with was getting on a plane the next morning.

Oxygen refused to completely fill his burning lungs when he accidentally caught sight of the illuminated coffee shop below. The lights from the copy machine flashed behind Peter's closed lids as his breathing shallowed.

How could he have let her go so easily?

She made herself vulnerable in professing her feelings and he had essentially laughed in her face. And yet, in that cruel moment, Ryleigh did not walk away. She remained at his side, even though he ruined their intimacy, despite his shouting and talking down to her, and through his breakdown as he laid bare his most hideous scar.

In spite of all of that, Ryleigh still loved him, still found something of value within him. What had he given her in return? Unreciprocated feelings, a broken heart, and an unofficial no-contact order.

"Any day, Rosenfeld," came the irritated intonation of Allison, their prissy finance columnist. Her gaudy cobalt, rhinestone-buckled high heel impatiently tapped on the cheap carpet.

Allison's thick Jersey accent jarred his brain into focus. The machine blared its continuous beep until Peter retrieved the papers from the tray and reset the digital menu. He turned his back to her, affixing a paperclip to the stack of documents and keeping his head down as he ducked out of the room.

Upon returning to his desk, Peter became lost in the framed photo of Ryleigh and himself, captured by Charlotte at graduation. At the last moment, he had placed his hands on her hips, resulting in a candid picture recorded mid-reaction. She looked up at him with an open-mouthed grin, burrowing her fingers between his while he met the camera's eye with a crooked smile.

Sitting there in his office, he could still feel the weight of her in his arms, still smell that fruity perfume that drove him wild, still hear her soft, teasing voice: 'Are you getting sweet on me?'

The fire crackling in his chest roared with an unbridled strength the longer he studied the photo. Peter had made the biggest mistake of his life.

His pulse accelerated as he regarded his phone's display.

7:26.

Peter lunged out of the desk chair, killed the lights, and fumbled with the set of keys to lock his office. A fluttering sensation in his stomach propelled him through the hallway, paying no mind to odd looks from passing colleagues.

All that mattered was finding Ryleigh.

He came across his boss chatting with Ms. Walters at the reception desk, muscles tightening as he considered the job offer. Not that there *was* anything to consider.

Not anymore.

"I quit," Peter said, as if it was not a loaded statement, and barreled past them toward the elevator.

Mr. Roberts cast him a slack expression. "I realize you're under quite a bit of duress, but quitting seems a little—"

"Can't talk, Cliff. I have somewhere to be."

Repeatedly pressing the elevator's button, he waited for the polished chrome doors to slide open.

After several seconds of bottled impatience, Peter opted for the stairs, descending their flights at a neck-breaking pace. He had to get to the Bransons' house, stat, for he could not go another minute with these waves of unspoken words threatening to inundate his insides.

When Peter stepped out onto the street, he froze. A light summer breeze sailed through his curls, but it was not responsible for the anxiety pricking his skin.

Though it was past closing, The Roast was lit up and a small group of people, most of whom were employees, were gathered inside.

And then he saw her.

The warm light in the shop bathed across Ryleigh's angelic face and added a layer of ambiance to her obvious boredom. She stood on the edge of the group, sporting frayed shorts and a hole-infested t-shirt, full lips closed around the straw in her frozen coffee.

Peter nearly dropped to his knees at the sight. But his relaxed muscles and easy breaths carried him to the other side of the pavement.

He noticed Kendall wrapped in one of Jake's tattooed arms and his heart thumped harder as the real reason for her text clicked into place.

That matchmaking little bitch.

Approaching the glass storefront, some of his previously steady confidence faltered. His knuckles gently rapped against the window, startling those inside.

Something tore at his chest when Ryleigh's gaze landed on him, her eyes brimming with hurt and lips slightly parted, like she was on the verge of tears.

Peter pushed on the front door.

Locked.

Ryleigh had sacrificed an enthralling night of stuffing her face with dark chocolate and crying over sappy rom-coms to attend the intimate going away party; emphasis on intimate.

Jake held onto Kendall like she was his center of gravity, and she looked at him as if he was the reason the sun rose each morning. Mr. and Mrs. Connor, the owners, sat at a cozy table for two, nursing lattes and playing footsie. And though Oscar and Andrea had exchanged few words, they had been eye-fucking each other since his arrival and would likely vanish to the bathroom at any given moment.

Maybe if Peter had slept with me, this wouldn't hurt so much, because at least then I'd understand on some fractional level how everyone else in the room feels.

Her stomach hardened and she clutched her plastic cup until it audibly crushed, prompting her to lessen the grip.

What was she even doing there?

The more Ryleigh thought about her presence in The Roast, the more absurd it became. There she was, holding a frozen coffee, mingling with a group of people whom she would never see or speak to again—well, other than Andrea.

She was confident the chocolate and cheesy movies would have provided better consolation than the current PDA-fest surrounding her.

Every so often, Ryleigh looked over at *The Chronicle*, curious eyes insistent upon betraying her aching heart. Was Peter thinking of her, or had he lost himself in work, unfazed by her departure out of his well-rehearsed life?

Moisture blurred the building out of focus.

You can't lose it. Not here.

"I'd like to propose a toast," Mrs. Connor announced. Everyone raised their caffeinated beverages in anticipation as she proceeded, "Ryleigh, it's been a pleasure having you as a member of our team this past year. The regulars won't be the only ones who miss you. I know you'll do great things in Michigan, and I want to wish you luck in whatever it may bring. And if you need a letter of rec, I'm always here. To Ryleigh."

Plastic and paper cups bumped together, lacking the pleasing 'clink' of glassware typically following a toast. Ryleigh raised her coffee in half-enthused participation.

As thoughtful as the party was, she hoped it did not carry on much longer. Her ability to hold it all together was dwindling at an alarming rate; she wished that the unavoidable breakdown heading her way staved itself off until she reached the safety of her car.

A rhythmic tapping on the window caught everyone by surprise, but no one more than Ryleigh, whose sweating drink nearly slipped out of her slackened grasp when she identified the source of the noise.

Seeing Peter standing beyond the glass made her shriveled heart reanimate and jump into her throat. And despite the dark circles and gauntness sharpening his already severe features, he was the most handsome man she had ever laid eyes on.

Curiosity guided her toward the entrance. They had already said their goodbyes, what the hell did he want, to revel in the satisfaction of ripping her heart out a second time?

Pulse quickening, her trembling hands struggled to unlock the door, and she almost grew regretful once the key twisted and she found herself on the sidewalk, a dangerous five feet away from the man who still gave her butterflies.

The man she was not supposed to see after last night and whom she may never see again.

Ryleigh bit her lip, glancing around the quiet street. "What are you doing here? I mean, how did you even know I was here?"

"I didn't. I was on the way to your house and then I saw you in the shop."

Her neck stiffened. "Peter, you can't play games with me. We've already been through this once and it was painful enough. Why were you going to my house?"

Pushing the sleeves of his dress shirt up his forearms, he blew out a concentrated breath.

"Because I'm done being an asshole. All I've done is push you away the last few weeks, and maybe it took me too long, but I realized it's because I'm terrified of losing you." Peter spoke with urgency, as if he were being timed.

The butterflies in Ryleigh's stomach multiplied, their spasmodic wings tickling the victimized organ.

"So terrified of losing you, that I just quit my job." Pausing, he repeated it like he was unveiling the bombshell to himself. "Holy shit, I quit my job."

"You said that." An accidental laugh slipped through her stern armor. A shrug repaired the crack as she prompted coolly, "Where are you going with this?"

Peter took a few steps toward her, leaving a shoe's worth of room between them. He gazed down at her, red eyes ablaze with yearning, and a weakness invaded Ryleigh's knees. She fought to stay afoot as he went on.

"What I'm saying is, I can't picture the rest of my life if I let you get on that plane tomorrow and pretend to feel nothing. The thought of being without you … I don't want that to become my reality, because I can't imagine losing my best friend." His voice shook on the last bit, and his Adam's apple bobbed as he glanced at the night sky. But the glorious forces of gravity soon returned the focus of his feverish eyes to Ryleigh. "If you're going to Michigan, I'm going, too."

Had she heard him correctly?

Surrounding noise and action swooshed by in slow motion. Inhabitants of downtown Harris carried on with their business, oblivious to the peculiar pair anchored outside of The Roast, staring at one another without a singular word passing between them.

"Why?" Adrenaline flooded her brain, coaxing any ounce of doubt to the surface.

A crooked smile hoisted its way onto Peter's face.

"I've never felt this way about anyone. I didn't think it was possible to feel this way. When I'm away from you, I feel sick. I get lightheaded whenever I see you. My stomach knots up and I can't breathe." He paused, exactly as she had during her confession. "You're all I think about."

Never had Ryleigh seen him more serious, devoid of any trace of sarcasm or humor. Flames engulfed her ears as she reeled at the borrowed dialogue. Peter had recited her romantic admission verbatim.

Amid the animosity that night in her bedroom, he had memorized her words as if they had been chiseled into his stony heart rather than fleetingly spoken.

"I love you, Ryleigh."

Tears sprung to her eyes as she jumped into Peter's unprepared arms, and he stumbled backward slightly while adjusting to support their combined weight. A commotion of applause and squeals erupted inside the shop, flooding the street with a muffled hum of celebration.

Any background noise faded into the ether when Peter's fingers tangled in her hair and he dipped his lips down to meet hers.

But no sooner than their lips brushed, someone vied for attention across the street. An older man with snow white hair bent over to catch his breath, palms planted on his thighs.

"Rosenfeld," he shouted, posture straightening thanks to an onslaught of coughing.

"My boss. Former boss, I guess," Peter mumbled to her. "Kind of in the middle of something here, Cliff."

"Rosenfeld, you don't have to quit, son." He threw up his hands. "You have *four* months of rollover vacation days." Pointing to the newspaper building, he continued, "So, get your scrawny ass back upstairs when you're done sowing your oats or whatever the hell it is you're doing."

Cliff pushed inward on the heavy door to *The Chronicle*, veiled in the arrogance of someone who refused to take 'no' for an answer.

Ryleigh raised her eyebrows, tightening her hold on his neck. "Looks like you got your job back."

"I got you back. Everything else is secondary."

The laugh lines around his mouth crinkled and happiness bubbled beneath her skin, knowing she no longer had to give him up, because Peter wanted her and loved her and would not have been able to live with himself had he let her go.

And that was enough. More than enough.

Heat radiated through Ryleigh's chest as his mouth covered hers, kissing her like her affection was essential to his survival, that without the reparative caress of her lips, he would perish.

He slipped a hand into her back pocket and Ryleigh jerked away, gaze flitting from him to the shopful of her former coworkers. "Careful, if you take this much further, it'll really make their week."

His other hand claimed the vacant pocket, grabbing her flesh through the layer of denim.

"I deserve an Oscar for that performance, or at least a bagel. Do you think they'd invite me in for one?"

"Well, the thing is, there's so many varieties of bagels to choose from. There's blueberry, chocolate chip, cinna—" Ryleigh smirked, only to be silenced by Peter's lips.

If you enjoyed the first installment of Rosenfeld, please consider leaving it a review on Amazon, Goodreads, or your vendor of choice. Reviews help indie authors gain visibility and expand their readership.

Sign up for my newsletter to stay up to date on new releases, cover reveals, beta opportunities, and more!

ABOUT THE AUTHOR

Leighann Hart is the author of the Rosenfeld duet and the Confessional trilogy. She is a huge mental health advocate and this sometimes—okay, oftentimes—bleeds into her love stories.

She consumes heinous amounts of espresso and pays tithe daily to the New York Times Spelling Bee. Her biggest regret is that she probably will not meet Rick Moranis before he dies.

Leighann lives with her husband, daughter, and Sugar the Shetland Sheepdog in a convection oven—er, Georgia.

Connect with Leighann Online

www.leighannhart.com
leighanniswriting@gmail.com
Goodreads @ Leighann Hart
Bookbub @ leighannhart